Chasing the Dragon

Kate Sherwood

PART ONE

.

Kate Sherwood

CHAPTER ONE

Hunter froze when he heard the muffled sound from somewhere down the alley. Years of training and his natural instinct made him ease back into the doorway he'd been about to leave. He pressed against the brick wall and made his eyes and ears relax, open to any new sounds instead of trying to chase down anything specific.

The sound came again. Movement, and then a muttering voice. As Hunter's eyes adjusted to the dim light he was able to see the shapes. Two people, one standing, the other.... Oh. The other crouched, head bobbing rhythmically. Another low mutter, and the standing body started to move, rocking forward and back in its own, rougher rhythm.

It was a blind alley. Hunter had no intention of going back into the building he was leaving; his business there was finished and there was no potential for socializing. And maybe it was a previously uncovered strain of prudishness, but he didn't think he wanted to walk by two people in the middle of a back-alley blowjob. Well, not prudish. His lips twitched. He was a romantic, that's what it was. Didn't want to interrupt something so beautiful.

He wondered how long they'd been going at it and whether he could expect a quick conclusion. He found himself easing forward, stepping carefully and keeping to the shadows. He was just curious, that was all. Gathering information.

As he got closer, the standing body's words became clearer. "Take it, you fucking whore. Yeah, like that. Fucking take it."

So much for romance. Hunter squinted, trying to make out where one body stopped and the other began. Well, that was clear in *one* area, but there was something odd about the crouched body, something that didn't fit the expectations in Hunter's mind. The crouched body was bigger than made sense. Hunter eased forward a little more and understood. A man. They were both men. The softer sounds came to him now, the wet slurping, the quiet grunts driven out of one of them with each thrust.

He moved closer. There was no excuse for it, but something about this was fascinating. Arousing, Hunter realized as he felt his cock shifting against his jeans. Well, that wasn't something he generally let himself think about. But here, trapped in a blind alley with all of this going on right in front of him, he didn't have much choice.

He realized his own breath was coming faster, and his mouth was dry as he tried to swallow his confusion. The stander was really going, now, fucking into the croucher's mouth with something close to violence. "Fucking choke on it, whore," he demanded, but somehow the croucher wasn't. He was taking it, absorbing it all, his posture still completely submissive, no strain or struggle apparent.

Jesus Christ. Hunter was rock hard. He stared at the scene, resisted the urge to reach into his pants, and then jerked his head back with a start. The croucher's head hadn't moved, but Hunter's vision had adjusted enough now that he could see details. He could see the croucher's eyes. And they were angled away from the man fucking his mouth, staring right at Hunter.

Hunter froze. Even as the stander's voice got louder, even as his curses turned into indistinct moans and a final shout of completion, Hunter stared into the eyes of the croucher, and the croucher stared right back.

"Oh, fuck," the stander said, staggering away, his cock dropping from the croucher's mouth. He braced himself against the brick wall and took a few deep breaths. The croucher broke eye contact then and rose gracefully to his feet. He was wearing a pair of ripped jeans and a too-small T-shirt, not enough clothing to keep him warm in the coolness of a fall evening, but he showed no sign of cold. He stood there, taller than the stander, lean to the point of skinniness, his eyes huge, his dark hair spiking out messily from his head. He looked like a teenager. There were so many reasons Hunter shouldn't have found him beautiful.

"That was good, kid," the stander said.

"Thanks." His voice was hoarse. He glanced in Hunter's direction, then turned his attention back to the stander. He held his empty hand out, palm up.

The stander snorted as if disgusted by the banality. "Yeah," he growled, and he reached for his wallet. He pressed a single bill into the kid's hand.

"No," the kid said. "Forty, not twenty."

Jesus. Forty dollars? Hunter hadn't been with a prostitute since he was about the kid's age, and even then it had been women, not men, but surely forty dollars was low for the kind of abuse the kid's throat had just taken.

"Take it or leave it," the john growled.

"The price is forty dollars," the kid responded. "That's what I told you." His voice was still hoarse, still low, but there was steel in it.

Hunter had the inexplicable urge to step in. He knew better. He'd seen worse than this, had kept himself neutral and uninvolved through countless horrors in various war-torn nations. If he could watch a country's army torch the grain reserves of an innocent village, he could watch a teenage hooker get stiffed out of some of his fee. He wasn't part of this fight.

And *fight* was starting to look like the right word. The john stepped forward menacingly. He wasn't as tall as the kid, but he was broader, a grown man with mature muscles. "Give me the twenty back, then, you little shit."

"No," the kid said. "The price is forty dollars."

"I'm not taking food out of my kids' mouths to give to a fucking whore like you," the man responded. Then he moved, fast for someone his size, reaching forward and grabbing for the kid, clearly ready to wrestle him to the ground and reclaim his cash.

But by the time he reached the kid's position, the kid wasn't there. He'd danced to the side, and he grabbed the back of the man's coat and shoved him forward, using the man's own momentum to bash him into the brick wall the kid had been standing in front of. The movement was quick, graceful, and efficient, and Hunter could appreciate it on a professional *and* aesthetic level.

"You won't take food out of your kids' mouths, but you'll put your dick in mine?" The kid bent over, quickly finding the wallet in the dazed man's back pocket. "Not for twenty fucking dollars you won't." He pulled another bill out of the man's wallet, then looked thoughtfully down at him. He turned toward Hunter and then pulled the rest of the bills out of the wallet before tossing it down on the man's head. "Service charge," he said.

The man was struggling back to his feet and the kid stepped back cautiously, keeping himself positioned toward the open end of the alley. For sure the kid could outrun the big guy, so it was another smart move.

"Give me my money," the man said.

Hunter had no idea what possessed him, but that was when he stepped forward. "I've already called the cops," he lied. "I don't want this shit going on in my alley. You need to clear out of here before they arrive."

"Who the fuck are you?" the man demanded.

"I'm the guy who called the cops. It's time to go."

"Fuck!" The man stared at the kid, then jerked his head. "Come on, we'll sort this out somewhere else."

"I'm good here," the kid said. He eased around, giving the man space to escape without getting too close.

"You're a fucking thief!" the man yelled.

"And a whore," the kid agreed. "You want to stick around and press charges? What would those hungry kids think about Daddy then?"

Felicitously, a siren sounded from somewhere nearby. It was the sort of neighborhood where a siren was hardly a rare event, but it seemed to be enough to kick the john into gear. "Fuck," he swore. He took a heavy step toward the kid and growled, "I'm not going to fucking forget this. Next time I see you, you're fucking dead." Then he turned and stalked away, a bulky silhouette against the streetlight at the alley's entrance.

They both watched him leave Then the kid turned to Hunter. "I could have handled that, but thanks. I guess you didn't really call the cops?"

"No," Hunter admitted. He knew the next logical step. He needed to get his ass out of there. being careful at the alley entrance to make sure the john wasn't sticking around and looking for revenge, and then he needed to forget all about this whole thing. He could put it out of his mind, if he just worked at it.

But he didn't move, and the kid drew closer. He had high cheekbones, making his face almost delicate, and lush lips that were possibly a little swollen from his recent exertions. Pale skin that looked like it would tan well if it ever got the chance, and deep, dark eyes staring at Hunter as if trying to understand the secrets of the universe. Then he cut his gaze down and took in the still hard bulge in Hunter's jeans. "Forty bucks," he said softly. "Eighty bucks to fuck me." He stepped closer and ran his hands down over his chest to the exposed inch of skin between his shirt and jeans. Hunter froze, and the kid smiled softly, as if he liked that response. "Or you can take me somewhere. Two hundred dollars for the rest of the night. You can have my mouth, my ass, whatever you want. You can fuck me blind, then wake up and do it again. Two hundred dollars. A bargain, right?"

Hunter knew he was staring. He knew what his answer had to be, but it took him longer than it should have to send the message from his brain to his dry, frozen mouth. Finally, though, he stepped jerkily backward and forced himself to laugh. "Sorry," he said. "No sale."

The kid frowned as if genuinely confused and looked down toward Hunter's fly. "Why not? You broke?"

Hunter snorted. "No. You're just not my type."

The kid grinned as if he knew how cheesy his next words were and just didn't care. "I'm everyone's type," he purred.

"I'm straight."

"Really?" Another look, this one more pointed, toward the erection that would not die. "So was it the violence, then?" He squinted at Hunter's face, then shrugged. "It'd cost extra, but you can beat me up if you want. Fuck me after or not, your call."

"Jesus Christ!" Hunter stared at the kid, and finally he could feel his arousal fading. "That's fucked up. You'd let someone beat you up for money? How much?"

The kid shrugged. "How hard do you want to go?"

"No, I don't want to go at all. I just... why would you do that? How much money does it take to let someone do that to you?"

"What are you, a reporter?" The kid didn't seem to like Hunter's attitude, which probably wasn't too surprising. "If you're sure you're not interested, then you're wasting my time." He took a backward step toward the mouth of the alley. "Last chance. You're going to pass?"

It shouldn't have been so hard to make himself say, "Yeah, I'm passing. Thanks."

"If you change your mind, I'm outside the Belvedere Hotel most nights. I'd show you a good time, man."

"Yeah, okay." Hunter just wanted the kid to leave. He had one more day of business in town and then he could escape, get back to his cabin where he could live in peace, without any of this shit breaking into his day and confusing him.

And the kid left. No backward glance, but Hunter was glad to see him approach the entrance to the alley cautiously and then break into a jog as soon as he was clear. It was a rough line of work, but....

Hunter had been about to decide that the kid could take care of himself, but as soon as he'd thought the word *rough* his memory had treated him to an instant replay of the john fucking the kid's mouth, the low, dirty sounds, the feral abandon, the unbelievable, undeniable hotness of the entire scene.

It was just sex, Hunter told himself, and he practically tore his fly open and reached inside to grab his insistent cock. It had appealed to Hunter as a pure, animalistic display. It wasn't like blowjobs were just a gay thing. A good blowjob was a good blowjob, and Hunter could appreciate seeing one without it meaning anything. He jerked himself hard and fast, smearing wetness up and down his shaft, gasping after only a few strokes. He tried to think of women he'd been with, the best mouths he'd experienced, the hottest, wettest, tightest, most feminine goddamn lips that had ever been wrapped around his cock. But as he came, spurting onto the dirty asphalt of the dark alley, he wasn't thinking about mouths at all. He was thinking about deep, dark eyes staring at him, watching him, *seeing* him for all he truly was.

He braced his forearm against the wall and sagged forward, trying to recover, trying to forget. He forced himself to laugh, a tight, unnatural chuff of desperate breath. It had been a quiet visit to town, up until that night.

Quiet, but important, he reminded himself. That was what he needed to focus on. He was trying to move on from his old life, but he didn't want to burn bridges. Retirement, even if that seemed like a stupid word for someone in his midthirties to be using. And it didn't make sense that he was working so hard to maintain his connections, not if he was actually planning to retire. A sabbatical, maybe. A leave of indeterminate length.

He did up his fly, trying to act as if he'd just taken a leak rather than masturbated to his fastest orgasm since he was a teenager. Yeah, he was taking a break. He rubbed his left shoulder, the bullet wound no longer painful but still a presence on his skin and in his mind. He was too old to think he was invincible, that was all. It made sense to look for a different role, or to take some time and figure out what he was after.

And what he was after was *not* a jailbait male prostitute. No. That had been a little glitch, but it didn't mean anything. Easier to convince himself of that now that the pressure in his balls had subsided.

So he headed back to his midrange downtown hotel and flopped down on the bed of his single room. Maybe he needed to go out. He could find some female companionship. Hell, he could *pay* for some female companionship. Maybe he didn't have a hard-on for gay kids, just for hookers. That would be easier to swallow.

Oh, fuck, *swallow.* The kid hadn't choked, hadn't seemed to struggle at all. He'd sucked that john dry, swallowed it all, taken it all like it was nothing. Hunter felt himself getting hard again, but this time he pulled himself to his feet and grabbed the bottle of Crown Royal from his dresser. Usually he wanted ice, but there was none in the bucket so he sloshed a shot into the nearest glass and knocked it back. Then another. Not quite drinking out of the bottle, but so close that he might as well have kept the glass clean. One more shot, then he let the burn in his throat and stomach distract him from the ache in his balls. He'd go out. He'd find a woman. It would all be fine.

He grabbed his jacket and headed for the door. Everything would be better in the morning.

"This is an interesting challenge for us," Trevor said. Considering his line of work, he was pretty damn pompous. Maybe it was because he was British. He looked around the boardroom, a location that had always struck Hunter as pretty damn pompous in itself. The people sitting around the table were wearing smooth and expensive suits, but the clothing wasn't enough to camouflage their true natures any more than the boardroom could hide the sort of business they were in. Not for long.

Trevor seemed satisfied that he had everyone's attention. "We want this company to be self-sustaining. We want it to fund our working lives *and* our retirements. So if Hunter wants to take some time off, this is a chance for us to work out the details of it all. What does it mean to be an active member of the firm? What does it mean to simply be a stockholder?"

"Well, I'm glad I could help you all out with that," Hunter said.

Bentick snorted. He was South African, older than most of the people in the room, someone who should have been looking at his own version of retirement but didn't seem at all interested in leaving the life. "It will affect the way the business is run," he said. "Imagine if we *all* walked away and expected the money to keep coming. It wouldn't work."

"But if having equity doesn't mean anything, why did we bother creating the company?" Larson was American, and had only agreed to base the company in Vancouver because it was close enough to the States for him to live on one side of the border and work on the other. "Sure, it's nice to have more control over the jobs we take, but we could have done that as independents."

"I don't give a shit about the money," Hunter said. He could see Larson rolling his eyes in disgust, but he continued anyway. "I need a break. I've got money saved. If you guys want to start declaring dividends, that's great, I'll take them. If you think you need to reinvest in the company, that's fine too. I'm not working, so I don't need a salary, I don't need combat pay, none of that shit that we worked out when we got started."

"But we don't want to lose you entirely," Trevor said smoothly. "We formed this company based on combining unique men with unique skills, working together, creating something bigger than the whole of its parts. Without you, there's a piece missing."

Hunter shook his head. "I'm a grunt. What's unique?"

Trevor's smile was almost oily. "You have a way of getting things done," he said. "The martial arts skills...." He shrugged. "Possibly we can find someone to match you there. Possibly. But you're resourceful. You're our man on the ground."

"I'm your man in the ground, if things keep going the way they have been. I care about the business, and I take pride in my work, but I'm heading for a body bag or an unmarked grave." He shook his head. "Fuck that. I've given you as many of my contacts as I can, and I'll stay in touch if you want. But in terms of boots-on-the-ground work? I'm out."

"I'm not sure we can accept that," Bentick said calmly.

Hunter scowled at him in disbelief. "What? What the fuck? You can't *accept* it? So get some fucking therapy, come back to reality, and fucking adjust." He shook his head. "I'm out. Maybe I'll be back, maybe I won't. You want to start making a fuss, acting like you have some sort of fucking *control* over me?" He glanced at Bentick, then turned to Trevor. "You try that, you'll see how fucking *resourceful* I can be."

Trevor nodded as if this was exactly the response he had expected. "Another one of your strengths. You're not easily intimidated." He smiled, then soothingly said, "We're all on the same team. And you need some time. We understand that. I think we should absolutely keep in touch, but get yourself healthy. Mentally fit. Then come back and we'll sort everything out."

Hunter didn't like the word choices. As if he were mentally *unfit*. But he was done with the conversation. He hadn't gotten much sleep the night before, too busy entertaining the laughing redhead he'd found in a downtown club, and he just wanted the meeting to be over. "Fine," he said. "I met with the Antonov guys last night, told them I was taking a break. Told them to contact Larson if they needed anything. Everything else is taken care of, right?"

"You'll be at your cabin?" Trevor asked mildly. "That's where we can reach you? I'm not sure we have an exact location on that."

"I'm planning to travel," Hunter Led. "Try my cell, or e-mail."

"And your sister?" Bentick said with a smile that showed he knew what he was doing. "She's still your next of kin? She's who we should contact if—"

"Stay away from her," Hunter warned. "*If* I come back, and *if* something goes wrong and you need to tell somebody, yeah, you tell her. But while I'm away?" He shook his head. It was a room full of hard men, but none of them could meet his gaze as he looked around and growled, "*Anyone* contacts her or goes near her while I'm away, there's going to be a serious fucking problem."

"Hey." It was a new voice to the conversation, but one familiar to Hunter from countless missions, the calm, controlled woman speaking into his ear in the middle of any hairy situation. Wendy Traynor leaned forward in her chair and said, "We *are* a team." She looked at Larson and said, "*That's* why we created the company. Because we wanted to be able to trust the people we worked with. Right?" She waited for everyone to process her observation. "So let's not let that fall apart now." Her voice had been soft to that point but it hardened as she said, "Let's remember that if *anyone* in this room takes advantage of the information we've shared with each other, if *anyone* betrays the trust that was the whole point of all of this, then that person will be facing all of the rest of us, combined. And even without Hunter's help...." She smiled proudly. "This is a group that gets shit done. So we should *not* be messed with."

"Fuck yeah," someone said, and there was a chorus of agreement.

It was Wendy's specialty. Kind of a cliché, probably, for a woman to be the emotional heart while the men dealt with the guts and gore and practicality. But Hunter had seen enough of Wendy to know that she was as practical as she needed to be, and her ability to manipulate people was just one more aspect of that practicality. Men expected her to live in the land of emotions, so she'd learned the terrain and figured out how to fight there like a native. Didn't mean she couldn't step out of that world anytime she wanted to. She'd go from a cooing mother to a demanding drill sergeant in the time it took to change channels on her radio set, if that was what the mission demanded. He trusted her as much as he trusted any of them, and he was glad she was speaking up for him. Further than that, he wouldn't go.

"So, we're good," he said, standing up. "I'm out for the foreseeable future. You'll contact me if I can help from a distance, but you won't bother me with requests to do fieldwork, 'cause that ain't gonna happen. Okay?"

"Take care of yourself," Larson said. He sounded genuine. "And keep in touch."

Hunter nodded and made his way out of the room. He tried not to think about the conversation that was probably going on behind him, but he had about as much luck dismissing those thoughts as he'd had forgetting about the kid in the alley.

There'd been a time when his brain was as disciplined as his body, but apparently that time was gone. Another damn good reason to get out of the field. He strode out of the building and took a deep breath of cool autumn air. He had his freedom; now he just needed to figure out what to do with it.

CHAPTER TWO

Hunter had paid a quick visit to his sister Hayley, a student at UBC, to give her an update on his plans. Now he had his bags packed and sitting in the back of his SUV. He'd done his shopping, stocked up on all the little things he'd gotten used to in the city but couldn't find in the country: a few cases of good wine; some Chinese jerky; some seasonings from the Indian market. He wasn't a versatile cook, but he knew the flavors he liked and he didn't want to give them up.

Now it was midafternoon. He had a four-and-a-half-hour drive to get to the cabin, and it was always best to arrive before dark, especially after a long absence. He'd grown up in the area and could have found the place blindfolded, but there was more to it than that. The cabin was remote and off the grid, and there was no anticipating the effects of weather, marauding animals, or destructive humans. If he showed up and there were repairs to be made, it would be easier to get started in the daylight.

Still, he lingered. With a sigh, he finally pointed the SUV's nose toward the east side of town. The Belvedere was a flophouse, and Hunter wasn't sure what to expect from any whores working the streets outside of it. He hadn't thought there even *were* many street whores left in Vancouver—hadn't they all gone into the escort services and massage parlors?

But that was what the kid had said: the Belvedere, most nights. He hadn't really said when *night* started, but Hunter figured maybe there was an after-work crowd to be tempted, a team of closeted suburbanites looking for a thrill before making their way home. Maybe something like that.

So he drove to the Belvedere and circled the block a few times before parking the SUV and making sure the alarm was activated. No sign of the kid, but there was a bar across the street from the hotel, one with a counter along the front window. Hunter had no idea what he was doing. Well, he knew *exactly* what he was doing, but he had no idea why.

He ordered a draft beer, found a stool in the corner by the window, somewhere he could have his back to the wall and still see outside, and he waited. He was trained to observe, to pay attention to little details that might end up being dangerous or useful, or both. But down here, with the street people and the lost tourists and the upstanding-but-impoverished citizens all living their lives, oblivious of him or his strange quest, he found himself wanting to observe without judgment. He wanted to soak things in, not analyze and classify them.

Mostly, he wanted to see the kid from the alley, wanted to realize that he was just another member of the struggling class, a too-skinny punk with a smart mouth and no common sense. Nothing special, nothing to challenge Hunter's understanding of himself or the way he related to the world. Nothing to worry about.

But the little bastard wasn't there. Hunter sat and watched the corner as another hustler came and found a client, came back and left again with another desperate john. Hunter ordered a greasy dinner from the bar kitchen, drank more beer, and watched as the corner grew dark. He gave up on driving to the cabin that night; he'd find a hotel or he'd sleep in the back of the SUV. It was stupid to get this obsessed, but he didn't like to abandon a task once he'd begun it.

The kid finally showed up around ten o'clock. He seemed different than the night before. Softer, somehow, less edgy. He stumbled a little as he hit the step at the hotel door, grinned easily at the blond kid, and casually stretched, running his hand up over his abdomen and pulling his shirt up a little as he did so. Hunter watched him, and he felt nothing. It was the same kid as the night before. Hell, Hunter was pretty sure he was wearing the same clothes, even. But today, there didn't seem to be anything special about him. There was none of the fire, the fierce beauty. Still a good-looking kid. But there was nothing feral, nothing that stirred a response in Hunter's cock.

Hunter snorted. Maybe the kid hadn't been wrong the night before. Maybe it *had* been the violence that had turned him on. Was that more or less disturbing than a same-sex attraction?

His musings were interrupted when a man approached the kid. He looked normal. The young side of middle age, casually dressed, nothing unusual or dangerous about him, but there was something... something Hunter didn't like. And apparently the kid didn't like it either. He exchanged a few words with the man, squinted at him, then stepped backward, shaking his head.

Good move, kid. Good instincts.

Maybe Hunter was just being a prude; maybe he wasn't going to trust *any* of the johns who approached the kid that night. But he didn't think so.

The man stepped forward again, the kid stepped farther back, and Hunter stood up. Then he sat back down. This wasn't his business. He didn't need to get involved. He'd come down there to see the kid, to try to understand the strange stirrings the night before had provoked, and now he knew it had been a weird aberration. Nothing to worry about. The kid was nothing to him.

But when the black SUV with dark-tinted windows pulled up in front of the hotel, blocking Hunter's view, he stood up again. And when the SUV eased back into traffic and neither the kid nor the man he'd been talking to were on the corner, Hunter moved fast. He sprinted across the street to his own vehicle, hopped in, and found himself locked in traffic about a half block behind the other SUV. That was okay; he was close enough to keep an eye on them. He couldn't be sure what was going on *inside* the vehicle, of course. He could call the cops, but what if the kid had consented to whatever this was? What if the kid was working? Whatever had gone wrong with his life, he probably didn't need an arrest to make things that much worse. So Hunter followed.

He managed to work his way up a few spots closer to the SUV and followed it into a light industrial area. He was pretty sure there was trouble when it turned into a dead-end street, an abandoned factory on one side and a shrub-covered slope up to railroad tracks on the other. And he *knew* things weren't going well in the SUV when the back door burst open and a body rolled out. It was the kid, and he was mobile, scrambling to his feet and then sprinting away from the SUV as the man from the corner fought his way out of the backseat and ran after him. The SUV was turning around, but it was slow, hampered by the tight quarters. Hunter spun his own vehicle around and let it idle. When the kid got close enough, Hunter leaned over to throw the passenger door open.

"Get in," he grunted as the kid stared at him. There was only a moment's hesitation before the kid made his decision, leaped into the seat, and slammed the door behind him. Hunter wasted no time getting out of there. He had no idea what was going on, but he didn't want to get killed on his first day off from a job he'd quit because it was too dangerous.

"How serious are they?" he asked the kid, not taking his eyes from the road. "They going to follow us? They armed?"

The kid turned around in his seat. "They're following. And the guy in the backseat had a gun. I don't know what kind."

"Do they want you dead?"

The kid frowned. "I don't know. I don't think so, but they said they were losing patience. Said I needed to hear their message."

He raised his hand to feel along his jaw and for the first time Hunter noticed the redness that was fading to a purple bruise.

"Which was?"

"That I need to stop fucking around and give them their money."

"Their money? How much?"

"Three grand. A bit less."

Okay, probably no one was going to get killed over three thousand dollars, not as long as they played this smart. "Where's the nearest police station?"

"I can't go to the cops!" the kid objected. "Then they really *would* kill me."

"What's the debt from?"

The kid was silent for too long, then said, "I was holding on to something for them. But I lost it. So now they want the money from it."

Holding on to something. "Drugs?" Hunter demanded. He took his eyes off the road long enough to give the kid a hard look. "Fuck, you're on something right now." That was where the edge had gone, that was why the kid had seemed tamed and softened on the street corner.

The kid just shrugged, staring out the window.

"Fuck," Hunter said again. He slowed down as they approached the next intersection. He'd be the first car at the lights, the guys following would be the third. He waited for the light to turn red, then floored it, making it through the intersection just before the traffic started the other way. He watched in his rearview mirror as the trailing SUV tried to maneuver around the car in front of it and then work through the intersection. Hunter took a quick left, then a right, then another left.

"Nice moves," the kid said.

"Fuck." Hunter probably needed to expand his vocabulary, but the word suited his emotions. He looked at the kid and saw his cheekbones accentuated by the streetlights as they passed each one. But that wasn't what he should be thinking about. "So what's your plan? How are you going to deal with this?"

The kid didn't even look at him. "Don't suppose you want to loan me three grand?" Then he squinted as if trying to see through some sort of haze. "Wait. You're the guy from the alley. What the fuck are you doing here? Were you following us? What's going on?"

"Let's not worry about *me*," Hunter said. Easier to deflect than to try to answer any of those questions. He looked behind them, then pulled into a multilevel parking garage, took his ticket, and drove to a spot near the exit. "They know where you live," he said quietly. "Where you work."

The kid nodded.

"You got somewhere else you can go? Family or friends to stay with?"

The kid shook his head.

"Is there anything really tying you to this town? I mean, if I take you to the bus stop and buy you a ticket to, I don't know, Calgary, or somewhere. Would that work?"

"Calgary?" The kid sounded lost. And stoned.

Fuck. It'd be like dropping a kitten off in the forest and thinking it could fend for itself. Hunter gave himself a moment to find another option, then took a deep breath and asked, "Have you ever used a chainsaw?" He couldn't believe he was doing this.

The kid slowly turned his head. "What? A chainsaw?"

"Any power tools? Any building experience?"

"No. Never even took a shop class."

"Okay. Good. So I wouldn't have to break you of a bunch of

bad habits."

"What are you talking about?"

"A job. Menial labor—I'd pay you minimum wage and take room and board out of what you make. I've got a cabin up north of Kamloops, and I'm doing some work on it. I could use some help."

The kid stared at him. "Why?" he finally said.

Excellent question. Hunter just shrugged.

"You looking for the Boyfriend Experience?" the kid asked, his voice suddenly harder than it had been. "You get turned on by sweat, want to make me work before you fuck me? Fine. But that's three hundred bucks a day, not minimum fucking wage."

"I'm straight," Hunter said. He was pretty sure that was true. The kid was doing nothing for him now. "I'm offering you somewhere to go until things cool off here. You can get yourself together, maybe save up enough money to pay these guys back, or to start a new life somewhere. Gain some skills."

"Oh, I've *got* skills, honey," the kid purred.

"Ones you could use for a more legit job."

"And what's in it for you?"

"I get to be a big fucking hero," Hunter said. Maybe that *was* what he was after. Maybe he'd turned away from too many people in need and had somehow decided that this time he was going to help. He had no idea, and it wasn't the kid's business anyway. "Take it or leave it."

The kid was quiet for a long time. Finally, he said, "There's something north of Kamloops?"

"Most of the province," Hunter confirmed. "Not a lot of people, but some real nature. Trees, mountains, bears, the whole thing."

"But you *do* have a cabin? Like, with a roof?"

"Yeah. It's not huge, but there's a garage with a space above it that I was planning to insulate and turn into a guest room. That can be your first job, if you want." Hunter had thought it would be a good place for Hayley to stay when she visited, but apparently he was going to rent it out to this punk, instead. Interesting.

A black SUV drove up behind them, slow and menacing, and then drove right by, the woman behind the wheel not even glancing in their direction.

The kid's shoulders had tightened when the vehicle approached, but now they slumped. "Yeah," he said quietly. "Okay."

"Okay," Hunter repeated. He had a feeling he'd just bitten off way more than he could chew. "We can leave tonight." He might need to stop for coffee, but he'd make it. Sleepless nights had come with the job, before he retired, and he didn't think he'd lost his discipline already. And it seemed like a good time to get out of town. "Is there a back door to the Belvedere? Some way to get your stuff without them seeing you, if they're watching the place?"

"There's nothing there I need."

"Clothes?" Hunter suggested.

"You're looking at 'em." The kid saw Hunter's frown and said, "Bad roommate a couple weeks ago. Moved out and took everything I owned. Everything I wasn't wearing at the time."

The logistics of laundry seemed a bit challenging, but Hunter didn't ask. The kid didn't smell, so that was something. "Okay," Hunter said. He tried to think of it as a fun adventure. "I guess we're ready to go, then."

The kid leaned his head against the window as Hunter put the SUV in reverse. "Fuck," he said quietly, and that was all.

They drove through the night, stopping once for takeout and again for coffee. The kid picked at the burger Hunter bought him, but probably only ate about a quarter of it; it was hard to get a good measure from the demolished remains the kid finally threw out the car window. And he didn't have any coffee. He dozed most of the way, which was a welcome relief from trying to make conversation. He startled awake when they turned off the last paved road onto the long rutted trail that led to the cabin.

"I only own a couple hundred acres, but we're in the middle of nowhere. If you go out for a walk, take a GPS with you because if you get lost you're going to stay lost for a long time. Closest neighbor is about eight kilometers away, and they're not home all that often. The main road's about ten kilometers, but it doesn't get a lot of traffic. We're forty kilometers from town. I'll go in tomorrow to get groceries, and you can come with me and get whatever you'll need too. You still have money from that guy last night?"

"Yeah, some," the kid said. He didn't seem dopey anymore; his smile was almost too sharp as he turned to Hunter and said, "Don't suppose the store down there carries heroin, does it?"

"Heroin?" Hunter hit the brakes and jerked his head around to stare at the kid. "*That's* what you're on? Jesus Christ, I thought maybe it was pot, or even pills. Not fucking heroin." His surprise made him quick. He reached out and grabbed the kid's arm, then pulled it toward him as he turned on the overhead light with his other hand. "No track marks."

"Safer to smoke it," the kid said. He leaned back into the seat, apparently not worried that Hunter's fingers were digging in to the skin of his forearm. "Safety is my watchword."

"How much do you take? I mean, how often? Are you going to go through withdrawal?"

The kid snorted, still staring out the front windshield into the darkness. "I expect so. I've never quit before, but, yeah. I think it might be a little rough for a while." Then he turned, his smile overly innocent, his eyes glittering with something close to malice. "Oh. Should I have mentioned that before we left town?"

"Fuck." Hunter let go of the kid's arm and turned off the overhead light. It was his turn to stare through the windshield. It wasn't enough that he'd decided to violate the sanctity of his wilderness retreat with a possibly underage whore being chased by angry drug dealers. No, the kid had to be a junkie too.

"You going to turn around, drive me back?" the kid asked. It sounded like he was making an inquiry about the price of potatoes. "Or just dump me here in the forest?"

Yeah, those were the two options that occurred to Hunter too. But he knew he wasn't going to choose either one. Instead, he took his foot off the brake and started driving again. "Anything else I should know?" he asked once he was sure he'd be able to speak calmly.

The kid had braced himself against the door and was openly staring at Hunter, clearly trying to figure him out. "I steal the covers," he finally said.

"Gonna be pretty hard for you to do that when you're sleeping on the couch and I'm in the bed."

"I'm very goal-oriented. I'll find a way."

Hunter snorted. Then they turned the last bend in the track and the headlights danced over the log walls of the cabin. He was home, and the knowledge let him relax more than he had in the whole week he'd been in the city. Even with the kid next to him, he felt like everything would be okay here.

"Come inside," he said as he parked the SUV. "We'll go into town tomorrow. I've got a friend who's a doctor; we'll see if she can fit you into her schedule. Get some information on the withdrawal thing."

The kid stared at him. "Seriously? You're going to.... No, man, you don't have to do that. I was kidding. I'll... I don't know, I can hitch back to town, probably get there before things get too bad."

"And go through withdrawal alone in the city?" No, that wasn't what the kid was suggesting. "Or just not do it at all. Go back to it, get beat up by dealers and johns, keep shooting shit into your veins—"

"I don't shoot," the kid said as if it mattered.

"Great, so you can get lung cancer on top of everything else."

"Jesus Christ, what the fuck does it matter to you?"

Hunter heaved a deep, dramatic sigh. "My brother died of an OD," he said gravely. "And I vowed that I'd never let that happen to anyone else."

The kid squinted at him skeptically. "Really?"

"No, not really." Hunter pushed his door open and looked back in at the kid. "Get out and go to sleep. We'll talk to Miriam tomorrow and see what she thinks about it all. She can tell you what to expect, and you can make your decision then."

He shut his door and headed for the cabin, and by the time he had the place unlocked the kid was behind him. Before they entered, Hunter turned around and held out his hand. "I'm Jack Hunter. Just Hunter is fine."

The kid looked suspicious, as usual, then slowly extended his own hand. "Christian Manning," he said.

"Nice to meet you. Come on in."

And Christian did. It was a bewildering turn of events, but apparently Hunter had a roommate, at least temporarily.

CHAPTER THREE

"What on *earth* are you thinking, Jack?" They were in Miriam's office at the medical clinic, and she was clearly torn between confusion, concern, and amusement. "He's just some street kid? Some stranger?"

"His father saved my life in Korea."

She shook her head. "No, he didn't." She sank down in her desk chair and glanced toward the door. Christian was off giving a urine sample so she'd called Hunter back for a little conversation. "He gave me permission to discuss his case with you," she said almost primly. She was a decade older than Hunter, fit and strong and beautiful, and they'd spent quite a few nights together before mutually deciding they were better as friends. So she probably *did* have the right to send him a disapproving glare, but he didn't really appreciate it anyway. "He needs more help than you can give him. But I've called around and there's no detox spots available for another month and a half; my feeling is that he'll have drifted off by then, back out of our reach."

"That seems likely."

She shrugged. "So possibly you're his best bet. But I really don't think he's your problem, is he?"

"I'm a grown man. I choose my own problems."

"You *create* your own problems."

"I didn't create this one."

"No," she said sadly.

Christian appeared in the doorway then. He was still wearing his own ripped jeans but he'd let Hunter lend him a sweatshirt and he was swimming in the fabric. It made him look even younger and more fragile.

"You want to come in and talk about your options?" Miriam asked.

Christian stepped tentatively into the room and perched on the edge of one of the leather armchairs. He seemed restless; not quite twitchy, but certainly not as relaxed as he'd been the night before. His natural state, or the beginnings of something?

Miriam smiled at him kindly. "You're in pretty good condition," she said. "A bit underweight, and obviously not completely healthy, not when you're drug-dependent. We have to send your samples away for full test results, but on an initial exam I don't see anything that would suggest that withdrawal would be life-threatening."

The kid didn't respond, so Miriam gave him a moment, then said, "But it will be *very* unpleasant. I admit, I don't have a lot of experience with heroin addiction, but I've helped a significant number of patients deal with oxycodone, and it's not dissimilar to heroin."

She leaned forward then and waited until Christian finally raised his gaze to meet hers. "If you want to get off this drug, I will help you, and apparently Jack will too. But you're going to need to be *absolutely* committed to getting clean, or you're wasting everyone's time and putting yourself through agony for nothing. Are you ready to get clean?"

Christian had stopped fidgeting. He sat still for far too long, long enough that Hunter was about to start shifting around himself, but finally the kid said, "I want to do it. That's why I came up here." His voice was low but sincere.

Miriam leaned back in her chair and looked at Christian, then turned to Hunter and raised her eyebrows. "There are places that keep you sedated for the entire detox process. I can't offer you that, and the findings are unclear about whether they're better or worse for your long-term success. If you do this now, you're looking at...." She made a face. "Probably at least a week of pretty acute misery. I can give you *some* medication to help treat the symptoms, but you're essentially going to be going cold turkey. You'll be restless, exhausted, depressed, and anxious, and you'll really, really want to take heroin. You probably already feel like you're coming down with a cold. You're not; that's the withdrawal starting. You'll have fever, diarrhea, nausea, insomnia, and some pretty serious pain. Five times worse than the worst stomach bug you've ever had, lasting far too long, plus some bonus mental symptoms."

She paused and her smile was kind but sad. "And when you're through with that, you'll still have restlessness, depression, anxiety, and heroin cravings. It's that second stage where most addicts relapse. After going through all the initial pain you'll feel like you deserve a reward, and instead you'll still feel really crappy. You might start worrying that what you're feeling is just normal life off heroin, but it isn't. It's your body adjusting to the new normal, that's all. You've taken out a serious loan against your body's pleasure centers over the last couple of years, and you need to repay at least some of that loan before your body starts letting you feel good again."

Christian was quiet for another long moment, then he looked her in the eyes and said, "Your sales pitch sucks."

She smiled. "I'm not selling, I'm warning. If this is what you want to do, I think that's great. I think it's the only way for you to really get your life back on track. But like I said, it'll only work if you stay strong. I don't want to put myself or Jack through all this if you're going to bail out partway through."

Christian nodded, then raised his head. "I won't let you down."

"Oh, sweetie," she said. "Don't let *yourself* down."

He smiled in response, but it was forced and empty.

Miriam tore her eyes away from the kid and looked back at Hunter. "I'll write a couple prescriptions, but mostly what you're going to want is over the counter—ibuprofen is the best non-opiate for dealing with this kind of pain. And some people swear by antihistamines, so pick up some allergy pills as well. They can't hurt. Gatorade, Pedialyte, Imodium." She turned back to Christian. "Flat ginger ale, crackers, soup— whatever your preferred sick-foods are. Be prepared to be very cold; the fever won't be doing you any good, so feel free to take something to bring it down. Some people find exercise helpful. Other than that?" She looked back to Hunter and shrugged. "I could write a prescription for marijuana, but it's a slow process up here, getting the approved stuff. You might be better off just stopping by Mike Talisker's and picking some up."

"Wait," Christian said. "I get to smoke pot?"

"It's the best anti-nausea drug we've got, and it will alleviate some of the pain," Miriam said. "If it helps a bit with the stress, that's an upside too. You'll want to avoid alcohol—a lot of addicts try to use it but it isn't as effective as other medications, and it adds to the nausea."

"She's not telling you to smoke pot, and she's not saying it's legal, not if it's unprescribed," Hunter said quickly. Miriam could sometimes be a bit idealistic and he didn't want her to get burned. "*If* you choose to smoke some, that's your decision and your responsibility. Right?"

The kid nodded seriously, then grinned and cut his gaze toward Miriam, then back to Hunter. "So you really *are* straight, huh?"

Hunter had no response. Damn, the kid was pretty perceptive. And Miriam just raised an eyebrow and started writing on her prescription pad. When she was done, she handed a couple of sheets across to Christian, then said, "You can go out to the front desk and finish up the paperwork for insurance, okay? It's a nuisance that you lost your insurance card, but you're still covered, even without it. Whoever's at the desk can give you the paperwork so you can contact the government and get a replacement."

Christian nodded obediently and left.

Once she was sure he was out of earshot, Miriam looked at Hunter and said, "He told me what he was doing for money, in the city." She looked almost gleeful. "Any reason why he might have thought you were gay?"

"Because he's got an overactive imagination," Hunter growled.

She didn't look completely convinced, but at least she let the subject drop. "I wanted to tell you, if you can keep him out of town, that's best. If you can't, make sure you're with him. The dealers up here—dealers anywhere, I guess—they're bloodhounds for desperation. And oxy isn't heroin, but it's close enough that he could get serious relief if he took it. Unless we want him to exchange one addiction for another, we need to keep him away from them until we're sure he's strong."

"You got a timeline on that?"

"Oh, *now* you're starting to worry about how long it's going to take?" She shook her head. "Too late, buddy. No backing out now."

"Not backing out. Just wondering."

"Seven to ten days for the first stage," she said, and she checked her watch. "Last dose about ten last night, so he's already got cravings, for sure. But the actual *physical* issues probably won't hit until late tonight, or maybe even tomorrow or the next day. It varies. Then after the first stage, probably a month or so for the second." She shrugged. "He's been using pretty heavily for about three years. It's not the worst-case scenario, but it's not a kid coming down after a spring-break bender, either."

"He's been using for three years? How old is he?"

"Nineteen. Almost twenty." Another strange expression as she said, "These are bits of information I would really expect you to know before you invite someone to live in your home."

"I have no explanation or excuse for my behavior." The line had worked the first few times he'd tried it when they'd been dating, but it had lost its luster then and didn't seem to have earned any back in the couple of years between.

She shook her head. "You don't need to explain yourself to me. But you might want to try to figure it out for your own sake, at some point." Then she was back to business. "I'll order a complete series of tests for him—for things related to the prostitution as well as the drugs, although there's a significant overlap between those areas. Results should be back in a few days. Still no phone out there?"

"Two-way radio, if you need to reach me."

"I'm not going to tell a kid his HIV status on a two-way radio." She turned to her computer, hit a few keys, and said, "I'll come out for dinner Friday night. He'll be in the middle of things by then so he probably won't want to eat much, but that doesn't mean you can't feed *me*. I can check on him, and assuming the test results are clear, I can talk to him about them then. If they *aren't* clear, I'll wait until he's feeling better."

"A house call. Very nice."

"I like that grilled salmon you make. Maybe with a nice Riesling?"

"It's starting to sound like a date."

"Nothing quite as romantic as dining with a detoxing junkie."

Hunter stood up. "Thanks for finding time for us."

"He seems like a nice kid." Miriam shook her head. "He's not going to seem that way for long."

"Yeah, thanks."

Hunter gave her a quick kiss on the cheek and headed for the front of the office. "Ready?" he asked Christian.

"Probably not," the kid replied. But he stood up gamely and followed Hunter out the door. He was quiet as they hit the pharmacy and the grocery store, barely seeming to notice where they were. On the way back to the SUV Hunter steered them into the town's small department store and said, "You should get some sweats, probably. Something comfortable. A few pairs." Enough to sweat through or puke on and still have something clean to change into. Jesus. Hunter felt like he was taking charge of an oversized infant.

Christian obediently pulled some clothes off the shelves, not looking too closely at anything about the items. He added a few packs of underwear and headed for the register. They'd picked up basic toiletries at the pharmacy, and Hunter racked his brain trying to figure out what else the kid would need. "Running shoes," he said.

Christian looked at him, then down at his sneaker-clad feet.

"Something with more support, something to work out in. Miriam said exercise might be good."

"These will work," Christian said.

"You're not going to get top-notch shoes in a place like this, but they'll have something better than those. A pair of work boots would be good too."

"I'm out of money," Christian finally admitted. "I have enough for the clothes. That's it."

"I'll advance you the cash. As soon as you're able, you'll be working, and you'll need boots for that. And you'll be able to work faster if you get some exercise while you're... sick."

The kid still looked reluctant.

"What size are your feet?" Hunter asked impatiently.

"I don't know. Twelve, maybe?"

Hunter strode to the footwear section and found a pair of running shoes and a pair of work boots for the kid, then insisted he try them on. The kid's socks had big holes in them, so Hunter grabbed a few packages of sports socks on the way to the cash register. "It's a long way back to town," he said as they stood in line. "If you're going to need something, it'd be a lot easier if you could think of it now instead of after we get home."

"I've never done this before. I don't know what I need."

"Okay, but you've been *alive*. What do you need for just, like, day-to-day stuff when you're leading a normal life?"

"I don't remember."

Not the answer Hunter had been expecting, but he supposed it made sense. "Okay," he said. He was tempted to reach out and put his arm around the kid's shoulders, but he restrained himself. Strange that he'd even wanted to, really; he wasn't usually physically demonstrative. Then again, he didn't usually take in detoxing junkies, either, so maybe he was just in the mood for trying new things.

They paid for their purchases, Christian contributing all his cash and Hunter making up the balance, then headed home after a quick stop at the Talisker place.

The cabin wasn't large. A bathroom, kitchen, and utility room at the front of the main floor, with Hunter's sleeping loft above it; the open living area was at the back with a wall of windows soaring to the peaked ceiling. Christian peered at the framed photos by the bookcase, and Hunter wanted to herd the kid away from them. Whatever was going on with Christian was separate from Hunter's friends and family, and it should stay that way. So he gestured toward the wall of windows. "I need to take down a few more trees," he said as Christian obediently redirected his attention. "Every couple years I cut them down so I can see the lake, and the bastards just grow back up again."

"Nature abhors a vacuum," Christian said softly.

It was unexpectedly philosophical and Hunter found himself wondering about the kid's background, his education, his family. How the hell had he ended up on the streets? But it seemed invasive to ask too many questions. Instead, he focused on the concrete things. "We're off the grid here, so you need to keep an eye on how much electricity you're using. Most of it comes from solar, but there's a generator that kicks in automatically if it needs to. But even with the generator, if you go crazy with electronics, you'll run out of juice. Oven, stove, dryer, and hot water are propane, but the microwave, washer, and fridge are all electric. So just take it easy. If you're doing laundry, hang it to dry. Or if you can't, if it's raining or something, use the dryer but not at the same time as the washer. You getting the general idea?"

The kid nodded.

"I've got a propane space heater you can use to heat the space over the garage, but there's no point doing that until the insulation is installed. I've got that bought and delivered, so maybe you can help me with it this afternoon. We'll see how much we can get done. We won't have time to put up wallboard or paint or anything, but the insulation is the main thing to make it livable, if not pretty."

The kid still seemed to be listening, so Hunter kept going. "There's a rough bathroom out there. I've got plans to make it nicer, but it's good enough for the time being. The water's turned off right now, but once we get the space warmed up we can turn it on."

"Okay," the kid said.

"Okay," Hunter agreed. "First, lunch. Get that bread cut up and we'll make sandwiches." He wondered if this would be the last meal the kid was able to eat and decided he should try to make it count. "I'll make a salad and heat up some soup. You like chicken noodle?"

"Sure."

What else was healthy? Milk. The kid should drink some milk. Or maybe juice. Nah, he could probably manage juice when he was feeling shitty, but milk would be harder to get down. So the kid should have milk now, while he still could. The bread was multigrain, and there were cold cuts for the sandwiches, so that was protein....

"I'm not actually a big eater," the kid said. "Just soup is probably good for me." He saw Hunter's expression. "Or maybe a bit of salad." He waited, then forced a smile. "Maybe half a sandwich?"

"What kind of nineteen-year-old doesn't eat like a horse?"

"The kind who gets everything he wants or needs from smack." Christian's eyes were a bit wild, suddenly, the muddled teenager fading away to be replaced by something Hunter couldn't quite classify. "I think you don't really believe it," he said softly, watching for a reaction. "I think you have some sort of... I don't know, some sort of fairy tale in your head where a good meal is going to make a damn bit of difference." He stepped closer, almost threatening in his intensity. "I'm a junkie. Food doesn't fucking *matter* to me. If I was drowning and there was a boat above me and smack below me, I'd fucking *dive* for it. I got kicked out of my house because I was stealing shit from my *family* to pay for junk. My friends? Anyone who has smack is my best buddy, anyone else is nothing. I suck cock, I get fucked, I do *whatever it takes* to get money to get a fix. Do you fucking understand that?"

"You say you want to quit," Hunter said quietly. The kid was right in his face, glaring, but Hunter kept his cool. "Where's that coming from? If *all* you care about is heroin, why are you trying to quit?" The kid eased back a little, but Hunter followed him. "Whatever that little part of you is, that tiny voice saying you can be something else, you can kick the habit... that part of you is *not* a junkie. *That* part of you is still you, whoever you were before all this started." He waited to see if the kid would respond, then stepped back and smiled. "So we just need to make that part bigger, and the junkie part smaller." Another pause to see if the kid would mock his simplistic argument, but he didn't, so Hunter pushed a little further. "The part of you that isn't a junkie? It needs a fucking sandwich."

The kid stared at him and as suddenly as the fierceness had arrived, it drained away. "Half a sandwich?"

"Make the whole thing. Eat half now and see if you want to finish it off later."

The kid exhaled sharply, not quite a raspberry but dangerously close. But then he went to the counter and found a bread knife and started cutting.

Hunter opened the carton of soup and tried to let his shoulders relax. One battle down. One battle more or less won. There would be more, he was sure. Many more. And he had no idea if the future ones would be resolved as easily.

CHAPTER FOUR

As expected, things went downhill from there. Christian helped Hunter in the afternoon, tidying up the future guest room and installing insulation, but as the day wore on Hunter could see the kid getting more and more restless. By the time they had the last rafter stuffed with pink fiberglass, Christian was shaking. Still trying to work, trying to ignore it, but shaking.

"You cold, or in pain?" Hunter asked quietly. "You want some ibuprofen?"

"I'd love some heroin, if you have any lying around."

"Don't think I've got any. You want to try the weed?"

The kid took a deep breath. "No. Fuck it, not yet. Let's keep going."

"Next step is doing the floor, from beneath. We can leave it for tomorrow."

"I could use the distraction," Christian said.

Fair enough. So they headed down the stairs and Hunter made sure he was the one climbing the ladder, but he kept Christian busy and tried to ignore the kid's weakness. By the time the floor joists were filled it was time to break for dinner, and Hunter was pretty sure he'd gotten all the work out of the kid that he was going to, for a while at least.

Christian struggled on, gamely following Hunter into

the cabin and sitting at the counter, but one look at the raw beef Hunter pulled out of the fridge had him sprinting for the bathroom. Hunter cooked his dinner to the sound of retching from the bathroom; years of living in suboptimal conditions had given him a pretty strong stomach.

Christian finally struggled out of the bathroom, pale and miserable-looking, and said, "I need to go lie down."

"Sleep on the couch," Hunter instructed. "I need to check on you, and I don't want to have to go out to the garage every damn time."

"I'm gross," the kid protested weakly.

Hunter agreed, but wasn't sure what conclusion he was supposed to reach based on the information. "I'll get a puke bucket. But you can't have much more left, I wouldn't think."

"I should—"

"Christian." It was the first time Hunter had said the kid's name, and it felt a bit strange in his mouth. "Do you honestly think you're in any condition to win an argument right now?" He waited until Christian's shoulders slumped in defeat. "Lie on the couch," he said more gently. "The sheets are still on it from last night. You'll be fine."

Christian did as he was told. Hunter cleaned up his dinner, then poured a little Pedialyte into a plastic cup and carried it over to put on the coffee table. Christian was huddled on the couch, shivering, and Hunter felt his forehead. Warm, but not scalding. It wasn't just fever making the kid shake. "Want another blanket?"

Christian nodded pathetically and Hunter pulled a couple of old blankets out of the linen closet. He felt helpless. Hayley was fifteen years younger than him and he'd helped to raise her, and he remembered this same feeling from times when she'd been sick.

So that was good, he decided, settling into an armchair and

trying to distract himself with the newspaper he'd picked up in town. He was feeling paternal toward the kid. Weird, but not something that needed to be analyzed or really understood. He was a good guy. He cared about people. Just because he didn't always act that way didn't mean the instincts weren't there; he'd just had to keep them buried in order to stay alive. Now that he was out of that line of work, he was letting a new aspect of his personality blossom. Miriam had said Christian had been borrowing from his pleasure centers and had to go through some pain to pay them back; maybe Hunter had been borrowing from his hardass center and needed to be a softy for a while until things evened out.

"Fuck," Christian gritted out. "How long has this been going on for?"

Hunter was pretty sure the kid wasn't going to like the answer. "The bad part? A few hours."

A long pause, then, "Fuck. It's not even really bad yet. Right?"

"I have no personal experience. But, yeah, I think it's going to get worse."

It did. Hunter tried to accept that he couldn't do anything for Christian and went through the motions of a normal evening at home. He washed his dishes, unpacked some clothes, and read a book, all while trying to pretend there wasn't a teenage junkie trembling on his couch.

When he couldn't pretend anymore, he gently said, "Christian?"

"Yeah."

"Do you want to smoke? Or some ibuprofen?"

"Yeah, okay." He slowly, tortuously worked his way to a sitting position.

"Which?"

"Both?"

So Hunter fetched the bottle of painkillers and shook a few into Christian's waiting, trembling hand, then rolled a thin joint and lit it, taking one quick puff for himself before handing it over. Christian inhaled deeply, let his head fall back against the couch, and groaned softly, the smoke filtering out of his mouth as he exhaled. "That might actually help," he said.

"I should have bought more of it," Hunter said. Christian waved the joint in Hunter's direction, offering it back, but Hunter said, "You keep it. Pinch it out if you don't want it all." He tried to tell himself that it was because he didn't want to share a joint with someone who may or may not have brushed his teeth after puking up everything he'd eaten in the last week. But really, there had been something about the line of the kid's neck, the groan of satisfaction, the way his lips had pursed around the joint.... Hunter needed to draw some lines, and one of them was that he wasn't going to be smoking up with the intermittently attractive junkie in his living room.

He waited until Christian had finished smoking, made sure the butt was extinguished, then said, "I'm going to bed. I'll check on you a bit later."

"You don't have to. I'll be okay." It almost seemed true; the shaking had almost stopped, and his color was better.

But Hunter didn't want to count on any magic cures. "I'll be up anyway," he said. "I'm not a good sleeper."

"You should try heroin. You'll sleep like a baby."

"Sleep like the dead," Hunter corrected bleakly.

Christian didn't reply, just took a careful sip of the Pedialyte and lowered himself back down until he disappeared from Hunter's view, blocked by the back of the couch.

Hunter slowly climbed the stairs to the loft: rustic wooden furniture, two skylights, and a king-sized bed that hadn't been used for much besides sleeping for far too long. That was the problem, he decided. The redhead in Vancouver had been a start, but he needed something more regular. Not Miriam; he wasn't looking for a girlfriend and he wouldn't risk their friendship with casual sex. But somebody. If he was getting laid regularly, if he *knew* where and approximately when he'd be having sex next, his mind wouldn't need to cast about so widely, looking for excitement from strange sources.

That was his best theory yet, he decided as he stripped off his shirt and eased out of his jeans. Yeah, he liked that one. He was going to stick with it for a while.

He hadn't been lying about being a bad sleeper, and when he woke sometime after two, he stumbled downstairs in the dark and peeked cautiously toward the couch. Christian seemed to be sleeping, at least. Miriam had said that insomnia was likely, but maybe she'd been talking about Hunter, not the kid.

He went out to the garage and peered at the bathroom. The stairs to the loft were on the inside of the garage structure, a nod to the cold climate, and the bathroom filled the space between the top of the stairs and the outside wall. He'd been planning to just throw a coat of paint on the rough walls and call it a day; the fixtures were functional, if not new, and it wasn't like he was trying to *encourage* visitors or anything. But maybe he could do a little better. Some tile, maybe something locally made if such a thing existed. And there was room for a better shower: Hunter could barely lift his arms to his head in the little prefab stall, and Christian's long limbs would have even less space.

He sat down heavily on a stack of dry wall. Christian. He was planning to redesign the goddamn bathroom for *Christian*? As if the kid would still be there by the time the project was complete. "I need to get a fucking dog," he said out loud. Or a cat, even. Hell, maybe he should tame a goddamn chipmunk and build a little guest suite for *it*.

He needed some exercise. *That* was what was wrong. He'd been stuck in the city, then driving, then coddling. He just had too much energy, with no appropriate release. He sneaked back into the cabin and got changed, found his headlamp, and set out on the rough trail he had to reclaim every year. He would damn well create a vacuum so he had room to run, whether nature abhorred it or not.

It felt good to move, good to breathe the cool night air and rediscover his forest. He did his five-kilometer route, enough for a good warm-up without exhausting him, then headed for the ground floor of the garage. He'd installed rubber mats over the entire concrete surface, then emptied the walls of anything sharp or unstable, and now it was his gym. He taped his hands and slid into his gloves, then did some work on the heavy bag in the corner. From there, on to the speed bag. It was old-school boxing stuff, but he still liked it. Then kicks, some stretching, and finally his favorite part of any workout. He'd never spoken the name out loud, but in his head he thought of it as *freestyle chaos*. Start with some sit-ups, then roll to his feet and attack the heavy bag, the hanging dummy, run up the wall and then backflip to attack an imaginary enemy on the ground. A few hits on the speed bag and then maybe back to the heavy bag, or some push-ups leading to a handstand. Whatever occurred to him, whatever felt right, as long as he was always moving.

The company had a gym in the city, but Hunter felt like he was being watched when he worked out there. Evaluated, assessed—when the company had first started it had been useful to get feedback on his technique from fellow experts, but now it felt like they were looking for weaknesses, things to use against him. It was much better to work out here, in privacy.

Or not quite privacy, he realized with a start. Damn, the kid was either really good at sneaking or Hunter was losing his alertness. There was no way a sick civilian should have been able to come into the room and sit down without Hunter even noticing. Well, he hadn't made it very far in, Hunter told himself. Christian was sitting on the bottom stair, just inside the door. And he was staring at Hunter with wide eyes.

"You're really good," he stuttered. "I don't know what that

was, but you're really good at it, right?"

Hunter eased onto the mats and stretched out his legs. It wasn't as easy to be flexible as it used to be, so he needed to work hard at it. "You feeling okay?"

"Better," Christian said. "Still not great. Wouldn't it be cool, though, if I just got a really light dose of it all? The doctor *said* it couldn't be predicted."

"That would be cool," Hunter said noncommittally. "She also said exercise would be good for you, if you can manage it. Feel up to that?"

"Not the way you do it," the kid said quickly.

"Want to just go for a walk?"

"It's nighttime." He looked embarrassed, then asked, "Are there bears?"

"Yeah, there are bears. But not many of them, and they're not looking for trouble."

"I don't think I'd *give* them much trouble. I'd just be dinner."

"You wouldn't give them much dinner, either," Hunter said. Damn, the kid was thin.

"I shouldn't go too far from the bathroom."

"Still puking?"

"Uh, no. I guess my body is emptying the crap from whatever orifice it can find."

"Nice. You drinking the Pedialyte?"

"Yeah. It's going right through me, but hopefully I'm soaking up *something* on the way."

"People pay a lot for cleanses."

"I'm gonna be scrubbed clean."

Hunter grinned. "Come do a few stretches, see how that feels."

Christian looked doubtful, but he stood up obediently and gingerly made his way to the mats. "I'm tired," he confessed.

"Yeah. Just stretch a little, keep it gentle."

The kid lowered himself to the mats as if he was ninety years old, but when he stretched his long legs out to the sides the angle was just as wide as Hunter's. Little bastard was flexible even with all the abuse he'd doled out to his body? Not fair.

They stretched in companionable silence for a while. Maybe Hunter should have felt as if his sanctum sanctorum had been invaded, but he didn't. The kid was innocent, at least in the ways that related to Hunter's combat readiness. At least, he probably was. "You're not a really skillful mole sent here to spy on me, are you?"

Christian looked startled. "There's people who want to send moles to spy on you?"

Well, that was a good point. Maybe Hunter's paranoia was a form of self-centeredness. Probably nobody really cared too much whether he was enjoying his workouts. "Aliens," he said. "We'll have to tinfoil the windows later on."

Christian didn't look convinced, exactly, but he let it go.

"I'm going to turn the water on out here," Hunter said. "We should have two bathrooms running if you're not feeling well. I don't want you busting in while I'm in the shower just 'cause you need the toilet."

"You need to preserve your virtue and modesty," Christian said solemnly.

"Something like that."

So Hunter showered in the tiny garage shower and decided he was definitely going to redo the bathroom; it was stupid to expect any full-size human being to use that stall. And it would give him something to do with his time. Getting shot in some off-the-map African village had been his wake-up call, and he'd started the retirement process as soon as he'd made the painful trip back to civilization and gotten out of surgery, but he hadn't really had a plan other than getting out before he got killed. Now, looking at a long winter of isolation and idleness, he figured he'd better work out something a bit more detailed. Home renovations would be a start.

He fell asleep easily and woke up to daylight. Daylight and groaning. Not the sexy kind. He rolled out of bed and jogged downstairs. The kid was on the couch, body so rigid it looked like he might be having a seizure.

"Hey," Hunter said gently. No response. "Hey," a little louder. "Hey!" He shook the kid's shoulder and his eyes jerked open, blurry and confused and drowned in pain. Hunter had seen eyes like that before, and he'd really hoped that he wouldn't see them again.

"Fuck," the kid ground out. He'd been sleeping, Hunter realized, the exhaustion enough to let him rest despite the pain. And Hunter had wakened him to this unpleasant reality.

"Shit, kid, I'm sorry." He felt useless. "I'll roll a joint, okay? Is it your muscles? You want ibuprofen?"

"I want smack," the kid gasped.

He'd been joking about it before, but this time Hunter was pretty sure Christian was serious. If there'd been a bag of heroin there, a lighter and some tinfoil and a straw, Christian would have been smoking it. And Hunter didn't think he could blame him. "Sorry, kid," he said. "Haven't got any."

Another seizurelike shudder ran through the kid's body, leaving him gasping. Hunter needed to do something. "Okay, that's your muscles. Ibuprofen, pot, and then we're going to try to walk around a little, okay? See if we can get them to relax." Hunter had no idea if any of that made sense. Hell, maybe the stretching the night before had set all this off. But Christian didn't argue, so they followed Hunter's plan.

All that day, through the night, and into the next day,

Christian suffered. Mostly in silence. Sometimes there were quiet but intense obscenities. Groans were reserved for times he didn't think Hunter could hear him, but he obviously underestimated the acoustics of the small cabin.

By Friday evening, he seemed to be getting better. The pain, at least, was fading, and he'd managed to eat a little soup midafternoon and keep it in his stomach for a couple of hours. But neither of them speculated about being on the downhill side of the mountain. They had no idea *where* they were, and they both knew it.

Miriam arrived for dinner and gave Christian a quick checkup, then let him sleep on the couch. "He's doing okay," she said softly as she sipped her class of Riesling in the kitchen. "A bit dehydrated, but not to a critical level. Obviously exhausted, but not much we can do about that, not right now. His tests came back clean, at least. I told him that but I'm not sure it really registered, so maybe you can remind him of it later, when he's less out of it." She smiled and reached out to brush the backs of her fingers against Hunter's stubbled face. "You don't look all that much better. You must have seen worse than this? Been around worse than this?"

Hunter nodded. Of course he had. Much worse. "It feels different when it's at home," he said tentatively. "I don't just mean in my actual house, I mean in this country." He shrugged. He wasn't sure if this was making sense or not, and if it *did* make sense, he wasn't sure what it meant about his capacity for compassion. "It's easier to keep it separate. I get on a plane, and I'm... I don't know, I'm somebody else. Somebody harder. And life in some of these places... everything's so fucking miserable to start with that you can barely notice a little extra pain dripped on top." He shook his head. "I don't know." Then he thought about it a bit more. "Actually, it used to kind of work in reverse when I was working. I'd see something beautiful—nature, or a mom smiling at her baby, or some kids playing—whatever—something that here I'd totally take for granted. And over there it would hit me like a fucking grenade."

"You compartmentalize," she said. "And when something doesn't fit in the compartment you've built, it shakes the structure of things. And you *need* that structure in order to do the job you do."

"Did," he corrected.

"Did," she repeated. "You're sticking with that?"

"It's been three days. You thought I was going to change my mind after three days?"

"I really didn't know. The whole decision caught me by surprise." She smiled, but there was too much wisdom in the expression for her to look truly happy. "Made me start wondering about what might have been, if you'd quit a few years earlier."

His smile was probably just as melancholy as hers. "We probably would have gotten sick of each other even faster."

"Yeah, probably." She took a longer sip from her wine, then said, "Do you need any help with anything?"

They ate their salmon and Hunter nagged Christian until he choked a little of it down himself, and then all three of them went for a slow, careful walk around the shortest loop of the forest. Hunter teased Christian about bears being attracted to the smell of salmon on people's breath, and Miriam told them about a yearling bear that had been hanging around the grocery store in town until it had been trapped and relocated. It took them about three times longer to get around the path than it normally would have and Christian collapsed on the couch as soon as they returned, but Miriam seemed pleased with his progress, so Hunter decided that he would be too.

Christian dozed while Hunter saw Miriam to her car, but he sat up when Hunter returned and nodded when Hunter waved the rolling papers in his direction. So Hunter rolled a joint, and this time he shared it, the two of them passing the burning ember back and forth as part of a worldwide ritual. "I used to be fascinated by people smoking," Hunter said. He'd never thought about it before, but now he could remember it as vividly as if it were yesterday. "They seemed like dragons, or something, bringing hot fire into their lungs."

Christian nodded thoughtfully. "That's what they call smoking smack." He looked at Hunter as if to be sure he wasn't sharing common knowledge. "Chasing the dragon. Because of the smoke, I guess, but also because the first time you smoke it...." He shook his head in fond reminiscence. "It's the best feeling you've ever had. Better than *anything*." Another look at Hunter as if to suggest the other excellent feeling that might rival it and making it clear that an orgasm wasn't quite on the same level. "But then every time after that, it's a bit... flatter. A bit less intense. So you take more and more, always trying to hit that one peak again, running after that one moment of perfection, enjoying the echoes but knowing they aren't the real music. Chasing after the dragon that you got to ride that *one time*."

Hunter sighed. "That's pretty poetic. Hard to reconcile that with the kid puking and shitting his way through withdrawal from his beautiful, spiritual experience."

Christian looked surprised, and maybe a little hurt. But he finally shrugged. "Yeah. It comes with a price, that's for sure."

There wasn't much to say after that. They went to sleep, and they made it through a few more days of Christian being pretty sick, and then one morning Hunter woke up and came downstairs to find Christian staring into the fridge like a lifelong Elvis fan who'd finally made it to Graceland. "I'm starving," he said. "Should I make us breakfast?"

"Sounds good," Hunter replied, and he settled onto one of the stools by the island. It seemed like one stage of life with Christian was coming to a close. He had no idea what the next stage would be like, but he was looking forward to finding out.

CHAPTER FIVE

By the time Hunter bought the materials for the new bathroom, Christian was ready to start working on it. Not full strength, maybe, but as Miriam had said, the issues now seemed more chronic than acute. The kid still tired easily, and his insomnia combined with Hunter's meant that some of their best work was done in the middle of the night, but the pain had dulled to an occasional throb, he was eating better, and most of what he ate stayed in his body for an appropriate period of time.

He started exercising with Hunter. At first he walked while Hunter ran and skipped the gym work entirely, but by the time they finished work on the bathroom he was running most of the way right along with Hunter, then doing some of the calisthenics with him too. By the first real snowfall Hunter had started showing Christian some basic martial arts moves, and the kid picked them up fast.

It was nice to have the company. Christian had moved into the garage shortly after he'd started eating, but he came into the house for breakfast and lunch, worked with Hunter through the day, and helped cook and clean up dinner. Sometimes they'd stay together and watch a movie or something in the evening; sometimes Christian would head out to the garage and read on his own, or whatever it was he did out there. Hunter was pretty sure there was some significant brooding and staring at the ceiling going on, but that was only fair.

Everything was good. They were getting work done on the house, cutting the brush on the paths and clearing the trees on the way to the lake, shoveling snow. Living. Christian had started taking more responsibility for meals, experimenting more than Hunter ever did. Sometimes he came up with brilliant flavors; only once had they had to abandon the meal and make grilled cheese.

Then Hunter started teaching Christian to spar and grapple, and everything went to hell. It caught Hunter by surprise. He'd honestly thought he was over whatever the hell that had been—the brief moment in the alley, the few flashes since then. But the first time he pulled Christian in tight against him, trying to show him a simple throw, it had all come back with a vengeance. A flash of want and need so strong he could barely understand what it was, a hyperawareness of the warmth and strength in the body next to his, and a dizzying, exhilarating rush of blood to his cock.

He was wearing a cup. It made it a bit less comfortable physically, but much less worrisome socially. Sure, maybe he was suffering through some sort of second adolescence where he got hard for weird reasons, but at least he didn't need to traumatize the kid with that knowledge.

He eased away from Christian and reached for his water bottle. He'd probably be better off just pulling out the waistband of his shorts and dousing the fire down below, but he squirted some water into his mouth instead. And then choked as he remembered Christian on his knees in the alley, swallowing....

"I need some air," he gasped, and he reeled out into the snow.

Of course, Christian followed him. "You told me not to do this," he observed. "You said it was bad to stand around in the cold without cooling down properly."

"It is bad," Hunter said. Maybe if he focused on the kid being a nagging little know-it-all he'd be able to get himself under control. "You should go inside and cool down."

"We're done?"

"For today."

Christian stayed a few moments longer, an awkward pause that suggested he wanted to say something, but he finally, mercifully, went back into the garage.

Hunter stayed out in the snow and tried to calm his racing mind. His cock could take care of itself.

It wasn't like he'd never gotten hard from grappling before. Especially as a teenager, any friction would create a natural response. And it wasn't like he'd never had flashes of attraction to men. Nothing frequent, but random, odd desires to kiss a friend when drunk had certainly occurred. And it wasn't like he was homophobic. There was nothing wrong with a man being attracted to a man. Hunter didn't have any gay friends, as far as he knew, but he'd never shunned anyone for being gay or looked down on them.

And, of course, it wasn't like he was gay. Even if this was more than some strange aberration, it would at most mean he was bisexual. He was still attracted to women. And there, of course, was his solution. It had been too long since he'd slept with a woman. That was all. He was back to the adolescent horniness stage. Almost two months since the redhead in Vancouver, and she'd been the first in probably four months before that. Nothing like taking a bullet to slow down your libido. But now it was back, and it was looking for any attention it could get.

So he'd go to town. He'd find a partner, maybe someone with potential for a repeat visit. It would all work out.

And it did. Christian gave him a bit of a weird look when he picked up his keys after dinner and said he was going to town, but didn't say anything. Hunter spent long enough at the bar to run into the ex-wife of a friend of a friend; a close enough contact so she didn't have to worry he was a psycho, distant enough that there should be no social recriminations. And she lived alone. The setup was perfect, the sex completely satisfactory, and they set a tentative date for a few days later.

It was all taken care of, he told himself, and then he pulled into the cabin's parking area and saw Christian chopping wood. The kid had filled out. He was still lean, but he had the start of a good set of muscles, and they were clearly visible through the thin shirt he was wearing in the surprisingly mild morning air. He was working hard, a steady, demanding rhythm, and when Hunter climbed out of the SUV he could hear a soft, muffled grunt with every stroke of the axe.

Fuck. Fuck. Fuck! It wasn't an aberration, and it wasn't misplaced horniness. Hunter wanted Christian. He wasn't exactly sure what he wanted to do once he had him, but it would definitely involve a demanding rhythm and muffled grunts. He leaned against the hood of the SUV and tried to cool his thoughts enough to figure it all out. He got nowhere, and finally Christian turned toward him impatiently. "There's fresh muffins on the counter, if you want. I baked." It should have sounded welcoming, but the undertone was clearly *stop watching me work and get your ass in gear.*

"I can clear for you first," Hunter said.

Christian shook his head and bent to start picking up the split firewood himself. "I can do it. I didn't get laid last night, so I've still got plenty of pent-up frustration to work off."

Hunter stared at him. The kid had a point. If Hunter had needed a break, at his age, what the hell was the kid feeling? He was nineteen... oh, fuck. "Did I miss your birthday?"

"What?" The confusion cut through the kid's irritation.

"Your birthday. You were almost twenty when you got up here. Did you already have your birthday?"

"Uh, yeah, I guess. A few weeks ago."

A twentieth birthday should have been marked by something. By someone. "I'm sorry Christian. I should have gotten you something."

"Are you shitting me?"

"What?"

"Hunter, you saved my fucking life. The way I was going I might not have *had* a birthday if you hadn't gotten involved. Or it might have been my last one. I don't think you needed to get me a card." Christian made a face. "And you don't need to worry about me getting laid, either. Sorry about that." He forced a smile. "The muffins are pretty good. I did that applesauce thing, so they're healthy. We need more applesauce, though."

Things were changing a bit too quickly for Hunter to keep up, especially after a night without much sleep. "I'll go try them," he said, grateful for an escape.

He went inside, ate a couple of muffins, and stared out the window, watching Christian work. Yeah, he wanted him. Absolutely. No point in dancing around that anymore. If it meant he was bi, then he was bi. Who the fuck cared about the label? The problem was, what could he do about it?

Nothing. The kid was... well, he was a kid. If he'd just turned twenty, he was almost fifteen years younger than Hunter. And he was Hunter's responsibility. Hunter's employee, even. No. Hunter would just have to man up and deal with the attraction, without turning it into the kid's problem.

So he tore his gaze away from the beauty out the window, had a shower, and went out to work on the snow blower, which had stopped working the day before. Christian saw what he was doing and said, "I can just shovel. It's good exercise."

"Yeah, okay, for now. But I should get this fixed sooner or later."

So Christian shoveled, Hunter tinkered, and they didn't talk. They went in for lunch and didn't talk much, either, beyond the necessities of sharing food. After lunch they usually took a little break, then worked out, and Hunter couldn't think of an excuse to break the pattern that day.

But now that he'd recognized his attraction, it was damn hard to ignore. They usually took turns running first on the path, one person doing the hard work of breaking through the fresh snow for a while, then letting the other take over. But it was pretty distracting to run behind Christian, watching his tight ass as he lifted his feet high enough to clear the fresh powder. So Hunter charged on ahead. Let the damn kid watch *Hunter's* ass and see how he liked it. Who cared if it meant Hunter was the one working harder for almost the whole run?

They got back to the gym and Christian said, "You're full of beans today. Lots of energy. You gonna show me who's boss in the ring?"

"There's no such thing as a ring," Hunter said seriously. "Fighting in a ring is for sports—it's a fantasy. I'm teaching you to fight for real."

"Okay. You going to show me who's boss *for real*?" And there was something daring in the kid's voice, something teasing, something that suggested he was willing to be bossed around in any way Hunter saw fit. There went all the benefit of not staring at the bastard's ass.

"Workout first. Save the fun for the end."

Unfortunately, there didn't seem to be any way to work out with someone you were attracted to without getting turned on. Every stretch, every movement reminded Hunter of the other ways Christian's body could function, and the light sheen of sweat on his skin was absolutely an invitation for licking. The heavy breathing was just a bonus torture.

When the time came for sparring, Christian pulled on his equipment with puppyish enthusiasm and Hunter knew he was doomed. There was no escaping the blue balls.

So they sparred, Hunter yelling instructions as Christian struggled with the basics, and they grappled, Hunter doing more yelling even though Christian's ears were almost always within a foot of Hunter's mouth. And Hunter got hard. Painfully hard. Which would have been bad enough, but the desire was affecting his brain, as well, and spreading through his whole body. Hell, Hunter was pretty sure his baby finger was turned on. His *spleen* was probably excited.

When he finally couldn't stand it anymore, he pushed Christian away and said, "Enough for today." Then he turned around, pretending to stretch, and tried to get himself under control. He thought about standing up and getting the hell out of there, but he needed to control this, not run away from it, so he stayed on the mat.

Christian was silent for quite a while. Then, out of the blue, he said, "You know I'm gay, right?"

Hunter froze. "I.... Yeah, I guess I do."

"Some guys on the streets aren't," Christian said calmly. "They go with guys for money, but if they had their choice, they'd be with girls. I'm the other way around, I'd say. It's not like I can't get it up with girls, but they're not my preference."

"Yeah. Okay."

"That's kind of how I got into it all," Christian said thoughtfully. Hunter really wanted to turn around and see the expression on the kid's face, but he didn't dare. "I mean, the drugs came first. Not smack, just... anything. You know. I liked the escape. So if there were two hot guys at a party and one of them had drugs to share, I'd go with the one who had the drugs. Makes sense, right?"

Hunter tried to do the math. If the kid was just turned twenty now and had been doing heroin for almost three years, but these parties had been happening before he started doing heroin—

"Right?" Christian prodded. "It makes sense to go with the guy with drugs?"

"Yeah, I guess. All things being equal."

"Yeah." Christian seemed satisfied with that answer. "The

problem was, it was kind of a slippery slope. You know. Like you said, all things being equal, it makes sense. But then it's hot guy with no drugs up against sort-of-hot guy with drugs. Once you choose the sort-of-hot guy once, you're probably going to do it again. Sometimes maybe I'd break the trend and go with the hot guy with no drugs, but more and more often the guy with drugs won." Hunter heard a flop and looked behind him to see Christian lying flat on his back on the mat, staring at the ceiling. "And then once the smack came along, forget it. Guy without drugs was absolutely out of the picture. All that mattered was who had drugs, or who had cash so I could buy drugs."

"Where were your parents during all this?" Hunter turned around; this conversation was interesting enough that he figured it deserved his full attention.

Christian looked startled by the question. "Oh. You know. Around. Busy. Whatever. But that's not the point. I was just trying to say... I don't know. I like guys. I like sex. I like sex with guys."

Hunter's mouth was dry, but he tried to sound cool. "Probably could have just stuck with 'gay.' Seems like a pretty good short form for all that."

Christian snorted. "Yeah, good point." He rolled over so he was lying on his stomach, staring right at Hunter. "I fucking love giving head," he said, his gaze never wavering. "One of my favorite things. I've blown lots of straight boys, and they liked it."

Hunter couldn't breathe.

Christian licked his lips, and Hunter realized that the kid was nervous, but he was clearly determined to continue. "So I'm just saying. If you've got some tension you want to get rid of.... Or if you're bored sometime and want to give it a try. Anything like that. You should let me know. It wouldn't have to mean anything. It could just be friendly. You know?"

Hunter managed to draw in a breath, but it was audibly shaky, and he could tell Christian noticed.

The kid grinned suddenly and finally broke eye contact, only to look back up with a more tentative expression. "I can't tell if you're turned on or totally disgusted," he admitted. "I mean, I know you were turned on before. And yesterday. You're not as sneaky as you think, I guess. But now...." Another nervous grin, and then Christian was moving. Slowly, cautiously, he was crawling across the floor toward Hunter. "If you're grossed out, you should tell me," he said gently. "Don't just break my jaw or something." He was still watching, assessing. "The doctor told me I'm clean. In case you were worried about that."

Hunter had no idea what it meant that the thought hadn't even crossed his mind. His oversight wasn't evidence of clear thinking, that was for sure.

Christian was so close now. One more cautious glance, and then he reached out and gently rested his hand on the bare skin of Hunter's thigh.

Hunter's muscle twitched involuntarily, but he was still frozen otherwise. Even his brain seemed stuck, locked between the extremes of *oh, no*, and *oh, please, yes*. He drew another shaky, gasping breath as Christian slid his hand up Hunter's leg, beneath his outer shorts, over his compression shorts, only to hit the hard plastic of his cup.

"*That's* no good," Christian muttered, apparently to himself. He pulled his hand back and threw a leg over Hunter's so he was on his knees straddling Hunter. He brought his hands to the waistband of Hunter's shorts. "Lift up," he ordered gently.

God help him, Hunter did it. He lifted his hips and let Christian ease his shorts down and deal with his cup, felt the cool air hit his exposed cock, and watched in horrified fascination as Christian licked his lips and then bent down to gently kiss the leaking tip.

"Very nice," Christian murmured.

Hunter fell backward onto the mat, trying to take his brain away from what he was allowing to happen, but then he propped himself up on his elbows. He needed to see. If he was damning himself, he at least deserved to see it happening.

And it was beautiful. Christian was either telling the truth about how much he loved cock or he was a much better actor than Hunter had ever seen him be. He was practically worshipping Hunter's cock with his eyes, his hands, his tongue, and finally his smiling, sinful lips.

It was hard to think about how Christian had gained his skills. Well, hard to think about anything with the perfect pressure, the active tongue, the suction, the fucking *vibration* he had going on. But even the part of Hunter's brain that was still somewhat under his control didn't want to think about how much practice the kid had done, with how many different men. But there had definitely been... *oh, Jesus, yes, just like that...* been some.... *fuck, yes...* some.... *Ah. God. Yeah....* Some practice... *Jesus, fuck, yeah.* It was too much. Hunter lost control of his thoughts, his body, every goddamn part of himself. There was nothing in the universe but Hunter's cock, Christian's mouth, and then the exploding pleasure of orgasm.

As he came down, he realized that at some point he'd fallen back on the mat, his arm crooked over his eyes as if to block out the light. The reality. He kept his arm there as he felt Christian drawing away, then carefully rearranging Hunter's clothes.

There was silence for longer than there should have been. Then Christian said, "It's not a big deal. It's just a blowjob. It doesn't mean you're a fag or anything."

"Jesus Christ, Christian!" Hunter's voice was a little muffled from beneath his arm, and he decided that he really needed to man up and at least make eye contact. So he sat up and stared at the kid, trying to ignore the slight gleam on his chin and the sated, cat-got-the-cream look in his eye. Cat got the cream. Jesus. But he needed to stay focused. "I don't care about being gay. I mean,

I'm not. Bi, maybe, but even that, I don't care." He paused. "Okay, maybe it's a bit weird. Strange to be discovering things like that at my age. But, whatever. I can deal with that."

Christian's eyes narrowed slightly as he smiled and said, "Okay, great. 'Cause I enjoyed that, and you seemed to enjoy that, so we can do it again whenever we feel like. Right?"

The kid didn't seem at all surprised when Hunter groaned and said, "No, we shouldn't. Fuck, Christian. Have you ever heard about patients falling in love with their nurses? Or, like, students getting crushes on teachers? People in positions of authority should not be messing around with people under their care. It's not a safe setup."

Christian narrowed his gaze even further, into a full-on squint of disbelief. "Are you fucking kidding me? Jesus Christ, Hunter, I'm not *falling in love* with you. I mean, I like you, man, and I appreciate what you've done for me, but this isn't about *love*. It's just sex. If you want something, and I want the same thing, we shouldn't have that thing because... because some idiot somewhere fell in love with his nurse? What?"

Hunter needed to have this conversation sometime when his brain was a little more functional, because he was pretty sure everything Christian was saying made sense. And he didn't move away when Christian eased along the floor a little, getting close enough for a long look at Hunter's face. "Seriously, man, it's just a blowjob between friends." He shrugged. "I make muffins, I do laundry, and every now and then I suck you off. Whatever."

"This is not... I'm pretty sure this is not following the rules."

"Fuck the rules," Christian scoffed. "What, are we in some ivory tower university somewhere? Some big corporation? The fucking *military*?" And there was a little extra emphasis there, an almost troubling acknowledgment that Christian was making reasonably accurate guesses about Hunter's past employment. But that was a worry for another time. "We're in the middle of the fucking forest. It's just you and me. I could go hook up in town, like you, but I figure it's pretty much even odds between me finding someone who wants me and finding someone who wants to beat the shit out of me, so I'm happy to stay here."

"Wait," Hunter said. "You didn't even…. I mean, that was… yeah, it was good for me. It was fucking *great* for me. But you didn't even come."

Christian's lips twitched. "I figured maybe I'd leave that for next time. I didn't want to freak you out all at once."

"Wait. You want me to… to reciprocate?"

Christian looked at him for a long moment, then shook his head. "No. If you *wanted* to, then, yeah, that'd be great. But a reluctant blowjob? One that's just payback, or whatever? That's not hot." He leaned back, stretching his lean body out as he said, "I could just jerk off while I'm blowing you. I'm not kidding, it really turns me on to suck guys off. The right guys. So, yeah, it'd barely affect your experience at all, as long as you don't freak out if you get a glimpse of some other guy's hard dick."

Judging by the stirring in Hunter's cock, a cock that should have been completely exhausted, he wasn't too concerned about any such glimpses. But the whole thing still felt a bit too good to be true, maybe. "Is there a gay version of Penthouse Forum? I feel like I should be writing them a letter."

Christian grinned tentatively. "So you're okay with it?"

"I don't know. I have to think about it."

"Think fast, Hunter. This grappling thing? It's fucking *hot*. If we're going to keep doing that, I want to be able to suck you off afterward. Or possibly during. Maybe before, just to take the edge off."

"I've created a monster," Hunter said, trying to laugh.

Christian's eyes were dark but dancing as he said, "You didn't create it, you just let me unleash it. And now it's free and it's *hungry*."

Hunter's cock liked the sound of that. But he forced himself to stand up and laugh it off. "I'm going to go shower. Then we can go clear those branches that are hanging over the driveway, okay?"

Christian didn't argue, so Hunter made his escape. He stood under the warm stream of water in the shower and let his mind play back over it all: Christian's lips, his mouth. And, damn it, his smile, his honesty, his courage. Hunter let his hand fall to his cock and thought about the ecstasy Christian had given him. Right or wrong, it had been incredible, and Hunter really wasn't sure he would be able to resist if Christian suggested it again.

Chasing the Dragon

CHAPTER SIX

"I'm at a loss for words," Miriam said. Hunter had sent Christian to the grocery store and stopped in to Miriam's office, convincing her secretary that he just needed a quick moment and could be fit in between Miriam's other appointments. But it had taken him longer than it should have to explain the situation to Miriam, and now apparently it was going to take her a while to respond.

She shook her head and stared at him. "Okay, it's not so much that I don't *have* the words, it's more that there are way too many of them and I can't get them all out at once." She paused, then reluctantly said, "And I don't think I'm the one who should be saying them. I'm your doctor, I'm *his* doctor, you and I have a history... I shouldn't be the one giving any kind of advice on all this."

"I didn't come to you as a doctor or as my ex," Hunter said. "I came to you because you're my friend."

She sighed. "Your friend who's also your doctor, his doctor, and your ex." She looked out the window as if hoping the billboard across the street might start flashing answers in her direction, then said, "Are you familiar with the campsite analogy?"

"The what?"

"The campsite analogy. When you're camping, you should always leave your campsite in the same or better condition than

– 63–

it was when you arrived. Right?"

"Okay...."

"Same goes for relationships. Especially those with an age difference, although I like to think it should apply to *all* relationships. You should leave the other person in better shape than when you found him." She shook her head. "I'm sorry, but it still seems weird to be using that pronoun with you."

"You've had five minutes to adjust. It's been more than two months for me, and I'm still not sure my head won't go spinning off my body."

"Months," she said carefully. "So is this the reason you brought him up here? You met him, you wanted him, you... you isolated him, groomed him, made him dependent on you, and now you're finally reaping the benefits?"

"No!" He searched his conscience. "No," he said more quietly, with more conviction. "I helped him because... because he needed help. The attraction was there, I guess, but it wasn't a deciding factor."

She seemed to accept that. "Okay. So in terms of the campground, he's definitely in better shape than he was when you brought him up here. But that was a separate relationship, I think. That was you helping him out. You did that. It's done. Good work. Now you're thinking about changing the relationship. I think the campsite rule should start from this point, not from when you first met him."

"Fine," Hunter said impatiently. "What does the campsite rule say about it?"

"Oh, I don't know. I just thought I'd mention the concept. You'd have to fill in the details yourself."

"What? You can't... come on, Miriam, give me a few hints, here!"

She smiled. "Well... ideas, maybe. First... you are a very handsome man, Hunter. Very fit. Your personality, when you're not being an emotionally remote asshole, is appealing. You are financially stable, although I'm not personally sure how long that's going to last, so possibly 'stable' isn't the right word. You have some money, we'll say, and you don't seem to be spending it very fast. So, you know... you're a catch. I don't think we need to worry that Christian is only attracted to you because of misplaced gratitude or anything like that."

"Okay. This is good. Everything except the part where you called me an asshole is excellent."

"But I'm not finished," she said gently. "Because Christian is a recently recovered *heroin addict*. He seems to be doing very well, but he's received no counseling and has rejected my attempts to get him *into* counseling. As far as we know, whatever issues sent him down the path to addiction are still present and have not been dealt with. That means that, despite surface appearances, he's likely quite fragile, emotionally. People leaving rehab are usually warned against entering any relationships for at least six months to a year. We're obviously still well inside that warning range."

Hunter felt deflated. "So it's a bad idea. I'd be messing up the campsite."

She shook her head. "That's the part that I really can't tell you. The problem with emotionally fragile people is the lack of resiliency. Things don't necessarily hit them harder, but they have more trouble bouncing back from things. It's like their misery canister is already filled to the top and the drain is clogged, so when even a little negative emotion is added, it ends up overflowing."

"Your analogies are killing me, Miriam."

She ignored him. "Eventually, he needs to get that drain unclogged. I think the best way to do that is through counseling, but apparently he's not ready for it yet. And, honestly, we're going to have a hard time finding anyone for him to talk to up here anyway. So maybe he can unclog it himself. Maybe you can help him unclog it. Maybe you rejecting him would add a little more misery to the cup and it will overflow. If you get involved with him now, maybe over the course of your relationship the drain will get unclogged and he'll be better able to deal with things ending in the future. Maybe you'll live together in bliss forever, or maybe you'll both get hit by a truck on the way home from town. I have no idea."

"You've given me two crazyass analogies, called me an asshole, and told me I might get hit by a truck. What kind of doctor *are* you?"

"Witch doctor," she said blandly. "You'd better keep an eye out for that truck."

"That's it? That's what you're leaving me with?"

"No. There's one more thing." She smiled at him and leaned forward. "Hunter, you're worried about this because you're a good man and you're trying to take responsibility for yourself. That's good. That's mature. But Christian? He's a good *kid*. I don't mean to get you worked up about the age difference again, I just mean that he's not worrying about your emotional state. He's thinking about himself. About what *he* wants, and what works for *him*. It's normal, and he's still young enough to get away with it. But that means that you're the only one really thinking things through. I'm sorry to add to your concerns, Hunter, but I don't think he's the only one you need to be looking out for. I think you need to be worrying about yourself, as well. You need to take care of your own emotional health, because I don't think Christian is going to."

"Yeah," Hunter said heavily. He'd been right to come see Miriam, even if she wasn't telling him exactly what he wanted to hear. "Okay." He looked at his watch. "Shit, I've messed up all your appointments again."

"I'll work through lunch, get caught up." She grinned. "This conversation was *definitely* worth it."

He headed out to find Christian waiting for him in the parking lot, the back of the SUV full of groceries. Hunter climbed into the driver's seat and started the engine.

"I got pork tenderloin," Christian said. "It was on sale. But I'm not sure. It looks kind of like... I don't know. There's something about it that makes me think of dick. Not necessarily in a good way."

And there it was. Hunter had felt it before, but not sober, and he'd always been able to dismiss it quickly enough. But this time he couldn't deny it. He wanted to kiss Christian. Just a friendly, "good to see you, you're a goof but yes tenderloin does look like a penis" hello kiss. Sure, maybe there'd be a suggestion of something else in there. A quick flick of their tongues to hint at what they'd get up to later on, but for now, it could just be a simple gesture of affection.

But Christian had never said anything about kissing. And Hunter hadn't really finished thinking about all of it, anyway. He backed out of the parking spot and headed for the road. "You need anything else in town?"

"Probably too early to suggest condoms and lube, right?"

"Jesus Christ, Christian, you shouldn't say that shit when I'm driving."

"It was the tenderloin, man. Got my brain going all kinds of weird places."

"It's going to be pretty hard to eat that if you keep going on about it."

"I think the *eating* will be okay. And I'm looking forward to slathering on the seasoning." He added a little extra sibilance to each s. "But I'm not sure how I'm going to feel about cutting it up."

Okay, if Hunter wanted to kiss Christian every time the kid said something funny or cute, he was going to have a hell of a time getting any work done.

It was just as well Hunter had kissing to worry about, he supposed, so that he didn't have to think about the condoms and lube comment.

The whole thing was getting out of control, but he didn't think he minded.

Still, he tried to be responsible. That day after lunch, when Christian turned to him expectantly, Hunter looked away and said, "I think we might need to do independent study for our workout today. You should do the usual routine. I'm gonna go for a hike, I think."

Christian's smile looked forced. "Nah, man, you don't have to. I can control myself." He held his hands up as if surrendering. "No more surprise blowjobs. I promise."

"It's not about you, Christian. I could have stopped you if I'd wanted to. And I'm not... I'm not running away. I'm not making a permanent change in the routine. I just need some time to think it over."

"What'd the doctor say?"

"I just had a regular check up with her," Hunter protested.

"Nah," Christian said simply. "What'd she say?"

Hunter gave up. He'd either lost his lying skills or Christian was overly perceptive. Or maybe Hunter wasn't really trying very hard to deceive him. "She was ambivalent. Worried that this isn't a good time for you to get into something. Apparently there's some rehab rule where you shouldn't be in a relationship for six months to a year—"

"A relationship? Fuck, Hunter, you should have found a gay doctor. Nobody's talking about a *relationship*! I keep telling you, it's just sex!"

Hunter thought of his kissing urges and nodded slowly. "She also said that I needed to look out for myself, and make sure I didn't get... I don't remember what word she used. Probably something about camping. But the point is, it might just be sex for you, Christian. But I'm not sure it would be for me."

Christian stared at him. He looked as if Hunter had confessed to being a Martian.

Hunter forced himself to laugh. "So, yeah, separate workouts today. I'm going for a hike. I guess you can do what you want, but I'd recommend the usual running and then calisthenics, and some time on the heavy bag. Watch your stance, focus on form, but try to build your power too. You're naturally quick and flexible, but you could use some work on strength." There, was that helping out the damn campground enough?

"Okay," Christian agreed slowly. He was still looking at Hunter a little strangely, but that wasn't something that needed to be resolved right then.

Hunter took the long route through the woods. It was about fifteen kilometers, and the trail hadn't been broken. He should have worn snowshoes, probably, but it wasn't as if he was actually trying to get anywhere. He just wanted some exercise, and some time to think. As it was, he didn't make it home until well after dark.

Christian was in the living room but stood up quickly when Hunter banged through the door. "You made it," he said. "I was thinking I might need to call in the search and rescue." Hunter didn't respond, so after a pause, Christian continued. "I made the tenderloin. It was pretty good when I had some, but it might not be all that *tender* anymore."

Hunter started shedding layers. He'd been dressed for the mountain winter, so there were quite a few of them, many of them a bit harder to peel off because they were damp with sweat. By the time he got down to his long underwear, he knew his erection was obvious, and he knew Christian wasn't looking away. "I've had that for the last five kilometers," he growled. It was true, and it hadn't been comfortable.

Christian grinned and tentatively walked forward, his gaze on Hunter's face as if waiting to be waved off. "I could probably help you out," he purred as he got closer.

"Wait," Hunter said. He'd decided that Miriam was right, and there was no real way to predict what was best for Christian. So Hunter would try to at least do what was best for himself. "I want to kiss you."

"Kind of hard to kiss someone when you're sucking them off," Christian explained as if speaking to a small child. Well, not that Christian likely discussed blowjobs with small children, but the tone was the same.

Hunter nodded. "Before, after, during breaks. Possibly at random times of the day. And I want to reciprocate on the blowjobs. I *want* to." He waited until Christian nodded his understanding, if not his acceptance. "I'm not saying you have to go along with that. It's your call. But I thought I'd put it out there. That's what I want from this."

Christian looked away for a moment as if suddenly shy. Or afraid? But when he looked back, his smile was calm and teasing. "You want a kiss? You think you're going to get one way over there?"

That was all Hunter had been waiting for. He shot his arm out and grabbed Christian's shirt, pulled him forward at the same time as they spun, so that Christian ended up with his back against the door, Hunter hovering in front of him like a cat who'd cornered his prey. Christian's eyes were wide, and he licked his lips nervously.

Hunter didn't want Christian to be nervous. So the first kiss was gentle, a quick exploration. Stubble and strength instead of smooth tenderness, but otherwise a kiss was a kiss. Hunter pulled away far enough to see Christian's face.

The nervousness was gone, replaced by his more customary grin. "*That's* what all the fuss was about?"

Hunter felt the tension drain out of him like water out of a shattered glass, and it washed his self-control away with it. The next kiss was primitive, savage, all the urges Hunter had been repressing since he met the kid, since before that, even, all the desire and frustration and need and hunger, all in one biting, sucking, punishing full-body kiss. And he wasn't going to run out of desire anytime soon. He pushed in, his hard cock pressing through his underwear to find Christian's straining against his sweatpants. He kept one hand on Christian's neck, the fingers wrapped behind and the thumb stretched out over his jaw, and used the other to yank their pants down. Hunter wanted skin on skin, and he wanted it now.

For the first time, he wrapped his fingers around another man's cock, and the heat, the pulsing vibrancy, the weight of it... it all felt *right*. He wanted to savor the moment, wanted to explore a little, but the beast he'd unleashed wouldn't allow it. It demanded to be fed, and he pulled Christian's cock over to his own and felt a jolt like an electric shock as his cock made the same discovery his fingers had made just moments earlier. He stared at Christian. He wasn't sure when they'd stopped kissing, but now Christian was watching him, wide-eyed, not looking nervous anymore, but maybe amazed.

The kid linked his fingers with Hunter's, wrapping both of their hands around both cocks, and whispered, "Like this," as he jacked them both, smooth and easy.

Hunter took the instruction, but as soon as his lips found their way back to Christian's, he abandoned the smooth and easy for something faster and harder.

He couldn't last long. Maybe a disgrace, at his age, to be coming so fast, but he'd been hard too long and this was all too new, too perfect. Christian slipped his arm around Hunter's back, helping to support him as his knees practically buckled, as his mouth opened in a wordless gasp and as his body released great white streams over their linked knuckles, over Christian's shirt, his own shirt. Everywhere. A baptism.

He giggled a little at the thought, and there was an answering vibration from the skin he found beneath his lips. He tried to straighten but his head ran into something. Christian's jaw.

Hunter had buried his mouth in the side of the kid's neck, gasping into skin that was now moist and a little red.

"That was quite a kiss," Christian said lightly, but Hunter could hear breathlessness in his voice.

Hunter fell to his knees. Partly because he wasn't sure his legs could continue to support him, but mostly because with the surface of his desire satisfied, he was eager to explore some of its depths.

He nuzzled in to Christian's pubes, letting Christian's hard cock rub along his stubbled cheek. There was an odor, musky and sweet, and he wanted to remember it. But he also wanted to do a lot more. He found Christian's balls with his hand, felt the weight of them, the firm promise. He had no idea why it felt more daring to run his hands behind to find the smooth skin of Christian's ass than it did to kiss his way along the kid's firm shaft, but it did. He didn't need to understand why.

He wasn't ready to delve any deeper into the ass crease, he decided, but he teased forward with one hand, slipping around and between the kid's legs until he reached his balls from that direction. He used his other hand to steady Christian's cock.

He looked up and Christian was watching him, his smile tight but encouraging. Okay. Yeah, Hunter wanted to do this.

He flicked his tongue out to taste the tip of Christian's cock. Bitter and salty, as he'd known it would be. But not unpleasant. Not at all. A wetter, deeper kiss, stretching his lips over the head until they found the widest part of the ridge, then backing off. He let his tongue explore the slit, slid down again, making it right off the head onto his shaft, and then pulled off. He might not have given a blowjob before, but he'd received them. He wasn't confident that he was going to be able to do anything too spectacular in terms of depth, but he could at least try to have a little technique.

"A fucking cocktease," Christian murmured above him. "I wouldn't have guessed that about you."

Hunter pulled away long enough to look up and grin. "You guessed a lot of other shit pretty well, so we'll let you off the hook on this one." Another wet kiss to the head that turned into something more, and Hunter slid his mouth as far down as it would go.

It wasn't very far. He wasn't gagging, he was just... out of room. He needed to figure this out, but maybe not right then. He used his hand to make up the difference, tried to get the rhythm right, and let himself savor the experience, the weight and texture and taste of another man's cock in his mouth. And then the sweeter experience of Christian tightening his fingers on his scalp, his murmured warning, and then the come spilling out over Hunter's tongue, down his throat....

Fuck, too much! Was there really that much come in a single orgasm? He pulled away, but he was already choking and Christian was still shooting, some of it hitting Hunter in the cheek, the rest of it going who knew where as Hunter turned his head and coughed, choked, gasped for air, and tried not to laugh.

Christian recovered first, and he was the first to let the laughter free. "Fuck, man, up until the end I thought you were lying about this being your first time! But that was a fucking mess!" He paused and Hunter could hear him trying to control his amusement as he asked, "Do you want some water or something?"

Hunter fell back on his haunches. His underwear was bunched beneath his knees, his face, his shirt, and possibly his hair were covered in come, he was gasping for breath, and he was kneeling in front of a male ex-junkie ex-hooker who was laughing at his inability to properly finish a blowjob. "I don't need water," he said. "I don't need anything. Everything's perfect."

And he meant it.

CHAPTER SEVEN

Workouts got a lot more interesting after that. So did everything else. Cooking breakfast, eating breakfast, cleaning up after breakfast... if they made it that far without at least one of them coming, it was a slow day. And Christian didn't seem too put out by Hunter's random daytime kisses. Sure, he often leveraged them into something more, turning what Hunter had considered a simple greeting into foreplay, but it wasn't like Hunter was complaining.

He wasn't complaining about much of anything at all. He tried to make it into town a couple of times a week to check messages on his cell and his e-mail, and every message that came to him seemed like it was addressed to someone else. The old Hunter. Harder, more guarded, less happy. Straighter, sure, but that was only part of it.

He typed messages back, conveying what he remembered about the military politics in some country he'd done work in or the terrain of a remote location where he'd spent time, and he had to stop himself from inserting happy little emoticons and comments everywhere. *The bunker was about 5 clicks to the southwest, just past a shale slope. LOL!*

Miriam was amused by it all, of course, but he could tell she was a little concerned too. She came out for dinner every now and then, usually unannounced because Hunter didn't have a working phone, and she watched the two of them fighting to keep their hands off each other and she shook her head.

"It's okay," Hunter told her as he walked her to her car one night just before Christmas. "I know, I'm taking a chance. I know I'm more attached than he is. But my misery jug is empty. The drain is unclogged. If something bad happens, I can handle it."

She shook her head. "You just *think* it's empty," she replied. "And maybe the drain isn't totally clogged, but it's slow. Why else did you quit your job and come up here to hide?"

"I quit because I loved life and didn't want it to end, and I came up here because this is where I live! I'm not hiding!"

"You're not hiding? You've been up here for almost four months, and who have you seen since you got here? Besides me and Kelli Fraser?" She saw his expression and rolled her eyes. "Yeah, I heard about that. But, seriously, you haven't gone out, you haven't looked up old friends, you've just holed up. That's what you do when you're stressed, not when you're feeling good."

He remembered Christian talking about heroin, and how he didn't need food because he got all he needed from the drug. It didn't seem like the best comparison, so he didn't mention it to Miriam. Instead he said, "I'm happy out here. Why would I leave somewhere that I'm happy?"

She just smiled and kissed him on the cheek, then got in her car and headed out, slipping only a little on the icy drive.

Hunter went inside and stood behind Christian as he did dishes. "Keep busy," he murmured, and then he did his best to make Christian disobey the order, running his hands everywhere, kissing him in all the spots that made him squirm. Rubbing up against his ass, two layers of denim making things less than efficient but not enough to completely remove the sensation.

"You can, you know," Christian said as he rinsed the last

plate and put it in the dish rack. "If you want to fuck me, you can."

Hunter froze. Christian calmly dried his hands and eased around, still braced against the sink, still within the circle of Hunter's arms and chest. "I bought stuff the last time I was in town. I'd be totally into it, if you want to give it a try. And you know my tests all came back negative. Miriam says I have to get retested again in a few months, but I've always been careful, and we could be careful." His shrug was overly casual. "If you want."

"I don't know."

"Don't know if you want to, or don't know how? Have you ever gone back door with a woman?"

"Uh, no. Never have. Front door always seemed pretty welcoming."

Christian grinned. "The back door can be friendly too. More casual, less formal." He lowered his voice to a whisper. "It's where friends come."

Hunter laughed. "Maybe we should try it." It wasn't like the idea hadn't crossed his mind. Repeatedly. But it also wasn't like he really needed anything more than what he was already getting.

Maybe it was all the talk of doors that did it, but Hunter jerked away from Christian, startled at a sound in the driveway. A sound like someone slamming a car door.

Christian frowned. "Is someone here?"

By the time Hunter smoothed his clothes and got to the door it was being pushed open, a gust of wintery air almost seeming to propel the parka-wrapped figure inside.

"Hayley," Hunter said. Hayley. His sister. At the cabin. What the hell was going on?

"Hey!" she said brightly. "Did you get my message?"

It had been several days since he'd been to town. "Sorry, no. But, hey, come on in." His brain was stuttering, struggling to make the necessary adjustments. "Hayley, this is Christian. He's...." What the fuck was he? What was Hunter supposed to say? How could he explain this?

"I'm staying over the garage," Christian said smoothly. "I'm kind of a refugee. You're Hunter's sister?"

Hunter shot him a confused look, and Christian gestured to the photo by the bookcase. "I've seen pictures."

Okay, that made sense. And Christian's powers of observation were the least of Hunter's worries right then. His erection was dying fast, thankfully, and Christian looked pretty respectable... no sign of what had been going on before Hayley opened the door. "What did your message say?" he managed to ask. "It's good to see you, but what are you doing here?"

"Frank was being an asshole," she said with an eye roll. "Again." Frank was their stepfather, and Hunter had to agree that the guy spent a fair bit of time being an asshole. Only a decade older than Hunter, he seemed to think that marrying their mother gave him some sort of authority over Hunter and, especially, Hayley. Hunter ignored his nonsense on the few occasions they had to be in the same room, but Hayley had been planning to spend Christmas at home with their mother and Frank. "He was all, *my roof, my rules*, and all that shit. You know?"

"What rules were you breaking?"

Another eye roll. "Apparently I get *one* glass of wine with dinner. I'm nineteen, Jack, I could go to the corner and buy my *own* damn bottle of wine. So I did. Then he said it wasn't about the expense, it was about me learning moderation. Like that's *his* fucking job to teach me. And come on, one glass of wine with dinner? Over the holidays? That's not moderation, that's deprivation. He's full of shit." She glanced toward Christian as if aware that she was airing dirty laundry in public, then smiled at him apologetically. Wait, maybe more than apologetically.

Maybe flirtatiously? "Sorry," she said. "You're Christian? And you're a refugee too? I guess we have something in common."

"I guess we do," he said, and his voice was warm.

Hunter resisted the urge to jump in between them and wave his arms in the air as a distraction. "Have you eaten?" he asked instead. Food was always a good way to catch Hayley's attention.

"And would you like a glass of wine?" Christian added. "Or the bottle...."

Hayley laughed a little sheepishly. "I'm not a raging alcoholic. There was just lots of little stuff like that. He's a control freak, and I'm not interested in being part of that." She looked at Hunter and said, "If there's food, that'd be great. I drove straight through." She turned back to Christian. "And a glass of wine would be lovely, thank you." Another smile, her gaze resting on Christian for just a little too long.

Jesus Christ. Hunter's baby sister was going after his man. This was... well, obviously it was unforeseen. Essentially unforeseeable, although when Hunter sneaked a look at Christian he realized that the gangly kid was gone, replaced by a lean, tall, well-muscled young man. So, okay, Hunter could have anticipated that Hayley might find Christian attractive, but he couldn't have anticipated that they'd be in the same room together. So, yeah, he was sticking with unforeseeable. What else was it? Creepy? Yeah, it felt a bit creepy. He stuck his head in the fridge to find leftovers and cool off. He was a bit concerned that the creepiness came at least partly from him being involved with someone young enough to catch Hayley's eye. The same-sex thing was... well, it was part of the problem, obviously, because if Hunter had been dating a younger *woman*, Hayley wouldn't have been attracted to her. Unless latent bisexuality was a family trait.... Fuck. He needed to get himself out of his head and his head out of the fridge.

He straightened and said, "There's pork. Christian likes to

cook, and he's been doing some really interesting things with tenderloin lately."

He shot a quick look in Christian's direction, forbidding comment, but it was Hayley who giggled and said, "Tenderloin? Is that the part that... you know...."

"Yup," Christian said calmly. "That's the part." He looked at Hunter, practically begging for permission to unleash the innuendo, but Hunter frowned back at him. So Christian smiled politely and said, "This round I tried for a sort of spicy sweet-and-sour thing. Asian-inspired, I guess."

"Sounds great," Hayley said. She hung up her coat and slipped out of her boots, then padded over to sit on one of the stools at the kitchen island. Hunter put a plate together for her while Christian pulled out three wineglasses and filled them up.

"So, Christian," Hayley started. "I'm escaping the authoritarian stepfather and uncaring mother; what are you running away from?"

"Dragons," Christian said, smiling to take any sting away from his evasiveness.

And Hayley didn't seem put off. "Dragons? Those can be nasty. Do you need a princess to rescue you?"

He had a *prince*, goddamnit. Hunter set the plate in the microwave with more of a clatter than was absolutely necessary. If they'd been alone and Hunter had gotten frustrated by something, Christian would have soothed him with a gentle touch, a teasing smile. Possibly a blowjob. But Hayley was here, so all Hunter got was a disapproving frown.

"You're staying right over Christmas, then?" Hunter asked, making himself smile at his sister and then taking a deep swallow of wine.

"Yeah, if that's okay. I could have set something up to stay with friends, but it feels a bit pathetic to do it now. School starts again after New Year's, so I'll head back down then."

It wasn't like Hunter'd had *big* plans for the holiday. He wasn't going to dress up as Santa, wasn't planning anything more than some champagne in front of the fire for New Year's Eve, but he'd wanted to spend the time with Christian. *Just* Christian.

But maybe it didn't have to be a total loss. He watched Christian chatting with Hayley and wondered what the holidays would be like if Hayley knew about them. If Hunter could still touch Christian even with her around. Okay, the fucking was probably out considering that there wasn't a real wall between the sleeping loft and the rest of the cabin. That was too bad, but fucking could wait. If Hayley knew about them, she wouldn't be surprised at the top-of-the-line MMA gear Hunter had ordered for Christian's Christmas present. She wouldn't be shocked if they kissed good morning, or if Hunter sneaked up behind Christian and nuzzled into his neck. She'd probably either make herself absent or at least manage to be discreetly distracted if they kissed at midnight on New Year's, a real kiss, full of the passion and affection that Hunter wanted to start the year with. And Hunter wouldn't have to feel that he was keeping a secret from his baby sister.

"Christian's actually been living up here for quite a while," he said in the next break in conversation. Hayley looked interested.

And Christian looked uncomfortable. "I'm working for Hunter," he said quickly. "You should see the guest room, and the trails are all cleared. I've really learned a lot."

"That's great," Hayley said. "And how do you guys know each other?"

Fuck. That was a natural question to ask, but Hunter couldn't answer it without giving away information that Christian might want to keep under wraps.

But Christian was ready. "Help-wanted ad. Seems like your

brother can't do quite *everything* by himself. Putting up a drywall ceiling is *not* a one-man job. And I needed a place to stay."

"So the dragon story wasn't real?"

"Metaphorical," Christian said.

"I don't remember you ever having a roommate before," Hayley said to her brother. "Is this part of your whole 'retirement' plan?" She looked back at Christian. "Can you believe that someone could *retire* at thirty-four? I mean, 'private security'— to me, that's a mall cop. But apparently it's really something a bit more lucrative!"

Christian nodded, unfazed, and Hunter squinted at the kid, trying to figure out how much he knew. They'd never discussed Hunter's profession, just like they hadn't talked about Christian's life before heroin. Maybe it was a sign they didn't trust each other, but Hunter preferred to think they were both focusing on the present, leaving the past behind. Or maybe it was because Christian had already figured out what Hunter did, somehow. Had Hunter left clues? Had Miriam spilled more than she should have? Did it matter?

Hayley was still talking, apparently to Hunter. "So, it's part of your retirement? You used to work so much and travel all the time, and then you stay put and realize that your mountain serenity is a bit lonesome?"

"Something like that," he agreed. "I had the space, Christian needed a place. It worked out."

"And he *cooks*!" she said, taking the last bite of her pork and smiling happily. "I don't care *what* that looks like when it's raw—you made it taste delicious."

They spent the rest of the evening chatting with only occasional periods of awkwardness. And apparently Hunter was the only one who felt those, because the other two seemed perfectly relaxed. When they started thinking about bed, Christian said he'd put fresh sheets on the guest room bed and sleep on the couch, and Hunter didn't argue; it'd be good to have Hayley safely out of the building, if possible. Maybe Christian could be lured up to the loft....

But Hayley, of course, refused. "I've slept on this couch lots of times, and it's got to be easier for me to fit—you're so tall and your shoulders are so wide, you need a full-sized bed, for sure. And the couch is what I expected when I came; Jack's been talking about turning that space into a guest room for years, but he's never gotten around to it until now."

Hunter had nothing to say to that, so he found sheets and a pillow for Hayley, and by the time he had finished with that Christian had disappeared, gone out to the guest room alone.

It didn't feel right, Hunter decided, lying restlessly in his bed. He needed to talk to Hayley, but he should talk to Christian first. So he waited until he was sure Hayley was asleep, then sneaked down the stairs and out to the garage. When he climbed to the guest room he found Christian lounging on the bed, lights on. Clearly waiting.

For once, Hunter didn't rush over and start fondling the other man. Instead, he hovered by the doorway and said, "I want to tell her."

Christian shook his head disgustedly. "I *knew* you were going to say that. Jesus, Hunter, is it really any of her business? What does it matter if you occasionally exchange blowjobs with your roommate? That is *not* the kind of detail people need to share with their little sisters!"

It stung. It always stung, every time Christian did it, but this time was somehow worse. Bad enough that Hunter was going to respond. "We're more than roommates," he said quietly but firmly. "We're doing more than exchanging blowjobs, and we're doing it a hell of a lot more often than *occasionally*."

Christian stared at him. "Okay, yeah, I'll give you the frequency thing. We're doing it a lot. But, Hunter, how many times can I fucking tell you this? It's just sex. It's not... whatever the fuck you're thinking it is, it *isn't*."

"It is for me."

"Well, that's unfortunate. But trust me, you'll snap out of it soon enough. And when you do, you'll be fucking sorry if you've dragged your baby sister into it."

"I'm a grown man, Christian. I know what I'm feeling."

"You're a virgin. For this stuff. And you just got out of some work trauma, and don't think I haven't noticed how fresh that scar on your shoulder is. You don't trust *my* opinion, you should at least trust Miriam's, and she's worried about you."

"What the fuck did Miriam say to you?"

"Nothing. She doesn't have to *say* anything, not when she's watching you like a... I don't know. Like a mix between a hawk and a momma bear trying to protect her cub."

That was a disturbing mental image. Hunter needed to get the conversation back on track. "It's not really your call," he said. "I just wanted to give you a heads-up so you don't come in for breakfast and get hit with a big reaction from her."

"No, Hunter, this is stupid. You're making bad decisions, here. And the fact that you think I don't get a say in what you do? That kind of *proves* that we're just fuck buddies, doesn't it? I mean, if we were... whatever the fuck you think we are... boyfriends, or something... then I'd have a right to make this decision *with* you, wouldn't I? I mean, you're not just outing yourself."

"That's ridiculous. She's *my* sister. You don't get to control what I tell *my* sister because *you* suddenly want to be in the closet. No way."

"Just give it some time," Christian said. He rolled over so he was on his knees on the mattress, his dark eyes almost pleading. "You don't need to decide anything right now. If she comes back for the summer and you're still feeling this way, okay, great, tell her then. If you're done with me and I'm long gone, you don't have to mention it. You can go back to the way you were, no harm no foul."

"I love you, Christian." He hadn't planned to say it. Not yet, not this way. Maybe in front of the fire on New Year's Eve, maybe some other time when it just burst of his chest and refused to be hidden any longer. Not like this. But he'd said it, and he wouldn't take it back. "If you don't feel the same way, I can deal with that. I mean, if you need to take some time, get used to the idea, that's fine with me. I understand. But—"

"Jesus Christ, Hunter!" Christian sounded almost pained. "Have you lost your fucking mind? You're straight, asshole. And I'm a junkie whore." He swung his feet off the bed and approached Hunter almost menacingly. "You think that's *fixed*? You think I'm *cured*?" He shook his head and his next words were almost a sob. "You think I don't wake up every single fucking day and have to fight with myself to stay here and do work with you, instead of hitching back down to the city and getting lost in the smoke? Are you that fucking *blind*, Hunter?"

Apparently Hunter was exactly that blind. He'd known Christian had moody periods every now and then, but nothing like this. "You're exaggerating," he tried.

"You know why I won't sleep with you? Why I come back here every night instead of staying in the house? Because I don't want you to see me lying here in a cold sweat, wanting smack so bad I can feel it in my lungs. I don't want you to see me almost cry when I wake up from a dream of being high and find out that I'm still stuck right fucking here."

Hunter licked his lips. "Okay. No, I didn't know all that. But it doesn't change how I feel about you. I love you, Christian. If you're going through all that... I don't know what there is that can help you, but we should look. And you *can* sleep with me, and if you wake up like that, I can be there—"

"Jesus," Christian said. He flopped back onto the bed in defeat. "You think you being there is going to do any fucking good? You remember what I told you? How if I was drowning and there was a boat above and heroin below, I'd dive for the heroin? You're in the boat, Hunter. You're the captain of the fucking boat, and you're cruising along like it's just a nice day for a sail, and you see me and you think you can just pull me on board. But you can't." His next words were barely audible. "But I can pull you into the water with me. And I don't want to do that."

"These are separate issues," Hunter said slowly. "A *lot* of separate issues. I mean, telling Hayley or not telling her—that's kind of a detail at this point, isn't it?"

"The more people who know, the harder it's going to be for you to move on," Christian said dully.

"Telling people is not the part that would make it hard for me to move on," Hunter said. He wanted to go to Christian, wanted to wrap him in his arms and hold onto him and squeeze out all the demons inside. But he knew Christian would shy away from that contact. "I have no idea what to say."

"So keep your mouth shut," Christian suggested. "And stop thinking stupid shit."

Stop feeling, stop loving. Hunter almost wished he could. For now, he was drained. Possibly in shock. He needed to regroup and find a new way to make things clear to Christian. And he absolutely, without a doubt, needed to figure out some way to help Christian move on from his past.

For the time being, though, he stepped backward. "I love you," he said quietly. Christian had his head buried in his hands and didn't respond.

Hunter went back to the house and lay in bed, unsleeping. He finally dozed off sometime around dawn and woke up a couple of hours later. He stumbled downstairs and found the couch empty. Hayley wasn't in the kitchen, and the bathroom was empty. Her parka was still by the door, so she hadn't gone for a walk. He knew where she was.

He walked out to the garage and opened the door. He felt like he was in a dream. A nightmare. No reason for this to be anything but innocent. Two young people getting to know each other in the only space where they could talk without waking up the old man. It didn't have to be something bad. But even before he heard the first moan, he knew that it was.

He walked up the stairs because he couldn't do anything else. As he neared the top he heard the murmured words, the throaty laugh, and the soft sounds of bodies moving together. He stood on the landing and looked into the bedroom. Hayley still had her tank top on, but Christian was naked, stretched out on the bed on his back, his hands on Hayley's hips as she rode him, slow and sensuous. He was looking up at her, but after only a few moments he turned his head and stared at Hunter, his eyes the same glittering dark pools they'd been that night in the alley, his face the same expressionless mask.

Then Hayley followed Christian's gaze and shrieked, grabbed the sheet to wrap around herself, swore at Hunter, told him to get out, what the hell was he doing, what was wrong with him?

Hunter asked himself the same questions. He couldn't tear his gaze from Christian, stretched out on the bed, cock still hard and ready. Waiting.

Hunter didn't make him wait too long. "Get the fuck out," he said. "Get out of here!"

"Jack! No! It wasn't his idea! And since when are you such a fucking prude, anyway?" Hayley still had the sheet wrapped around her but apparently she'd gotten over most of her shyness.

Hunter didn't look at her. "Get out," he repeated, staring at Christian.

Christian swung his legs over the side of the bed and pulled on the underwear and jeans that were waiting nearby. His shirt was close too, and his socks and boots.

"This is crazy, Jack," Hayley said. "Why are you being like

this?" She stepped between Hunter and Christian, trying to break Hunter's stare. "You're being just as bad as Frank! Seriously, Jack, if you kick him out, I'm going with him!"

"No," Christian said softly, and she whirled to look at him. He smiled gently. "This isn't about you. It's something else. It's been coming for a while." He picked up the knapsack waiting by the door. Already packed, some part of Hunter's brain registered. "It's time for me to go."

"This whole thing is crazy," Hayley said. She was crying now, and Hunter knew he should comfort her, but he couldn't make himself do it. And when Christian approached him, needing to get by in order to leave, it took every ounce of self-control Hunter had to step aside rather than throwing the bastard down the stairs and chasing after him to finish the job.

Christian seemed to realize the danger and moved fast, down the stairs and out the door before Hunter really understood what was going on. He stared after the kid for far too long, Hayley yelling at him and crying and demanding to know what the hell was going on. He couldn't tell her. He could just stare at the closed door and wonder what the fuck had just happened, what freight train had plowed through his life, and how he could ever recover from the carnage it had left in its wake.

Kate Sherwood

PART TWO

Kate Sherwood

CHAPTER EIGHT

It was by far the weirdest job interview Christian had ever been to. They hadn't even called it an interview. Just a "meeting to discuss employment opportunities". He kind of liked the sound of that, like *both* sides got to feel the other out and make a decision, but there were other things he didn't like at all. He especially didn't like it that he'd been approached out of the blue, at the gym after a sparring match. The two men in suits hadn't seemed like thugs, exactly, but there was something off about them. If they were looking for hired muscle, they were looking at the wrong guy.

Because Christian was strictly legit these days. He'd been clean for more than three years, working construction most of the time, and if his jobsite hadn't just closed, leaving him laid off until something new came along, he would have told the guys in suits he wasn't interested. As it was, he wasn't desperate for money, but he needed to stay busy. Even after being off the junk for so long, free time was not a good thing for Christian. Not at all.

So he showed up to their hotel conference room in downtown Calgary, wearing dress pants and a shirt and tie, and sat down when they invited him to. Then he waited.

The first guy to speak was British and sounded like he'd gone to all the right schools and did all the right whatever the hell they needed to do in England to qualify as posh. He didn't offer a name but he extended a well-manicured hand. "Thank you for coming to see us."

"Thanks for inviting me," Christian said. He guessed he was grateful. Maybe.

The other guy just nodded a wordless greeting, so Christian nodded back. Neither one had offered him a name, which was a bit weird and worrisome, but he was in a pretty public space, so he didn't let it make him paranoid.

"We're founding partners and members of the board of a midsized private security firm. Do you know anything about private security?"

Damn, it had been long enough that Christian should have gotten over it, but there was still an unpleasant twinge at the memory. "Mall cops?" he asked innocently.

The English guy didn't look impressed. "Not quite. Something a little less routine than that, generally. Although we do some domestic work in the area of protection for vulnerable citizens—bodyguarding, you might call it—most of our work is international. The globe's natural resources do not always fall into geographic areas with great political stability. The people of the world need these resources, and the corporations of the world wish to help extract them. But in order to do so, they need some level of safety and order for their employees. A significant part of our business involves providing that safety and order."

Christian nodded. It was probably a pretty careful way of describing what they did, but he got the general idea.

"Most of our staff is recruited from the world's militaries," the man continued. "These bodies provide excellent training and discipline, as well as valuable experience. If a man or woman can be an exemplary soldier, he or she will probably also be a good member of our team."

"Yeah." None of this was exactly news. Not to Christian, and probably not to anyone else who'd heard of Blackwater or any of the other big mercenary outfits. "I've never been in the military, and I'm never going to be."

"Because of your father," the man said smoothly.

Okay, that was surprising. And unsettling. These guys had a lot more information about Christian than he did about them. But they couldn't see inside his brain. "Because of me," he clarified. "I don't do well with that kind of authority."

"You'll follow someone who's earned your respect, but you won't follow someone who's just been given a rank for no reason you can see."

"Something like that, yeah."

"Nevertheless, your father's military leanings have had *some* influence on you. We understand you're a skilled marksman."

"I haven't held a gun in eight years, at least. I did the junior stuff because my dad wanted me to."

"You did very well at it."

"Seriously?" Christian wasn't sure how much longer he wanted to bother with this conversation. "There are guys coming out of the military who are experts at practically every weapon invented, trained snipers, whatever, and you're pretending to be impressed by some bullshit junior trophies?"

"You're also a skilled martial artist."

"Not in the same league as some ex-military guys. Hell, I'm working hard just to match some of the guys at my gym."

The man looked at his colleague and finally the other man spoke. His accent was hard to place, with weird vowels and kind of harsh on some of the consonants. It sounded like a German pretending to be an Australian. South African? "You have other qualities that interest us."

Christian waited, and finally raised an eyebrow. "Can you be a bit more specific?"

"Ex-military recruits tend to be used to working as part of

a team. A hierarchy," the English guy said. "They take orders, and they follow through. This can certainly be valuable. But there are times when we need someone who can work better alone. Someone with intelligence and initiative. Someone who's willing to be flexible and do what it takes to get things done."

"What evidence have you seen that I'm intelligent?" Christian asked. "Why do you think I have initiative, or that I'm flexible?"

"Prior to your difficult years," the man said with a somewhat greasy smile, "you excelled academically. This shows intelligence and initiative. And during your time off the grid, you... well, you survived. You did what you had to do. That shows flexibility."

That was pretty weak evidence, and Christian felt like these guys should realize that. Judging by their expressions, the possible South African totally did.

"We have no idea if you'll work out," he said. "Personally, I have serious doubts. But if the experiment were successful, you'd be useful. That's all."

"Why me? There's no way I'm the only—"

"You're the one we're talking to right now," the South African interrupted. "But, no, you're *not* the only one. You won't be the only one at training, and if you fail there, I have no doubt you won't be the only one going home."

"You guys do this kind of recruiting as a regular thing? The background checks and all that?"

"You actually came to light as part of a different background check," the Englishman said.

Christian wouldn't let his mind go there, wouldn't wonder about who he had any connection to that might be involved in a private security company—

"Apparently your father is exploring his options for after retirement," the man continued, and Christian tried not to react. *His father?* "The general wouldn't be a member of our day-to-day operations, but we're discussing the possibility of some sort of relationship with him."

Well, that made things simple. "I don't think I'm interested."

The man raised an eyebrow. "Really? Still? After all these years, he still has that kind of hold over you? You'd walk away from the possibility of a lucrative and rewarding career just because you don't want to run into Daddy?"

"You wouldn't be working near him anyway. Not at his level." The South African sounded amused. "We really don't anticipate you making contributions in the areas of military strategy, government contacts, or corporate relations."

"Think of it as a training opportunity," the English guy said. "You aren't working right now, so you've got nothing to lose. You'll be fed and housed, paid, and you'll have access to excellent instruction in a variety of areas, including martial arts. If things work out, you'll have a job that pays three or four times as much as your current work. If things *don't* work out, you come back here a little fitter and a little better trained and pick up your old life where you left it."

"I'm gay," Christian said. "In case that gets in the way of anything. I've got no plans to start hiding it."

"We have no plans to ask you to." The man's smile was a little tight. "As we said, we're interested in you because you're *not* the cookie-cutter ex-military type."

Christian was tempted. He wanted to ask about Hunter, but he couldn't find the words. These guys wouldn't tell him anyway, probably—personnel records had to be top secret, he was sure. Would Hunter have shown up in Christian's background check? Probably not. There were lots of people who'd seen him screwing up in high school and selling himself on the streets, but hardly any who'd known about the time he spent at Hunter's cabin. And using Hunter's name here, with these people—would that be violating a confidence? What if Christian's big mouth ended up getting Hunter in trouble? No, Christian had been weak three years earlier, and he'd dragged

Hunter too far into his mess; he wouldn't do the same thing again. Christian had cared about Hunter, cared enough to get the hell away from him. He wouldn't go back on that now. "Can I think about it?" he asked.

"Briefly," the one with the weird accent said. He passed a thin envelope across the table. "We have a training camp starting in two days. It's residential, so you wouldn't have to worry about finding a place to stay. It will last for two months, or until you are asked to leave." He cast his eyes up and down Christian's body, then added, "Or until you quit. If you wish to attend, be at the address outlined in that envelope by zero eight thirty hours, Monday. Local time."

"We'll reimburse you for travel costs," the other said. "Keep your receipts."

It was such a mundane touch. It actually made Christian a bit more comfortable about the whole thing. He was pretty sure movie henchmen didn't submit expense reports to their overlords. "Okay, thanks," Christian said. He stood up and they did too, they all shook hands, and he headed for the street.

Once he was out of view of the building, he pulled the paper out of the envelope. The address was in Richmond, a suburb of Vancouver. Another possible connection to Hunter's company. Or his ex-company.

Christian wanted to go. He had no right to be chasing Hunter down; he'd dynamited that bridge and scorched the land on both sides of it. But Hunter had quit, and this might not even be his company. And even if it *was* his company, that didn't mean Christian was chasing the guy. It was just a weird coincidence. Christian had moved on. Maybe he hadn't settled down and gotten married or anything, but he'd gotten his share of action over the last few years. He was a young guy, having adventures and learning new stuff. This would be a great addition to that. Yeah, he wanted to go. It wasn't like there was anything holding him where he was.

It wasn't hard to pack up his life in Calgary, wasn't hard to make it to Vancouver. He rode his motorcycle instead of flying, and wondered if he was allowed to claim for the gas he spent. The training facility was in a clean modern building that looked like it should be used for making thermostats or something, not for housing a team of international mercenaries. Private security consultants. Whatever.

A coolly efficient woman checked his identification and directed him into the main room of the building. There were huge garage doors at one end, obviously for loading manufactured goods onto trucks, and no windows until about twenty feet up the high walls. A warehouse, the shell of a factory; he didn't know enough about industry to know which was which. But whatever purpose it had been built for, it was clearly something else now. There was a gym area at the far end, with mats and weights and three full-size boxing rings. The closer end had a seating area, thirty or forty folding chairs arranged in a loose cluster facing a long table with chairs behind it and a screen behind the chairs. And along one of the side walls, to Christian's consternation, was a double row of cots, each with a military-style footlocker. That was supposed to be their accommodations? Christian didn't care about comfort, but he'd like a little privacy, and he'd like to be treated with a little respect, not like....

Not like a grunt at boot camp. There were other men in the room, some sitting in the chairs, some moving around like Christian, taking it all in, and most of them looked military, to his reasonably trained eye. It wasn't just the haircuts or the fatigues, but the way they carried themselves. Fit and ready, but also a little too obviously alert, as if they didn't just have to *be* on their toes, they had to be *seen* to be on their toes. Christian dropped his duffel bag with a thud that drew more attention than it should have; these guys were jumpy. Then he hooked his foot around the leg of one of the metal chairs and drew it to him. He enjoyed the clatter and the dirty looks it earned him. Yeah, he hadn't been lying when he'd told the guys in Calgary that he didn't do well with military-style structure. And it didn't do well with him.

He looked behind him at the one part of the building with two stories. On the bottom level there were a few solid doors; he suspected they led to bathrooms or utility areas. Above that was a wall of windows, but these were glossy and reflective, not the clear ones that let natural light in from outside. Offices, he was guessing. Reached by a staircase he hadn't found yet. There might be people up there right now, looking down on them, watching, evaluating. Maybe one of them was Jack Hunter.

Christian tried to push that thought out of his mind. That wasn't why he was doing any of this. He'd done the right thing, getting out of that mess before Hunter got even crazier. There hadn't been that many times in his life when he'd done the right thing, and he hadn't done this one pretty, he had to admit. The look on Hunter's face... better not to think about that. The point was, Christian had gotten out of there for a reason, and it had been for Hunter's sake. Well, for both of them—for the good of the planet, really, because Christian was pretty sure that if he'd let himself get in any deeper with Hunter, the explosion from their inevitable dissolution might have created a supernova. It would cheapen the good deed if Christian tried to go back on it now. That was the rationale that had kept him out of British Columbia for the last three years, and it was the reason he shouldn't be hoping to run into Hunter now.

Not to mention that Hunter would probably punch him in the face.

A burly man who looked like a movie drill sergeant came to the long table and blew a whistle, calling them all together, and Christian sat with the others and listened to him explain the setup. They were all going to sign a confidentiality agreement, and the company absolutely expected them to respect it. They'd refer to each other by last name only and were discouraged from giving any other identifying information or details of their history. They were not to fraternize in groups when outside of the building, and they were not to be loud or obvious or do anything to call the attention of the neighbors to them. Their activities were not illegal, but they were absolutely confidential.

They'd do preliminary training and evaluating here, then move to other locations. Everything they needed would be provided, so they could use their footlockers to stash whatever they'd brought. Every day was an evaluation, but there was no precise scoring system, no number that would determine a pass or fail. They should focus on the training for its own sake, without worrying too much about their chances of earning employment.

Christian liked the sound of that last part. He looked around, wondering about the background of the others. All men, he noticed. Different heights, different builds, but all of them fit and hard-looking. What could he learn from them? What could he learn from the trainers?

He'd given his clothing size to the woman at registration, and now the men were directed to find the piles with their names on them that had been placed alphabetically along the far wall. They were allowed to use their own running shoes, since there was no opportunity for getting things customized, but otherwise they should wear what was provided.

Everyone else seemed used to this idea and when the not-quite-a-drill-sergeant told them to, they jogged to the far end of the room to find their piles. Christian trailed along behind them. They were being issued jogging uniforms? Seriously?

He heard the surprised murmurs before he arrived, and his interest was piqued. He peered at the piles the others were uncovering and headed more quickly toward the middle of the wall where his clothes should be. He stared down at the pile with his name on it, then bent and shook the clothes out. A University of Maine T-shirt? Red Nike shorts?

Up and down the row, guys were pulling out random pieces of clothing. Some of them were holding up concert shirts with the arms cut off, others sleek running gear. The shorts were just as diverse, and the underwear and socks, while still in their original packaging, were also varied.

"You're not *in* the military anymore, boys!" the not-a-drill-sergeant yelled from right behind them. "No more uniforms, no more looking the same! No more running around in a big gang with some asshole yelling out cadences for you! Wipe that shit out of your mind and start thinking for yourselves." He lowered his voice only a little as he said, "When you leave here to go for a run, you're either on your own or with *one* other person. If you meet up with someone else from the company while you're out there, you nod hello and you take a different route if needed to avoid traveling in a pack. You do not fucking salute! You do your best to pull the fucking sticks out of your asses and walk around like normal people!" He turned suddenly and focused on Christian. "You, son! Where did you serve?"

Christian shrugged. "I did some bartending at a place called Tony's a couple years ago. Other than that, never been a server."

"Are you being a smartass, boy?"

"Yeah, I am." It was hard to maintain his casual attitude with the guy drill-sergeanting as hard as he could. Christian didn't know if he'd seen too many movies or was channeling his childhood in ways he never had before, but he was absolutely fighting the impulse to snap to attention and start yelling out, *Sir, no sir.*

"I will ask you once again, son, where did you serve?"

"Buddy. You *just* told us not to give out details of our history. Wouldn't me telling you where I served be that kind of detail?"

The sergeant-guy looked down at the slip of paper that had fallen off Christian's pile of clothes. His last name was clearly visible. "Manning, huh? I've got my eye on you, Manning."

Christian resisted the urge to blow the guy a kiss.

"The locker room is behind the blue door at the far end of the room," the guy half yelled. "Get changed *quickly*. The first to get to the front door will be the first to leave on his run. The rest of you will be sent out at two-minute intervals, so if you don't want to be stuck waiting around for a long time, you will *hustle*."

The rest of the guys moved, fast. Christian knew he was being a smartass again, but there was just something about the whole military thing... he stayed right where he was, stripped off his shirt and replaced it with the University of Maine one, then kicked off his boots, peeled off his socks, and dropped his jeans and underwear. He pulled on the supplied clothes, dragged his shoes out of his bag, and jogged to the front door. He was standing there, stretching, before the first man came out of the locker room.

"It's like that, is it?" the not-a-drill-sergeant asked quietly.

Christian shrugged. It wasn't like he was there to make this guy's life difficult. "I don't know, man, I just want to work out and learn some stuff."

"You didn't serve *anywhere*, did you." There was no question in the man's voice. "I heard they were trying to recruit from a different pool."

"I was told there'd be others. I didn't expect to be the only one."

"Maybe the others had sense enough not to show up." The man made the suggestion sound like a threat.

"Maybe," Christian agreed. But there was no point in dwelling on that. "How does this run thing work? We just go where we want, or—"

"You'll receive instructions once your colleagues are all here!" the man barked.

Christian nodded his understanding and stepped back, trying to disengage from the annoying conversation. He just wanted to train, and learn. And maybe hear something about Hunter, even just see his picture or his name on a file or something. Just one quick reminder that the man really existed and hadn't been a figment of Christian's drug-addled imagination. That was all.

Instead, he was stuck in some sort of anti-boot-camp boot camp. It was a peculiar turn to his life, but maybe he'd been ready for a change. "Could have bought a fish," he said quietly, mostly to himself. The recruit standing next to him frowned in confusion. "If I wanted a change," Christian said in polite explanation, "I could have bought a fish. Having a pet is a big responsibility."

"Shut up, asshole," the man grunted. He was about six foot six and made of solid muscle. He looked and sounded like the Russian in *Rocky IV*. Christian shut up.

The drill sergeant explained the three different routes they would follow: first out to take route one, second to take route two, third on route three. The fourth out would go back to route one, but he'd be well behind the first out by that time, so there wouldn't be much chance of contact between them. The company was obviously going to some pains to remain unobtrusive in the neighborhood. "Each route has been carefully measured. They are all ten kilometers long. You will complete this route in under fifty minutes."

Christian wasn't used to measuring his distances too precisely. He could certainly run for fifty minutes straight, but he had no idea how much ground he'd cover in that time. He guessed he was about to find out.

The not-a-drill-sergeant consulted the list he'd been making as men arrived from changing and said, "Okay, first man here with his clothes tidily stowed away was Stickle. Stickle, you're runner number one." He nodded Stickle toward the door and smiled at Christian. "What kind of place would this be, Mr. Manning, if *everyone* dropped their bags on the floor and left clothes scattered everywhere?"

Christian shook his head. "It'd be absolute fucking chaos, sir. The laws of the natural world would cease to have meaning in a place like that. Anarchy, sir."

"I agree. I think you should complete the first assigned task of your time here with a little more pride and precision, don't you?"

"Absolutely, sir. Thank you for giving me the opportunity to make amends from the shame I've brought on—"

"Shut up, fish boy," the six-six guy grunted. "Go stow your shit."

And so it began. Christian wasn't sure what he was doing there, but he wasn't going to leave just because he was unpopular. Hell, being unpopular actually made the whole thing a bit more fun. So he stowed his shit, and he ran his route, and he went through all the other drills and exercises they expected of him. He ate the healthy but not especially tasty food they provided and thought about breaking into the kitchen to add a little flair to things, and he slept on his narrow cot with twenty other men snoring and grunting beside him.

On the third day they started their martial arts training. All of the men knew at least the basics, but Christian was pleased to find that he was among the top few in terms of more varied and advanced moves. He got to know his colleagues a little better, figuring out how to irritate each of them in turn as well as collectively. He learned that the not-quite-a-drill-sergeant's name was Bob, and he tried to use the name whenever possible, sometimes three or four times in a single sentence.

The trainers started teaching them random things: how to take apart and reassemble a horse's bridle, how to do a pirouette, how to edit video footage. It wasn't about the skills themselves, Christian realized. Well, unless he'd accidentally joined some sort of cavalry ballet company that liked to make films. He was pretty sure they were just being evaluated on their ability to learn entirely new things in areas where they had no prior knowledge.

On the fifth day, whoever was making decisions started

making them, and six men were sent home. To his surprise, Christian wasn't one of them. When they packed up their gear that night and climbed onto their school bus with tinted windows, heading for the next stage of their training, Bob sat sideways in front of Christian's seat and looked back at him. "You're still here," he grunted.

"Bob, don't pretend they didn't ask for your opinion on that, Bob. I know my friend Bob would say nice things about me, Bob."

"You're fucking peculiar," Bob said. But he didn't explode the way Christian's father would have; whatever Bob's background was, it had apparently given him more control than could be expected from one of the highest-ranking officers in the Canadian Armed Forces.

"Bob, Bob, Bob," Christian said, each syllable making his disappointment clear. He was pretty sure it was his best work yet.

"You ready for the next step?" Bob asked.

It was a real question, not a barked order or a sarcastic comment, so Christian tried to answer with a little less insolence. "No idea," he said.

Bob looked at him and nodded thoughtfully. "I have no idea either," he said. "But I'm interested in finding out."

CHAPTER NINE

It turned out that Christian *was* ready for the next step, to the surprise of himself and pretty much everyone else in the group. He knew they'd given him grudging respect for his fitness and martial arts, but he also knew they were all expecting him to crash and burn when they got to the more military aspect of things. On arrival at the company's training camp in the remote BC interior, they started using guns, running combat drills, and generally acting like soldiers. Christian was braced for failure. But apparently he'd retained most of the target-shooting ability he'd had as a kid and was a fast learner with the new weapons. The precise combat drills were new to all of the men, since they were coming from different militaries all over the world, so while he had a disadvantage, it wasn't huge. He wasn't the best at any of it, but he didn't really expect to be, not in a crowd like that. He was just pleased to be keeping up.

He started taking the whole thing more seriously. He still wasn't sure he actually wanted the job he was auditioning for, but he'd at least like to be the one turning them down instead of the other way around. As he dropped his smartass comments, though, he found that the other men didn't get any friendlier. Before, he'd been an annoying distraction; now, he realized, he was their competition.

Alliances had formed in the first few days of the program, subteams within the larger group, like contestants on a reality show. And Christian had been too busy being rebellious to have been included in any of them. Not that they would have likely wanted him anyway, he consoled himself. Even if he wasn't *trying* to stand out, he didn't have the same background any of them did, and he couldn't fake it.

So he worked alone. Hadn't the men in Calgary said they were looking for someone who could work alone? But the more he watched the others, the more he realized that they weren't mass-produced grunts, pushed through basic training and then sent out to follow orders in the field. These guys were elite soldiers from all over the world. They could work alone if they needed to. And they could work as part of a group, which Christian apparently couldn't.

One Friday night about six weeks into the program, the men were sitting around their barracks, drinking the beer they'd gotten as a reward for spending three nights hiking through the wilderness. Christian came in from a long shower and every head in the room turned to stare at him. Obviously they'd been talking about him, and obviously they weren't ready to stop. But he wanted a beer and then his bed, and he wasn't going to be chased out of the room that held both of those things. So he pulled on a pair of nonmilitary sweatpants, added a T-shirt, and walked over to the fridge.

"Why the fuck are you still here?" Despatis asked him. The man was French-Canadian, a possible ally, but he apparently either didn't recognize that Christian was a fellow countryman or didn't give a shit.

"This is where my *bed* is."

"Not here in this room. Here at camp. Why the fuck haven't they thrown you out yet?"

"I kicked your ass in the ring Monday, asshole. If they're keeping you around, why would they get rid of me?"

"I'm a sniper, *asshole*. I'm not supposed to be good at hand-to-hand. What the fuck is your specialty?"

It was a pretty good question, really, but Christian didn't have an answer. So he shrugged and said, "I keep my ass nice and tight for Bob, but if I was going to say what my *specialty* was, I'd have to go with blowjobs. I think it's definitely the blowjobs that are making him want me around."

There was silence. Then Volkov, the guy from *Rocky IV*, nodded and said, "That was one of the possibilities we were considering." He didn't seem hostile, exactly. More amused.

But Despatis wasn't interested in letting the tension disappear. He stood up, grabbing his crotch, and stared at Christian. "You going to blow *me*, pretty boy?"

"Do you have something I want? Because your microdick isn't really enough of an incentive."

"Fuck you!"

"Again, with that dick? I don't think I'd even notice."

Despatis charged then. It was stupid. As Christian had already pointed out, he'd kicked the other man's ass in the ring earlier in the week, and every other time they'd come up against each other in the rotation.

He didn't see the bottle in Despatis's hand until it was almost too late. A beer bottle. What the fuck? He managed to dodge the attack anyway, but Despatis recovered easily and turned around, bottle still in hand. Christian could hear the words floating out of his memory. *There's no such thing as a ring. I'm teaching you to fight for real.* This was what Hunter had meant. The sport fighting Christian had been doing in Calgary had taught him some tricks, but nothing like this. Christian needed to remember what Hunter had taught him, and what he'd learned for himself, trying to stay alive on the streets.

And as Despatis charged again, Christian jumped. High enough that he found a good grip on the exposed I-beam that formed the rafters of their barracks, and fast enough that he got his feet high and even managed a bit of a swing, ramming his heels hard into Despatis's face. The momentum of the man's charge was enough to jar Christian back, but the effect was much more dramatic on Despatis. He was knocked backward, flat out on the wood floor, and the beer bottle shattered on one of the footlockers it hit on the way down.

If they'd been in the ring, that would have been the end of things. But they weren't in the ring. Christian scanned the floor to make sure there was no broken glass where he intended to walk, then scooped up the biggest part of the beer bottle and grabbed the front of the still stunned Despatis's shirt. He brought the jagged edge of the glass up to Despatis's eye and twisted it a little, letting it catch the light without actually touching the skin. "I have no idea why I'm still here," he said quietly. "But I'm pretty sure it isn't so I can blow you. So chill out, leave me alone, and we'll be okay."

He pulled away and stepped back, keeping his eyes on the other man, glad that his back was to the wall so he didn't have to worry about any of his other "teammates" sneaking up to try to finish Despatis's job.

Despatis scrabbled clumsily to his feet, still looking a bit dazed, and stumbled over toward the chairs. But before he could sit down, Volkov reached out a huge hand and caught him. "You need to clean up the glass," he said. "People don't want to wear shoes all the time."

And that was the end of it. The next day when Bob asked Despatis how he'd gotten two black eyes, Despatis said he'd fallen down. Bob nodded and said, "Uh-huh," and then he let it go. Three days later, Despatis and another man were sent home from camp. Two weeks after that, camp ended. The men were bussed back to Vancouver, asked to hand in the clothes and equipment they'd received, and thanked for their time.

It was anticlimactic. Christian was in the best shape of his life, he'd learned more about fighting and weapons and communication equipment than he'd ever thought he could possibly care about, and then... nothing.

He comforted himself that none of the men had heard anything from the company. Or maybe they had and were just being instructed to keep quiet about it. Things had gotten better between Christian and the other men after the Despatis fight, but there still wasn't anyone in the group he'd call a friend. Volkov was probably the closest thing, and he made it pretty clear that he thought Christian was an idiot.

So Christian sat on the saddle of his motorcycle outside the building that should have been a warehouse, stared at the formal record of employment he'd been given, outlining his hours worked and money made so he was eligible for employment insurance, and felt lost.

The last two months had changed him, and he couldn't imagine going back to Calgary and looking for construction work as if nothing had happened.

Volkov was driving by in a beat-up pickup, and he rolled down his window and looked out at Christian. "Go home," he said. "Get that fish. Get a whole aquarium. You earned it. Forget about this business."

Christian nodded slowly. "Yeah. I guess so. Hey, I'll name one of the fish after you."

"A good one," Volkov said seriously. "And name him Anatoli, not Volkov."

Great. Now Christian actually had to get an aquarium. "Anatoli," Christian said. He was too far away to shake hands, and he was pretty sure that by the time he climbed off his bike Anatoli would have driven away, so he flipped him a quick, not entirely disrespectful salute. Anatoli returned it, then left Christian alone in the parking lot again.

He needed something to *do*. The call of his past was always strongest when he had free time. He'd managed to shrink the part of him that was a junkie, but it was always still there, and when he didn't have anything else to occupy his mind and body, its tiny voice started getting stronger and more insistent. And this time, when he was so close to his old stomping grounds, when it would be *so easy* to just point his bike toward the East Side and find what he needed....

Yeah, he'd been hoping to be offered a job so he could keep his mind on that. But it hadn't happened and he couldn't just stay there in the parking lot. Couldn't camp out, making a nuisance of himself until they invited him back in and offered him some sort of job that would allow him to keep using his hard-earned skills.

Maybe that was his problem. He was thinking of this place as being the only show in town, but maybe it wasn't. His skills were transferrable, surely. He wouldn't have much on his resume to impress anyone at a similar company, but maybe he could *get* something on his resume.

Jesus, he was actually thinking about joining the army. He wondered what his dad would think about that. Then he wondered whether his dad actually *was* signing up with this company, and whether he'd be able to pull any strings to get Christian on board. *Then* he wondered if he was losing his mind.

Thinking about asking his dad for a favor? That was definitely a sign of a break from reality. He needed to get the hell out of the parking lot. Probably right out of Vancouver. He'd go back to Calgary and pack up his stuff, settle with his landlord, and go wherever he wanted. He'd made good money for the last couple months and hadn't had a chance to spend any of it. Instead of going full soldier, he should go full hippy, traveling around the country and seeing what there was to see.

It wasn't all that appealing, but he definitely needed to get out of the parking lot. So he turned the engine over, walked the bike backward, and headed for the road. A black sedan pulled out as he approached it, blocking the way, and Christian waited impatiently for it to move. Instead, the driver's window rolled down and a hand waved him forward. What the hell?

He wheeled up to the window cautiously, and when he got to it he saw the English guy behind the wheel. "I was getting bored, waiting," the man said. "I'm glad you finally got moving."

Christian had no idea what to say to that. "I was just figuring out where to go."

The Englishman said, "Whatever you decided, I think you should rethink it. We'd like to meet with you. Follow the car, please." Without waiting for Christian's agreement, he pulled away. Christian thought for about half a second, then got moving.

They didn't go far. Richmond was flatter than the rest of the region, its grid pattern clearer, with fewer interruptions, and the next location was two large grid squares over, one and a half down. A five-minute drive took them to another anonymous-looking building, this one with more rows of windows, suggesting, Christian supposed, that there were more individual floors inside rather than one large open space. The parking lot was almost full, but the Englishman pulled into an empty reserved space and gestured for Christian to take the one next to it.

"Not every time you come here," he said, as if he suspected Christian of having gone through all of it just to get a crack at a good parking spot. "But I've waited for you enough today, so I don't want to waste more time watching you find parking."

Christian didn't make any smart comments. Whatever was happening, he wanted it to continue, and his mouth could only get in the way of that.

He hung his helmet on the handlebars and followed the Englishman through the main doors of the building. The place looked like a lawyers' office. Lots of glass, lots of wood, some comfortable leather chairs in the waiting area and a well-groomed woman behind the reception desk. "Good afternoon, sir," she said to the Englishman.

"Good afternoon. I need a visitor's pass for my guest, please."

"Of course." She smiled at Christian and handed a clipboard across to him. "If you could write your name here, and sign here, please?"

He did as he was told. "Now, please, if you'll come over here and stand with your toes on the red line," she said, and he realized she was taking his picture with a machine like the one at the DMV. Damn. He was pretty sure they didn't do that at lawyers' offices.

And when he took a moment to look around the room, he realized there were two large men sitting on the leather sofas, one on either side of the door, not reading, not playing with their phones. Just waiting. Security guards, he'd bet. More subtle than having them standing by the doors wearing uniforms. These guys were there for action, not appearance.

The woman gave him another friendly smile as she handed over a little plastic envelope with a clip on top, his printed photo and name inserted into the flap. "Please wear it at all times while in the building," she said pleasantly.

"Okay," he agreed. Whatever.

He followed the Englishman up a broad flight of stairs, then another, climbing closer to the skylight that brightened the central part of the building. Everyone they walked by had a nod for the Englishman but kept their attention directed away from Christian. Discretion, he supposed. Clients probably didn't want a lot of eyeballs on them, not in this line of work.

The Englishman rapped on an office door as they passed, leaned in, and said, "He's here." Christian didn't have the angle to see who was being spoken to. He followed the Englishman down to the end of the hall and into a bright glass-and-chrome conference room.

The man with the unfamiliar accent came into the room right behind them; obviously he'd been the one the Englishman had summoned. "Sit down," he said. No handshakes, and still no names. Christian really wasn't feeling the love, but he did as he was told.

"We're interested in hiring you," the Englishman said. "You'd be on retainer. It's about forty thousand dollars a year. Enough to live on, but not enough to get anyone rich. Your time would be your own, although we'd expect you to keep yourself fit and continue developing your skills. You could use our facilities as convenient for those tasks. The condition is that you are ready to drop everything, at a moment's notice, to work on a job for us. You'd need to stay in the Vancouver area or one of our approved training facilities, and you'll carry a pager. If we believe you would be an asset for a certain project, we'll call you in, and you'll go on active duty. There's a complicated pay scale for that, based on a variety of criteria, but most of our active employees make well over a hundred thousand dollars a year. Some make almost three hundred thousand."

"And some don't make more than the retainer," the South African interjected. "If the team leaders don't want you, they don't select you, and you don't get paid. You catch their eye by training hard, doing well when we have in-house competitions, and doing a good job when you're *on* the job so they'll choose you for the next time they go out. If nobody wants you after a year or so, we stop paying the retainer."

Christian frowned at him. "What kind of training could I be doing?"

"You'll have access to our facility here, and the remote basic training facility you've already been to. In addition we have a facility in Virginia for more advanced training: urban combat simulations, water combat, crowd-control techniques... things like that."

"Just access to the *facilities*? Or to the trainers too?"

For the first time, the South African looked vaguely approving. "We were told you were eager to learn. Very motivated to improve."

"Yeah, well...." Christian debated how much to say. "Are you hiring anyone else from my round of training? Because, honestly, if I was a team leader and I was going to choose between any of those guys and *me*, I think I'd choose any of those guys. So if I don't get some serious training in, I think I'm going to sit around for a year and then go back to my old life."

"You should train," the man agreed. "But you'll still have a difficult time catching up to them. If we want someone to work in a military capacity—someone to ride around in a jeep and look intimidating, someone to work according to accepted procedures in a firefight, anything like that—we're not going to be calling you. That's true. But if we want someone to blend into the crowd at a café in order to perform surveillance, or to charm a young lady into leaving a window open, if we want someone to go back after dark and climb into that window and then retrieve valuable information that could be used to save the lives of those men riding around in the jeep... then we might look in your direction."

"Like a spy, more than a soldier."

The South African shrugged. "More like that, yes."

Christian felt a bit deflated. He wanted to be one of the guys in the jeep. "I could train for whatever I wanted? Like, if you kept me on retainer because you thought I might be a spy, but I took all the training in order to be a soldier...."

"Many of the skills are transferrable," the Englishman said. "You could train according to your interests." He waited for more questions, then said, "You should think about this. We'll expect you to sign another confidentiality agreement before we show you our contract, and then if you want to get legal advice on the contract we'll ask that you give us the name of your lawyer so we can more effectively trace any security breaches."

"Is this legal?" Christian asked. He supposed he should have thought about that a couple of months ago.

"Yes. We are very careful not to violate the laws of our home countries. Internationally? Well, there are countries where men can be killed for performing homosexual acts, countries where women can be executed for being raped. We don't necessarily follow *all* laws in the countries we work in, but we are careful to follow most of them, and to be very judicious in any breaches."

"Okay," Christian said. He knew he should do what they'd recommended. He should think it over, and probably get a lawyer to look at things. But he needed something concrete. He needed to be anchored, and by something more than a damn aquarium. "Okay, I'm in. I'll do it."

The Englishman looked at him for a moment, then nodded. "If you'll stay here, please, I'll go and get them started on drawing up the contract. It's fairly standard, so it shouldn't take long." He stopped then, and extended his hand. "I'm Trevor Allen. Welcome aboard."

The other man rose to his feet and waited his turn for a handshake. "Willem Bentick. I handle most of the jobs that are more suited to your qualities. We have some special trainers who may be valuable for you. Language specialists, psychologists... that sort of thing. I'm busy today, but set up an appointment for next week, and we'll go over your current skills and see what needs augmentation."

Christian felt a bit overwhelmed. He felt as if he'd been accepted, made a member of a secret club. It was a good feeling, and he wanted to savor it. Like most good things, he didn't count on it to last.

CHAPTER TEN

The work was good. Christian found an apartment not far from the basic training building, and he figured out a good running route, one that gave him a workout but still left him with enough energy to spar effectively when he reached the facility. Sometimes there was someone looking for a partner as soon as he arrived, sometimes he'd do weights or hit the bags or do calisthenics or kicking drills or whatever it took to fill the time until there was someone to spar with. He'd go up against anyone, and mostly got his ass handed to him, but that was the only way to learn.

He also got his firearms license and bought a membership to a firing range. He wasn't sure how he felt about the gun part of the job, wasn't sure if he'd be able to pull the trigger if he was aiming at a human being instead of a paper target. But he enjoyed the target shooting, and decided not to think too much about the rest.

And he had his meeting with Bentick, got hooked up with an assortment of other trainers, people who were helping him learn different languages and some computer skills and pretty much anything he could find to keep his brain busy after he'd worked his body as hard as he was able. He was exhausted almost every night by the time he fell into bed.

On those nights when he *hadn't* managed to tire himself out, he'd get on his computer and browse through local men, thinking about making contact, but then not doing it. He'd never been much good at the premeditated aspect of sex; if he was out and he met someone and there was interest and attraction, great. But there was something about online dating that felt a bit too much like shopping, and he'd had his fill of transaction-based sex. If the connection wasn't organic, he wasn't interested.

Which meant that he spent his first three months in Vancouver without getting laid. He might have found that frustrating if he weren't distracted by a much larger failure on his part: he also wasn't getting picked to go on any jobs at work. He was training his *ass* off, but nobody seemed to notice or care.

"You're working hard," Nadira said. She was the person in charge of his languages training, and they weren't friends, exactly, but they were friendly. "That's all you can do."

"What about this 'company picnic' this weekend? That's, like, a bunch of contests, right? A chance to show what I can do?"

"But what *can* you do?" Her soft accent didn't do a lot to make the words more palatable. "Can you shoot better than the best shooters? Fight better than the best fighters? There won't be a contest for 'has learned a lot about a lot of things'." She shrugged. "You're not even my best languages student. You work hard and you're doing fine, but you're not a natural."

He groaned. "It's kind of hard to stay motivated for practice when you don't think you're ever going to get to play in a game."

"You're, what, twenty-two? You've been training seriously for five months? And you're upset because you're not better than thirty-five-year-olds who've been working toward this their whole lives? Give me a break."

"I'm twenty-three. And I only have nine more months. They said that if I wasn't getting chosen for jobs after a year, they'd take me off the list."

"And you'd go find a job somewhere else, and get more training, and keep working until you got good enough. Or until you decided this isn't the job for you."

Christian couldn't argue with her, but that didn't mean he was convinced. Allen and Bentick had *seen* something in him. They'd given him a chance, and he'd made it through the training camp, and they'd offered him a damn job. He hadn't seen any of the others he'd trained with, so it looked like he was the only one who'd made it through. Allen and Bentick must have thought there was something unique about him, something that could make him useful. He just needed to figure out what it was so he could find a way to showcase it for the team leaders.

So he signed up for the company picnic. Cute name, but not much of a disguise; he didn't think there were many companies having their picnics hours away from the city, in the middle of nowhere, in early October. The festivities were scheduled to begin in the early morning, so he drove up to Lillooet, the nearest town, the night before. He'd already asked about sleeping at the site and been told that the beds there were booked months ahead of any event. The picnic was open to all employees, but in practice it was mostly for those who weren't on active assignment, since they were the only ones close enough to participate. But any active unit of more than ten or twelve men had sent at least one man back to participate, so there was also a bit of a reunion happening, as Christian understood it. Even in town, the motel parking lot was full of Humvees and Jeeps and pickups with off-road packages; apparently the company wasn't quite as committed to being unobtrusive when they were out of the city.

Christian got one of the last rooms at the motel and parked his bike in front of it. There was someone standing just inside the doorway of the room next door, looking out at the night, and Christian kept half an eye on him while he unlocked his room door.

The voice came out of the shadowed door, and out of the past. "You planning on riding that bike out to the site tomorrow?"

Christian froze for a moment, trying to give his mind a chance to sort it all out and be sure. "Hunter?" He stared into the room, trying to see the shape in the darkness.

And Hunter obligingly stepped out into the thin glare of the overhead light. "It's twelve kilometers of logging road, and ten kilometers of rough track after that. You're not going to make it on a street bike." He shook his head in disgust. "What the fuck are you thinking?"

That was an excellent question. It sure wasn't anything about rough roads or his bike's capabilities. "Shit, Hunter. I didn't.... This *is* your company, then? I wasn't sure. I wasn't, like, *stalking* you...."

"Why would you be?" Hunter looked different. A few years older, but nothing obvious, agewise. His body looked just as hard, as much as could be seen beneath jeans and a flannel shirt, and his face didn't seem to have any more lines.... It was his eyes, Christian realized. Hunter's eyes were cold, staring at Christian as if he was the enemy. No, not even that, because Hunter probably had some level of respect for his enemies. He was looking at Christian as if he was... as if he was a smack-addict hooker, a piece of street trash that nobody had gotten around to throwing out. Ironic that when Christian actually *had* been that, Hunter's eyes had glowed with affection.

"Right," Christian said. He wasn't sure what he was commenting on. "Okay. Uh, thanks. I'll try to figure out something else, with the bike. Thanks." He turned back to his door. He was getting exactly the reaction he deserved from Hunter, but knowing that didn't make it any easier to take.

"You're making a fool of yourself, you know." Hunter sounded as if he were discussing something of purely academic interest.

Christian was pretty sure he didn't want to hear any more,

but he couldn't help himself. "What do you mean?"

"Pretending to be a soldier. You don't know what you've gotten into, and you're...." Hunter shook his head in disgust. "You're acting like you belong, but you don't."

"I know I have work to do. I know I have to get better."

"You don't, actually," Hunter said. He lifted his hand, and for the first time Christian saw the glass of amber liquid he was holding. After a sip, Hunter said, "You could sit back and do nothing, and if they decide the time is right, they'll put you on a job. Or you could work your ass off, get way better—still not good enough to belong here, but way better—and they'll ignore you if they decide the time is wrong. And the time being right or wrong? It doesn't have a fucking thing to do with you. It's all about me."

"What? I don't understand. You're... you're blackballing me, or something?"

"No, you *don't* understand. You are in way over your fucking head. You're a fucking pawn that doesn't even know it's on a chess board."

Christian fought to keep his voice level. "What are you talking about?"

"The company doesn't recruit random assholes with junior marksman trophies and three years of sports MMA training. They don't, not without another reason."

Christian could feel the truth of those words. He'd made the same argument himself, after all, but he'd allowed Allen and Bentick to convince him he was wrong. "What other reason?" he asked, and he didn't like how young and insecure he sounded.

Hunter shook his head and took another sip. "They think they can use you to get to me."

Christian stared at him. "What? I don't... what? How do they even...? And why would they think...?"

"They were watching me," Hunter said. "After I left the company, when I went up to the cabin... when you were there. They think...." He shook his head impatiently. "I don't know *what* the fuck they think. I guess they're just desperate, grasping at straws."

"No. They said... they said they found me when they were doing a background check on *my father*."

"That probably *was* how they found you. They wouldn't have known much about you after my place. Some photos. Maybe more, if they bribed someone at Miriam's office; I've got her looking into that. They would have had a hard time tracking you down. But you'd have been entered somewhere in their fucking *database*." He spat out the last word like *it* was the obscenity, then took another sip of his drink, as if to rinse his mouth. "If they were looking into your dad, they must have stumbled across something that pinged the connection to your picture or whatever they had from when you were with me."

"But my father doesn't know where I was living. How would *they* have found out?"

Hunter shrugged. "How'd they *say* they found you? But I wouldn't be so sure about your dad not knowing. From what I've seen he was pretty good at playing the game, making things look good; if I were a man like that, and I had a son like you, I'd want to have some idea where he was at, just so I could be ready to do damage control as needed."

A son like you. A fuckup. A mistake. It was nothing. Compared to what Christian had done to Hunter, it was nothing. But it stung, one more bit of pain to add to all the rest. "So they don't think I might be useful," he said dully. "They said...." But what did it matter what they'd said? What Hunter was saying made more sense. He remembered the others in the initial training period, amazed that he'd made it past each round of cuts. And he remembered the pride he'd felt, the sense that he was finally *doing* something, achieving something, not just sitting there watching his life happening. But the pride was gone, and it was replaced with emptiness.

He knew exactly what would fill that hole. He could almost picture it, the smoke working into every nook and cranny, expanding and warming and making him not care about what used to be in that part of him. Making him not care about a goddamn thing.

He pulled the key to his bike out of his pocket. He had no idea where to find heroin in Lillooet, but Vancouver wasn't that far away, and it would be so, so easy down there. So easy to score, so easy to go back to his apartment and smoke, so easy to live off the company for the next nine months, doing nothing and feeling nothing. So *easy*.

He looked at the key, then thrust it out toward Hunter, keeping his eyes on the door to his own room. "Take this," he said, his voice so tense he barely recognized it. "I know you don't owe me, but please, take it. You can just leave it on the doorstep tomorrow morning, or on the bike. Whatever. But please, now, just fucking take it."

It took a long time for Hunter to respond, but finally he did, reaching out and plucking the key out of Christian's hand as if his skin were contaminated. "Look," Hunter started, but Christian was already moving. He couldn't stand still, couldn't hear any more of the truth Hunter was so eager to share.

He had no idea where he was going, but that really didn't matter. Hunter was right; he was an idiot. He'd *known* he wasn't good enough, but he'd wanted to belong, wanted to have some sort of fucking purpose, and he'd let himself believe. Damn it, he was too old for that shit. Too old to believe people's lies, to trust them when they said kind things, to let them *use* him like he was... like he was a pawn who didn't even know he was part of a chess game. Yeah, Hunter knew the score. Christian was stupid, naïve, fucking *unable to learn*.

He walked all night, letting the defeat sink into his bones.

It ached at first, but by dawn it felt natural; he'd gotten used to something else, but this feeling was familiar too.

He made his way back to the motel. The trucks were starting to pull out, driven by proud, skilled men who'd trained hard and were ready to display their abilities. One pulled to a stop beside him and the window rolled down. "Hey, Christian," the driver yelled. He peered inside and saw Lance or Larry or something, a guy he'd sparred with a few times. "You want a lift, man? Your bike's gonna have a shit time on those roads."

Christian hadn't been planning to go to the picnic. There was no need to wallow in his humiliation, now that he was aware of it. But he could still feel the craving thrumming through his body, and he knew that if he got on his bike now, if he headed back to town, his first stop would be the East Side, and if his old dealer wasn't there anymore, he knew he'd have no trouble finding someone new. "Yeah, okay," he said. He swung up into the truck and only then realized he was still wearing the light pack that carried his gear. He wiggled it off his shoulder and stuffed it into the back of the truck.

"You pumped?" Lance-Larry asked. "You know what events you're going to sign up for?"

"As many as I can," Christian replied. He needed to be busy. Sitting around waiting for other guys to do their thing? That wasn't going to help distract him. He was past the embarrassment, the humiliation of realizing that all the time he'd been trying so hard, the others had just been laughing at him. Let them laugh. After this weekend, he'd never see them again, and he didn't have energy to worry about *them*. He needed to worry about himself. So he'd enter every event, and he'd put everything he had into each one, and sure, he'd lose, but with luck he'd be too exhausted and beat up to even think about heroin. Fuck, if he was lucky maybe he could get a concussion in the sparring. That'd be helpful, for sure.

The first event of the day was prone shooting. There were

snipers there from all over the world. Christian came in second to last; the one who'd come dead last said there was something wrong with his scope, and people seemed to believe him. Still, the soldier was responsible for his weapons, so the guy lost. After that, paper targets from standing, kneeling, and prone. Christian managed to be third from last on that one, with no real excuses from the two below him. Still, in a field of more than twenty men, he was doing about as well as Hunter seemed to expect him to do. And he really didn't care. The focus required by shooting was good for his brain; it made him shut off all his emotions, all his thoughts, and let his body do what it had been trained to do. He wished he could keep going all day.

The hand-to-hand was being judged in a single-elimination tournament. Everyone drew random opponents for the first round, and as soon as you lost a fight, you were out. It was the most time consuming of the events, so it was scheduled to take up most of the afternoon on both days of the picnic. The first round matchups were posted right before lunch; Christian glanced at his opponent's name but didn't recognize it, then went to stand in the food line. He tried to keep himself distracted while he stood there, felt himself start fidgeting and getting restless, and tried to stomp it all down. He was thinking he might need to leave the line and go for a run when a familiar face appeared beside him.

The quick flash of pleased recognition was immediately doused when he realized what a pain in the ass he'd been to Bob. All the guys in training. Fucking Despatis, asshole that he was, had been right. It *had* been a joke that Christian was there with them all, and they'd been right to object. "Hey," he said quietly.

"What? No 'Bob, it's good to see you bobbing along like you do, Bob'? No 'Bob, thank you, Bob, I appreciate it, Bob'?"

"That was fucking obnoxious, man. I'm sorry."

Bob raised an eyebrow. "What the fuck is wrong with

you? You look like you haven't slept, you're talking like a little pussy... what's going on?"

There was no way Christian was getting into all that, so he forced a smile onto his face. "You are quite a sweet talker," and then, just to get the guy off his back, he added, "Bob."

But Bob obviously wasn't satisfied. He waved his full plate in front of Christian and said, "Get your food and come sit with me, over under that canopy. I'll make sure you know people."

Well, there was no fucking way that was going to happen. But Christian smiled and said, "Yeah, I'll try to make it over. Good to see you."

Bob still didn't look convinced, but he limited himself to one more skeptical look and then headed for his table. Christian focused on the ground beneath his feet, trying to count each blade of grass that was crushed as he stepped forward, watching the pine needles bend under the edges of his boots. It wasn't exciting, but it kept him from taking off in search of heroin, so he called it a win.

He got his food and ducked behind one of the prefab buildings to eat in solitude. He'd missed breakfast, and he was always hungry, as if making up for the meals he hadn't bothered with as a junkie. The food tasted like cardboard, but he choked it down anyway. He was tempted to go back for more but he didn't want to fight if he was too full. He could try to scrounge something up after he got eliminated.

Unfortunately for his stomach, he won his first match. And his second. Both were unanimous judgments and the crowd didn't seem to disagree, so he figured they hadn't been rigged. That was something, at least. He hadn't dominated, but he'd gotten by. That was what he could hold on to.

And it was enough, he realized. He was okay. Not great, but he wasn't going to do anything stupid that night. If nothing else, he was too damned tired for it

He looked around the camp, and it made him sad. He'd wanted to belong, but he didn't. He was a kitten trying to hang out with pit bulls; he might survive, as long as he didn't piss one of them off, but he was never going to be part of the pack.

Well, too fucking bad, he told himself. He was a grownass man, and he needed to stop being... what had Bob said? He needed to stop being a little pussy. Kind of fit with his own analogy; that was nice. He pulled off his sparring gear and tossed it to the side of the ring. He found his pack and pulled on jeans and a sweatshirt, and then he started walking.

"Hey, man, solid fight," someone said from nearby. "You're gonna get your ass handed to you next round, though."

Christian didn't look at him.

"What the fuck, man, you leaving? Jesus, you afraid of him? I mean, Hunter's good, but he's not an asshole. He's not going to fuck you up or anything."

Hunter. Christian's next opponent was Hunter. A guaranteed loss, obviously. Maybe Christian should stick around. He bet Hunter wouldn't mind taking a few swings at his head. Christian smiled without any joy. It was a long walk back, and he needed to get started. "He wins. I'm out."

CHAPTER ELEVEN

Christian ended up hitching a ride most of the way back to town. He walked to the motel, checked the bike, checked his doorway, then checked them both again a bit more frantically; the key wasn't there. Fuck. Hunter must have left it that morning but Christian had left it out all day, and somebody must have come and picked it up. But the keychain *said* Triumph, there was a Triumph bike parked right in front of his door... what kind of asshole would just walk away with the key? Stealing the bike, okay, that would make sense. But taking just the key was fucking annoying.

Maybe some good Samaritan had turned it in to the office, he figured, but when he went to check they said they didn't have anything. He opened his motel room door, checked the floor in case Hunter had somehow slipped it inside... nothing. Fuck. Fuck. *Fuck*. He just wanted to get away. He was done with all of it, and he'd used up all of his fucking self-control and there just wasn't anything fucking *left*. "Fuck!" he roared, slamming his palms against the wall. The volume didn't help, but it was probably responsible for the polite tapping on his door moments later. "Son of a bitch," he muttered. A noise complaint? Yeah, that felt about right.

He yanked the door open. Oh. Maybe not about the noise. "Hunter. Wait, what are you doing here? Aren't you supposed to be at the picnic?"

"Aren't *you?*" Hunter asked.

"I think we both know I'm *not* supposed to be out there." A ray of hope pierced the darkness in Christian's mind. "There's no chance you still have my bike key, is there?"

Hunter reached into his pocket and pulled the key out, but he didn't extend his hand to return it.

Christian wasn't sure whether to be relieved or annoyed. "Okay, thanks," he said, reaching for it.

But Hunter pulled his hand away.

Christian wanted to punch him in the face. He really, really didn't have the strength for whatever the fuck Hunter was up to. But he also didn't have the strength to get the shit kicked out of him by an angry martial-arts expert, so he just stood there instead.

"You need to talk to somebody," Hunter finally said.

"Somebody specific?" Or was this one more of Hunter's never-ending attempts to get Christian to go to a counselor? Well, not never-ending, because they had ended pretty damn quickly when Christian had fucked Hunter's sister. And remembering that little detail made Christian a bit more understanding of Hunter's current bitterness.

"Somebody next door," Hunter said. "We were supposed to be having a private meeting, but since you're here anyway... let's go." He stepped backward, making room in the doorway for Christian to get by.

There was enough room to close the door, if Christian moved fast. He could slam it shut, fall on the bed, cover his ears with pillows, and get some fucking sleep. Instead, he followed Hunter out of the room like an obedient fucking puppy. No, what was it he was like? A kitten. Except those little bastards weren't obedient. But they chased string. So he followed Hunter like a kitten chasing string—

"Christian?" Hunter said. He wasn't looking Christian in the eye, focusing somewhere around his cheekbone instead. Hadn't really looked at him the day before, either, Christian was pretty sure. Too angry, too disappointed, too disgusted. Now Hunter's voice was sharp and impatient. "Focus, asshole. This is Wendy Traynor. She's the chair of the company's board of directors. She wants to talk to you."

Christian looked at the woman. She didn't seem like much— small, wearing jeans and an oversized work shirt, nestled in one of the room's ragged upholstered chairs like a little elf in an acorn. "I quit," Christian told her.

"No, I don't think you do," she said quietly.

"I'm pretty sure."

She sighed with a vehemence that seemed out of place in someone so small. "Hunter," she said with a glare in his direction, "you are a pain in the ass and you should have kept your mouth shut." Then she smiled more calmly and said, "Bring me a scotch, dear." She turned to Christian. "I suppose I should offer you a needle? Oh, that's right, you smoked it, didn't you?"

What the fuck was that about? Christian just stared at her, waiting. She watched him for a moment, then said, "I thought we might as well get that out of the way." She watched him a moment more before adding, "I know things about you that you might not tell me. That's all. Sometimes things like that can be a bit of an elephant in the room, all of us wasting time pretending we don't know things when we really do. I don't think we have the luxury of that sort of thing, not today."

"Okay," Christian said. He had no idea what this woman was up to, but he had a feeling he was, once again, in over his head.

Wendy nodded, as if Christian's response had been somehow profound. She accepted her glass of scotch from Hunter and sounded genuinely sad when she said, "Hunter shouldn't have told you what he did yesterday."

"You saying it wasn't true?"

"Of course it was true. It's self-evident. You're an amateur, and we're a professional company. We don't recruit amateurs, not without a compelling reason. You're just not good enough."

Nice to hear it one more fucking time. Christian forced himself to sound calm as he said, "So why shouldn't Hunter have told me?"

"Because there was no point. Because it would make you want to quit, and we don't want that."

"Who's 'we'?"

"Well, me, mostly. But also Bentick and Allan and their cronies."

"Why don't you and they want me to quit?"

"Because you have not yet served your purpose," she said, as if it were obvious.

Christian supposed it *was* obvious. But also stupid. "They're trying to use me to control Hunter? Why the fuck would they think that would work? I mean, three years ago I was his handyman for a few months? Big fucking deal."

"Oh, there's that elephant!" Her smile seemed kind, almost gentle. "We all know you were quite a bit more than a handyman, dear."

"Not much more," Christian insisted. That was what he'd told himself three years ago, and there was no reason for him to change the story now. "And it was a long time ago. I'm sure there are more recent... whatevers." Exactly how much did this woman know about Hunter's activities? How much did *Christian* know? "What's the big deal about me?"

"It *is* something of a mystery," Wendy said dryly, with an affectionately impatient look in Hunter's direction. Then she returned her gaze to Christian. "Regardless of their reasoning, they think it will work. They think they can use you to make Hunter more compliant. So they won't want you to quit. They went to all the trouble and expense of finding you and recruiting you and training you, and there's been no payoff whatsoever. Well, except for the satisfaction I'm sure they took from seeing Hunter's face when they mentioned your name. He'd been out of the country for months, and when he got back they were very pleased to see him and share their news. They can be a little vindictive, those boys."

"Well, obviously they can go fuck themselves," Christian said. "And no offense, but I'm not sure why I'm supposed to care what *you* want, either."

Her smile was no less sweet than it had been earlier, but her tone was steel. "You should care what *they* want because if they don't want you to walk away, you won't be *allowed* to. There are contractual terms, obviously, things that they might use. Tell me, Christian, did you *read* your contract? Are you aware of the terms around terminating your employment?" She shook her head sadly. "They are not employee-friendly, I'm afraid."

"What, seriously? They're going to, what? Sue me?" He guessed it would suck to lose his bike, but he didn't have anything else of significant value. "They can go for it."

"Sweet boy," she said as if the words were an insult. Then she cocked her head to the side like a fierce little bird. "Yes, they would threaten to sue. And threaten to sue anyone who dared to hire you until the terms of the contract were finished, and in every other way make things unpleasant. And then they'd offer you one simple solution to it all. A tiny job. Nothing big, but something that needs to get done. If you do that, you're free. And you'd agree, of course, because deep down you know that we're all wrong, you know that you *are* good enough and you *could* do this job if someone would just give you a chance." She squinted at him, watching him react to her words, and even though he fought to keep his face blank, she nodded slowly. "Ah. Right. That's how *most* people would react. You, though... you'd *accept* that you aren't good enough for this job. You're not good enough for anything, really. But what the hell, you might as well do it because it doesn't matter anyway. Nothing really matters. Right?"

Christian turned to Hunter. "This is really a fun time. Thanks for inviting me."

Hunter just stared past him, and Wendy started talking again. "So for whatever reason, you agree to do that one job and they ship you off to Afghanistan or Somalia or wherever, send you out in the middle of nowhere, and then they decide how to use you. If they want a message sent, they put a bullet in your head." She watched his reaction. She saw him blink, hard, and he wondered if she could somehow see the same bullet he was imagining, going through his skull, exploding in his brain, ending all of this. She smiled, as if she was pleased with his vivid imagination, then said, "Of course, they would never say that *they* did it. That would be the sort of thing that could pull a company apart, not to mention lead to criminal issues. You were just one more casualty of a dangerous line of work. But we'd all know why it happened, and we'd all be a little more careful not to cross them." She shrugged. "Or maybe they'd hold you there for a while, try to use your safety to get Hunter to comply with their *requests*. I'd like to think it wouldn't work— I'd like to think Hunter's been around long enough to know that you were doomed the moment you stepped on the plane and nothing he could do after that would save you." She smiled gently. "But Hunter's not really known for his cool analytical skills."

"Okay," Christian said. His head was spinning. Too much to think about, and hearing his death discussed in such a casual manner was disconcerting at best. "Okay, so when they say I just need to do one more job, I say no. I stay here, take the heat from the contract stuff for the rest of the year, and move on. That's easy, right?"

"Well, not easy. But could it happen that way?" She squinted at him thoughtfully. "I don't know, Christian. It's *possible* that it might work. They *might* just let you walk away. But I doubt it. They have reputations to protect, after all, and as I said, they were quite pleased with themselves when they got you on board. I don't think they'd be able to just let that go."

"So... so what are we talking about now?" He was pleased that his voice came out reasonably level. He might not be able to fool the woman, but at least he could maintain some level of dignity in front of Hunter.

Wendy said, "One of the disadvantages of your past indulgences, Christian, is that everyone knows about them. Everyone who matters. And everyone knows how very, very difficult it is for junkies to get clean and stay that way. If one of them came to your apartment this evening and when the door opened there was already a smoking... what is it, a pile? A line? Whatever. A little bit of heaven, right there in front of you, *waiting* for you, so close you could smell the smoke... would you give in?" She shrugged. "That would be the tidy way. Have you smoke voluntarily, then, when you were sleepy and happy, stick a needle in your arm and give you the rest of it. But if you were able to resist the first temptation, they'd just hold you down and jab you anyway. No one's going to question a few bruises on an OD'ed junkie. No one's going to question much of anything, Christian, because no one cares. You're just one more junkie who couldn't quite get clean."

Hunter moved then, shifting around to look out the window. Christian followed his gaze and thought about leaping through the glass, trying to escape that way. It wasn't that the door was blocked; he could have left the room anytime he wanted to. But the jagged glass in the window frame, pressed against his throat—*that* would be the real escape.

Instead, he made himself look back at Wendy and said, "Okay. That's why *they* don't want me to quit and that's what *they* are maybe going to do if I try. What about you? Why do *you* care about any of this?"

"They're trying to take over the company, Christian. We formed this organization as a team, a cooperative venture between equals. We take turns being chair of the board, but the position is meant to be mostly ceremonial and bureaucratic. It's mostly a nuisance, really. We're supposed to be equals. But now, Bentick and Allen want to *run* the company. They want to take over." She shook her head softly. "My dear boy. If *anyone* is going to take control of this company, it will be *me*."

It was a little chilling, how she could sound so soft and so ominous all at the same time. Christian tried not to be thrown off. "You think *I* can help you get that somehow?"

She looked toward Hunter, who was still staring out the window. "Keeping Hunter out of their clutches is important to me. He's very useful." She turned back to Christian and added, "And I'm beginning to think you may be of some use as well." Hunter turned to stare at her, and she smiled. "Not as an active participant. Just as a distraction."

"The point of this was for you to get him *out*," Hunter growled.

"No," she disagreed politely. "I'm sure that's why you contacted me, but that's not why I agreed to meet with you. I came to see what was going on, and to determine how I might arrange things to my advantage. As always." The last words were mildly scolding, as if she thought Hunter really should have learned that about her by now.

"So what are you saying?" Christian wasn't sure he wanted to know, but he asked anyway. "What is it you expect me to do?"

"Stay alive." She shrugged. "Everything after that is a detail."

"And how do you... I mean, they know where I live. If all this stuff about them showing up at my door isn't just a scare tactic...."

"They know where you *lived*," she said firmly. "I had someone collect your personal belongings earlier this afternoon. Apparently it wasn't a big job. We'll put you up somewhere else. You should still train more or less the way you always have. Honestly, the safest place for you to be is on company property, with all our surveillance and our dedication to being low-profile. You'll need to change your running route in order to be less predictable. And you'll need to stop running alone." She stopped pointedly and looked in Hunter's direction.

"No," he said firmly. "I am *not* his babysitter. If you want to adopt a little orphan, you go for it, but I'm not part of your game."

"Of course you're part of it," she said, sounding tired. "And now Christian is too."

"This is crazy," Christian said. He was trying to ignore the invasion of his privacy, the totally callous way she'd violated his rights and sent someone to his home. He could be outraged about that later, but for the time being, he needed to get more information out of her. "There has to be... there's a plan, right? I mean, if they're pushing people around, there's a plan to push back? Something?"

"There's always a plan," Wendy agreed. "But not one you need to worry about. For now, you'll live where I tell you to, and you'll do what I tell you to. That will keep you alive. Probably."

Christian knew he had no right, but he also had no other options. "Hunter," he said quietly. "Is this what I should be doing?"

Hunter's gaze found Christian's cheekbone again, then drifted away. "I have no idea," he said.

"I need more than that."

"We don't always get what we need." Hunter seemed to take a vicious satisfaction in saying that to Christian. Then he pushed away from the wall, restless and tense. "I don't like this," he told Wendy.

She nodded placidly, but spoke to Christian, not Hunter. "Everything should be fine while we're up here—nobody wants an incident that would call attention to us. But still, don't be foolish. Don't be lured away from the main areas, and don't go anywhere with anyone you don't know and trust. Which means Hunter. Don't go anywhere with anyone but Hunter."

Christian tried to ignore the pained expression on Hunter's face. "If Bentick tells me to go somewhere with him and I say no, he's going to know something's up."

"He already knows," she replied. "You and Hunter *both* missing your fight time today? Sloppy."

"I didn't know he wasn't going to be there!" Christian protested.

"So why'd you miss it?" Hunter asked. He didn't bother to look at Christian's cheek this time, just glanced at his shoulder and turned back to the window.

"I was... I didn't need it. I didn't need to be distracted anymore. And I was planning to quit, so I just... I quit."

"Distracted from what?" Wendy inquired.

"Elephants," he snarled.

This time, Hunter didn't even turn in his direction. "I'll give you your key back tomorrow night," he said.

"Fuck you. Give it to me now."

Hunter turned, one arched eyebrow clearly questioning whether he'd heard correctly. "You think you can take it from me?"

Of course he couldn't. Christian'd had an older cousin who would play games like this, taunting young Christian into tears and tantrums by refusing to return something Christian wanted, something he knew was rightfully his. Adult Christian wasn't going to fucking cry about it, but he wondered what it would feel like to have a tantrum. Throw the TV through the damn window, tear the mattress off the bed and use it to club Hunter, run out into the parking lot and start screaming at the top of his lungs, sharing whatever secrets he knew or could invent. Doing whatever he had to in order to make it clear that he was fucking upset. The past six months of his life had been a lie, he hadn't slept, his life was being threatened for reasons he didn't really understand, his apartment had been invaded, the one man he'd ever really cared about hated him and was trying to make him suffer, and all Christian wanted was the key to his fucking bike.

But he couldn't have it. Because Hunter wanted to push him around and show him who was boss. Hunter wanted to make Christian feel small the way Christian had made him feel. That was the worst part. Hunter's behavior was all totally Christian's fault.

"Fuck it," he said. He pushed away from the wall he'd been leaning on and headed for the exit. He opened the door, turned to Wendy, and said, "Fuck you." Then he turned to Hunter and added a little more venom to, "And fuck you too." He went outside, walked the two steps to his own room, and turned the doorknob. The door was locked. And Christian's key was inside.

He leaned forward until his forehead thudded against the door. He pulled away and let it thud forward again, a little harder. As if he was knocking on his own door. As if there was someone inside to let him in.

He knew Hunter was watching him. Judging him, thinking he was stupid and incompetent and pathetic. The worst part was knowing that Hunter was right.

CHAPTER TWELVE

Christian eventually pulled himself far enough out of his little misery wallow to go get a spare key from the front office. They just gave it to him, without asking for ID or anything, and he wondered what would happen if someone else came by and asked for one, and then let himself into Christian's room. He bought dinner from the diner attached to the motel and took it back to his room, and he ate it while sitting on the floor behind the bed, with the lights turned out and a chair braced against the doorknob.

When the motel got loud, with music, yelling, and laughter, he lay down on the floor and wished he were somewhere else, and when a few people came by to bang on his door, yelling his name and telling him to come outside and have fun, he jumped every time.

He was exhausted, but he didn't get much sleep and woke up feeling worse than when he went to bed. Well, went to floor, because he'd never really felt safe enough to make the move up to the furniture.

He didn't want to shower; he'd *seen* the movie, he knew what happened when you showered. He managed to force himself in for a quick rinse, at least, although he didn't close his eyes and kept the shower curtain half open so he could see the bathroom door. He pulled his underwear on and headed for the main room, then jumped back into the bathroom when he heard someone walking past the door of his room.

His shower hadn't been long enough to steam up the mirror. He leaned on the counter and stared at his reflection, saw the wide eyes, the tense shoulders... the scared little boy.

Fuck it. He pushed away from the counter and headed for the door of the room. He wasn't going to live like this. He threw the door open. The bright sunlight burned his eyes, the cool wind stung his bare, wet skin, but he didn't stop moving. He found the middle of the parking lot and raised his hands out to the sides. Unarmed, undefended. He turned slowly, eyes closed, exposing all sides to all angles. He wondered if he'd feel the bullets or if they'd kill him instantly. One minute here, the next gone. That wouldn't be so bad. It'd suck if there was pain, but he could handle that. It would be fine. He kept his eyes shut and kept turning.

"Tanning?" The voice came from nearby, but Christian didn't jump.

"Yes," he said. Easier to agree than to try to explain this to Hunter.

"You're starting to get a bit of attention."

"From snipers?"

"From a family of four."

Christian opened his eyes a little, and Hunter jerked his head toward the diner. Sure enough, a mom, a dad, a boy and a girl, the perfect little family, were staring at him as if he were putting on a Vegas show.

"Get some clothes on," Hunter said, "and get some breakfast. I'll drive you out to the site."

"I can get a ride with someone else."

"Wendy made it clear to you. Christian. Don't bend the fucking rules. You don't get in a vehicle driven by anyone but me."

"What about a police officer? Or Wendy? Or, like, Chuck Norris. If Chuck Norris offers me a ride, I'm taking it."

"Did you sleep? Seriously, when's the last time you slept?"

"I napped. I'm good." He actually meant it. Maybe he'd just needed a little sunlight, a little fresh air. "Nobody's shooting me. Everything's cool."

"Fine." Hunter didn't sound like he agreed, but he also didn't sound like he was interested in arguing. "Get some clothes on, get some breakfast, and meet me at the truck in fifteen minutes."

Christian did as he was told, but he did it with a light, bouncing step. Sure, his little test hadn't proved that people weren't trying to kill him; Wendy had *said* they weren't going to call attention to the company by killing him at the picnic. But it had proved that if death came, he could face it. He wasn't going to sneak around. It just wasn't his style.

"That is the brightest shirt I have ever seen on a man who wasn't going hunting," Hunter said as he closed his motel room door and walked to the driver's side of his SUV.

Christian pushed off the bumper he'd been leaning on and headed for the passenger side. "I just bought it; they have a little gift shop by the office."

"I think it may be a woman's shirt."

"This shirt is 100 percent cotton, exclusive of trimmings. Cotton doesn't have a gender, Hunter."

"I know this is a bit of a sensitive topic, but are you high right now?"

Christian grinned. "Are you upset because I didn't buy a shirt for you? I can go check, see if they have another one."

Hunter didn't respond, and Christian figured it would be better not to push him too much. They were on the highway headed for the site when Hunter finally said, "This thing is serious. It's real. Don't play with it."

"You haven't given me anything to do *except* play," Christian said. "If it comes down to sitting around and waiting to get shot or playing? I'm going to fucking play." And then because this was Hunter, even "three years later and super grumpy" Hunter, Christian added, "I can't do nothing. I mean... for me. For... for how I am, for how I stay clean. I need to be *doing* shit, not sitting around *worrying* about shit. You know?"

Hunter looked genuinely startled. "I hadn't... I didn't think about that."

"No reason you should have. It's my problem, not yours."

"And this shit with the company is *my* problem. But somehow it got turned into yours."

"Well, yeah. So now I'd really like to be part of the solution. Whatever that is. I mean, like I said, I'm going to be doing *something*. The more I know, the better the chances that I'll do something that's maybe a little useful. Or at least not totally disastrous."

Hunter shook his head and didn't say anything for quite a while. Finally, though, he said, "I'm almost as much of a pawn as you. Wendy's the chess master. But, yeah, I'll try to keep you in the loop."

And there was almost peace. So of course, Christian had to push it a little further and screw everything up. "Look, Hunter. About before. You know, when I... before. I'm sorry."

As soon as the words were out of his mouth, he knew they'd been a mistake. Hunter's fingers tightened on the steering wheel, and his voice was tight and angry when he said, "Sorry for not loving me? Or sorry for finding such a chickenshit way of showing it?"

Christian could still remember how safe he'd felt at Hunter's cabin, how wonderful it had been to walk into a room and know he would be welcome in it. How warm it had been when he leaned against Hunter's chest, and how hot it could get when he did just a little bit more. And he remembered the look on Hunter's face when he'd come up the stairs and seen Christian and Hayley in bed together. "Both," he almost whispered. "I'm sorry for both."

Hunter didn't answer him, and Christian somehow found the sense to keep his mouth shut, at least for a while. But when they were almost to the site, bouncing over a rutted road that was hard going even in an SUV with an off-road package, Christian said, "Is Hayley okay?"

They were stuck behind a line of slow-moving vehicles, and Hunter turned to stare at Christian. "You think she's been pining for you for three years?"

"What? No, of course she'd be okay about *that*." Hayley hadn't been exactly virginal when they'd gotten together, and she'd known it wasn't a big emotional scene; that was at least one thing Christian didn't have to feel guilty about. "I just meant is she *safe*? I mean, you have a family. You have friends. Well, Miriam, at least. Maybe other friends, I don't know. If Bentick and his guys are going after someone as distant as me, they must be going after those people too. Right?"

"I'm worried about it," Hunter admitted. "But I don't think they'll go that far. If they went after family it'd be an open declaration of war. Something like that would tear the company apart. And the rest of them—Hayley, Miriam, my mom— they're respected members of the community. There'd be a hell of a lot of attention if a law student, a doctor, or a middle-class housewife disappeared or got killed. You, though? Nobody's going to make a fuss if something happens to you."

Luckily they'd reached the parking area then, and Christian was out the door before the vehicle had come to a full stop. Hunter hadn't said anything new; Christian shouldn't be a princess about it. There was nobody who'd miss him if he disappeared. He knew it was true, and he couldn't blame Hunter for answering a question honestly.

Didn't mean he had to like hearing it, though. He tried to put everything out of his head and focus on the events. He came in fourth to last in the three-gun competition, and when they picked teams for the paintball tournament, he was the very last one chosen, even after some guy who looked like he was about sixty years old and had a beer gut hanging halfway to his knees. When the game started, that guy was Christian's first target. His first kill. Suck on that, team-pickers. After that he just hid, letting the other players pick each other off. Then, when the battle reached its final moments he sneaked out and his pellets found three of the enemy players while his remaining teammates finished off the rest. The rest of them all celebrated and high-fived each other, but Christian had been at a distance when he was shooting and he didn't get any closer for the wrap-up. He'd enjoyed the game, but it had just been luck that he'd stayed alive. He hadn't been part of their strategy. He hadn't really been part of the team.

He was standing in line at lunch when Bob found him again. "You didn't join us yesterday."

"Bob, hey. Sorry about that, Bob, I guess I got a bit distracted, Bob. Bob, you know how it is, Bob, I had to get psyched up for my fight, Bob. Bob, I had to get ready to bob and weave, Bob."

"You're feeling better, I guess." Bob smiled easily. "Good work this morning."

Christian snorted. "What, the part where I came in almost last or the part where I hid my way through the paintball game?"

"The game," Bob said seriously. "You stayed alive. You took out enemy troops. You didn't have a job assigned to you, so you improvised. Did you know you had the highest head count in the whole game?"

"By sneaking up on people who didn't know I was even playing."

Bob looked at him in disbelief. "Yeah! It was beautiful. They underestimated you, overlooked you, and you took advantage of it." He shook his head. "It was good to see. Nicely done."

"I think you might be a little biased, Bob."

Bob looked at him slyly. "What, because you kept your ass so tight for me? Or because you *specialize* in giving me blowjobs?"

Christian froze, then turned guiltily in Bob's direction. "You heard about that?"

Bob grinned. "Yeah, I heard." He shook his head. "You have got a mouth on you, son...."

"Well, you'd know, Bob," Christian said, and he licked his lips lasciviously.

Bob grinned at him, then clapped him on his shoulder. "Good work this morning," he said again, and this time Christian didn't argue with him.

The afternoon was the finals of the martial-arts tournament, and Christian hoped maybe he and Hunter could leave early since they were both eliminated. But Hunter seemed intent on watching the others spar, so Christian didn't interrupt. He wondered how pissed Hunter would be if he hitched a ride home with someone else and decided it would probably not be a good idea to find out.

So he was sitting on the grass, waiting for the final matchup to begin, when he felt someone standing behind him and turned just as there was a sharp nudge to his ass from the toe of someone's boot. Bentick. Fuck.

"We need to talk," Bentick growled. He stepped back far enough to give Christian room to stand, but no farther. Christian looked to Hunter, but he was deep in conversation with one of the men about to enter the ring, clearly not paying any attention to Christian or his issues.

So Christian stood up. Wendy had said Bentick wouldn't pull anything at an event like this. Of course, Wendy was almost certainly a psychopath without emotions or remorse, so Christian shouldn't really be trusting her for information relating to life-or-death situations. He followed Bentick through the crowd and realized he only had Wendy's word to prove he was even *in* a life-or-death situation. Well, Hunter seemed to think it was pretty serious too, but he'd admitted he was just following Wendy's lead.

Maybe the whole thing was just a misunderstanding, Christian thought. Then Bentick turned to glare at him, his eyes glittering dark and sinister, and Christian was pretty sure Hunter and Wendy were on the right track. "You had a little meeting yesterday?" he asked. They'd taken a path into the forest, not far from the crowd, but out of sight. Out of earshot? "You and Hunter and Wendy, sitting down for tea?"

"Scotch," Christian said. "And not exactly a meeting. More like... scotch."

"Oh, just a casual get-together between friends, an untrained nobody hanging out with two members of the board of directors."

Christian could have deflected, or he could have joked it off. Instead he decided for a more direct approach. "Based on what they said, I think you know I used to have a bit of a connection to Hunter. They weren't evaluating my training, they were explaining why I got hired in the first place."

Bentick's eyes still glittered. "And what did you think about that?"

"I decided I should quit. There's no point wasting everyone's time and energy on a game I don't want to play."

"Your contract doesn't really allow you to quit. Not without some serious penalties."

Christian nodded. "Yeah. I guess I should have read that more carefully. But who am I kidding? I would have signed it anyway."

"And now you want to break it. After all the time and energy we put into you, you want to walk away, without completing a single assignment for us."

"Well, yeah." No point in beating around the bush. "That's what I'd like."

Bentick nodded. "You could pretend all this never happened. Move on with your life."

Go back to working dead-end jobs and fucking random strangers to distract himself from how empty his life was. Yeah, Christian could do that.

"I can't let that happen," Bentick said. "Not without getting the company *some* level of return on their investment. But if we could get one job out of you, just one assignment...."

So there it was. Christian wondered if Bentick was going to suggest Somalia, Afghanistan, or some other lawless place where an extra body would barely be noticed. He braced himself and wondered how to best phrase his refusal.

Then Bentick said, "This whole thing has gone too far. We're squabbling with each other when we should be focusing on business. And all we really need to do is sit down and talk it all over. But Jack Hunter is being... well, he's being Jack Hunter. A sullen, stubborn pain in the ass. And as long as he's behaving that way, the rest of the board feels like they have to too. Don't even get me started on Wendy. She's a piece of work, huh?"

Christian stared at him. This was so much more reasonable than he'd been expecting. Jack Hunter—the current version, at least—*was* a sullen, stubborn pain in the ass. And "piece of work" didn't even begin to describe Wendy. "They can be difficult, I guess," Christian said carefully.

Bentick smiled at him. Maybe the glitter in his eyes was just... well, maybe it was just moisture or something. Was Christian a witch, thinking he could read someone's thoughts based on a tiny feature of their appearance? "We just need to sit down and talk," Bentick said again. "That'll solve this whole problem, and, seriously, kid, if you can get us working together it would *more* than make up for the expense of your training. I'm wondering if you could be a sort of mediator. A peace broker."

Christian had to admit that sounded like exactly what they needed. "I'd help any way I could," he said.

"Excellent. Don't mention this to Hunter. He'll just... well, you know how he is. He'll overreact, twist it into something it isn't, get his back up and be determined to make it fail before even giving it a chance." Christian nodded his agreement, and Bentick said, "I'll contact you in the next day or two, give you a time and a place. I'll just need you to get Hunter there. Just Hunter and me. So he and I can really talk things through."

"And when I do that, I'm done? You'll rip up the contract?"

Bentick nodded. "All done," he agreed.

They separated then, taking different routes back to the event. The final match was almost over, two strong men moving so quickly Christian could barely follow them, trading blows, grappling, one finally being dragged to the mat and forced to submit, his body arching in resistance that looked almost exactly like ecstasy. Christian's eyes moved without any instruction, his gaze finding Hunter. And Hunter was staring right back at him. Christian's mouth was dry, his body tense, and he could not or would not look away. Fifty feet between them, but they might as well have been right next to each other. Christian could feel it all as if it were happening right then: the heat from Hunter's body, the smell of his sweat and arousal, the taste of his skin, his mouth, his cock. Most of all, though, the solidity of him. The knowledge that if Christian pushed, he'd meet something gentle but unyielding, soft but strong. If he fell, Hunter would catch him, and if he ran, Hunter would keep up.

Except he hadn't, Christian remembered, and he forced himself to look at the fighters, at the sky, anywhere but at Hunter. Christian had run, and Hunter had let him get away. Hunter had *wanted* him to get away. Because Christian had pushed way too fucking far.

There was no going back and no point thinking about things he couldn't have. Things he'd smashed and abandoned and destroyed. So Christian turned and walked away, following the crowd down to the parking area, then waiting by the SUV for Hunter to show up.

But apparently the festivities weren't quite over. Everyone gathered around as some guy Christian didn't even recognize climbed up into a pickup bed and gave a little speech about how good it was to have these events and how valuable it was to meet in friendly competition.

Then it was time for the awards, of course. Christian just wanted to get out of there, but Hunter was nowhere in sight, and it wasn't like they'd have been able to get the SUV out through the crowd anyway, not without drawing a lot of attention and resentment. So he stood and listened and applauded politely as all these men were celebrated for their skill, and he felt even stupider for having ever thought he could have aspired to join their ranks.

They ran out of events to celebrate, thankfully, and that was when the man in the back of the truck said, "And as usual, we have a few special awards this year." Jesus, there was more. So Christian stood there and watched as men were presented with lifetime achievement awards, special merit awards for things he was pretty sure had happened in the field, not in the contests, and then, finally, the man said, "Just one more. One more. It isn't that often that someone takes on every single event at one of our little gatherings. Not too common to see that dedication to being a true warrior instead of a specialist. But this guy is working on being a man on the ground, someone who just gets things done, and we appreciate that ethic and the development of that skill set. So, Christian Manning, come on down and pick up your all-rounder award."

It was a joke, obviously. Or else they thought they could still manipulate him, still fool him into thinking he had anything of value to them. But there was no way to refuse the award without making a scene, drawing more people into the little drama than really had to be. So Chr_stian pasted on as much of a smile as he could manage, made his way to the front of the gathering, and grabbed his award. It was a little chunk of metal with the company logo on it. They probably had them made in batches of a thousand.

He saw Bob at the edge of the crowd, grinning and clapping like he actually thought it was real. It was nice to know Bob wasn't in on it all, at least.

By the time he got back to the SUV Hunter was waiting for him. There was still a bit of a wait before they could go anywhere but they climbed into their seats anyway, both of them staring out the windshield like they were at the drive-in watching a great movie.

Finally Christian said, "Bentick wants me to set up a meeting. I'm not supposed to tell you about it, and he says it's supposed to be just you and him so you can get stuff figured out. He's going to get in touch to tell me when and where."

Hunter turned to stare at him. "That's what he said?"

"Yeah. You figure he's going to ambush you, take you out?" Christian shook his head. "Why are you acting so shocked? You think I'm maybe going to get killed, but you're the mighty Jack Hunter, you're immune from it all?" It was kind of satisfying to say, "I guess he doesn't think you're all that special after all. I guess he's decided he doesn't need to *control* you if he can just eliminate you."

"And what does that mean for you?" Hunter growled. "You think he's going to let you skip away from all this?"

"No. Nothing's changed for me. But it's a bit of a shake-up for you, isn't it?"

"Did he tell you roughly when? Like, he's going to contact you today, or...?"

"What's that short story called? 'Appointment in Samara,'

or something? About the guy trying to run away from Death?"

"Fuck, Christian! Shut up!" Hunter was yelling, but he brought his voice back down quickly and looked around to see if anyone in any other vehicles had seen. Luckily, they were all in single file, nothing on either side of the SUV but trees. "Listen to me. If this happens... if he decides to take me out... that means he's going nuclear. *You're* not safe, my family isn't safe, none of the board members are safe...."

Well, Christian didn't care that much about the board members, and he'd already been in danger before all this, but he didn't like thinking about Hayley or Miriam being in trouble. "What if there's, like, a subnuclear option? What if he just wants to kidnap you or something? I mean, I get it, you're Superman, you're the best, you're invincible... but really, if he just wanted you dead, a sniper outside your house would do it, wouldn't it? Does he really need to set up a special meeting just to knock you off?"

"A sniper outside the house would be tricky. I picked my place to make sure of that. But, yeah, outside the next board meeting, or some other place he'd know I'd be...." He shook his head in frustration. "I fucking hate this. I need to call Wendy, get her brain on it."

"You want me to drive while you dial?"

"No, I want you to shut up." Then Hunter huffed out a sharp breath. "Fuck. Sorry. You... he told you not to tell me, right? He sold this to you somehow?"

"Yeah. He said I could be the peacemaker, the diplomat, the one who solved it all for you guys. Like Wendy said, I guess: I was supposed to think that this was my chance to show what I could do and impress you all. But she was right. I didn't think that, I just realized how impossible it would be for *me* to do all that when none of *you* guys were able to do it." He glanced over toward Hunter as he added, "She was wrong about the last part, though. The part where I don't care. I want to get out of this alive, if I can. I really want that. And, you know, if at all possible, it'd be nice if you got out too. I care about that."

"Yeah," Hunter said dully. "That'd be nice."

Christian had probably said enough, but he didn't want to lay all that on Hunter as if it were his responsibility or something. "But, listen. If things *do* go wrong? I mean, if you get out and I don't? Don't feel bad, okay? You saved my life three years ago. I absolutely believe that. So if things go wrong now, at least I got an extra few years."

"Shut up, Christian."

Not exactly the response Christian had been hoping for. "I just wanted to be sure—"

"No!" Hunter said, louder this time "I'm not going to hear that shit."

"Well, you heard it once, so you probably don't *need* to hear it again. But remember it, okay? In case anything happens."

"Jesus Christ," Hunter said. He didn't sound angry anymore, just sad, and tired. So Christian left him alone, and once they hit the main road, Hunter pulled out his cell phone and called Wendy. Christian leaned his head against the side window and looked at the trees flashing by, half-listened to Hunter's side of the telephone conversation, and waited for the bullets to find him.

CHAPTER THIRTEEN

"It's like camp!" Christian said, peering into the windowless room and trying desperately to maintain some level of positivity.

"A POW camp, maybe." Apparently Hunter didn't share Christian's feelings about the importance of a good attitude. Which was fair, since Christian's devotion to the idea was more than a little itinerant itself.

There were two bunk beds, two footlockers, and two night tables. No other furniture, no decoration. Even the walls were a gloomy, mossy gray. It was pretty clear that the chief attraction was the heavy door they'd just come through and the heavy door on the wall between the beds. Two escape routes, in case anything happened. And a small bathroom, its doorway just beside the one they'd used. "It's well lit," Christian said. "We can read."

"Shut up, Christian."

Christian tossed his gear bag on one of the lower bunks, then heaved the boxes he'd been carrying over into the corner. Whoever had packed the stuff up from his apartment had been really efficient; he'd peeked inside one box to find clothes neatly folded that he was pretty sure had been balled up in his laundry basket before he'd left. Another box had his dishes and food, and there was a plug-in cooler holding the contents of his fridge. Two more boxes in the SUV probably had the rest of his clothes and his linens or whatever, but he hadn't bothered to look into them to be sure. He was actually surprised by how much stuff he'd accumulated over the past few months. Probably more than he'd ever had before in his life. Of course, it was all junk, but still. He had stuff; if he disappeared, someone would have to notice, even if only to figure out what to do with it all.

"We could brighten it up a little. Some posters. Hey, maybe an aquarium!" He still hadn't bought his Russian fish.

"We're not going to decorate the bunker."

"Well, maybe you're not going to decorate *your* side. But then it's gonna look pretty crappy compared to mine. Brace yourself."

"This is not a new apartment. This is a short-term arrangement. *Very* short-term. Hopefully just for tonight." Hunter sounded like he was working hard to keep his words even marginally polite.

"They emptied my apartment for one night? No way, I don't think so."

"*You* might be here for longer," Hunter admitted. "Or you might get shipped somewhere else. I'm talking about *me*. I'm only here short-term."

"I wonder what would happen if they locked us in," Christian mused. "Just decided to give up on the whole thing and get rid of us. We'd have water, unless they turned it off. The place isn't airtight, and we'd have *some* food. I mean, it's mine, but I'd share. Some of it, at least."

Hunter was staring at him like he wanted him dead, but Christian was pretty much past being intimidated by the other man's grumpiness. So he said, "I guess that'd be the first thing to go, right? We'd run out of food? One of us would have to kill the other and butcher him. Use the cooler to keep the meat fresh."

"Please shut up."

Christian grinned. "Yeah, you're thinking that you'd be the one to kill me. And, sure, okay, if it was a fair fight, you'd be right. But if I was the first one to think of it... if I caught you by surprise... I could take you out before you even knew what was happening. I bet I could."

"You're threatening to kill and eat me," Hunter said quietly, "and I would like it if you would shut up."

"Not threatening. Just... musing. You know?"

Hunter sighed. "Blowing the element of surprise, that's what you're doing. I mean, now that I know you're coming, I'll be ready. Waiting."

Christian tried not to smile too widely. He'd sucked Hunter in! Hunter was playing! Christian had no idea why it made him so happy, but it absolutely did. He made himself sound casual when he said, "But you still have to sleep. We're both vulnerable, here. It'd be a question of commitment, probably. Which one of us would be the first to decide that the time had come?"

"Just to be safe, I'll probably kill you as soon as the door locks. No waiting whatsoever. That way you'll still be full-sized, with a nice bit of marbling. I could eat you while you're fresh and tasty, and then move on to the dry goods later."

Christian squinted at him. "Well, not *right* as soon as the door locks. I mean, what if it's just a drill?"

"That would be unfortunate." Hunter turned to stare at him, his eyes cold and fierce. "Unfortunate for you."

It sent a chill down Christian's spine. Then Hunter grinned. That same old Hunter smile, the one that lit up his eyes, the one that made Christian feel as if the two of them were the only ones in the world that got the joke. Their gazes held for one beautiful moment, then Hunter blinked and looked away. "Good thing for you the doors only lock from the inside," he said. "I checked."

Oh. Yeah, that was a good thing. Christian lay back on the bed and looked up at the bottom of the bunk above his. He needed to get his thoughts away from Hunter's smile. "Why does this place even exist? I mean, is it really just for times like this? Or was it for drug mules, or human trafficking or something? How did you know to come here?" They were in the basement of an abandoned factory in Surrey, and Hunter had been just as dependent on directions to find the place as Christian had. Clearly not somewhere he'd been before.

Hunter shrugged and lay down on his own bed. "Wendy." He seemed to think the one-word was answer enough. But after a while he added, "She's not as wired in to the company as the rest of us. I mean, I don't have a single place the company doesn't know about. We could have gone to a hotel or something, but every credit card I own, they could track. I have one under a fake name, but the company guys were the ones who set that identity up. They could find me, for sure. Wendy, though? She probably has five different IDs all lined up, ones she set up on her own or through someone independent. She's been preparing for something like this since the day the company opened its doors."

"And you're sure you can trust her? You're *sure*?"

"I'm not sure of a goddamn thing." Hunter was sounding tired again. "But her motivations make sense, I think. Keeping Bentick and the rest from taking over the company."

"Why do you care? Why don't you just let them take over? I mean, if they did, how would that affect you? Since when do you care that much about the company? I thought you were retired."

"Things change," Hunter said, his voice clipped and tight. "And I don't want Bentick in control because he wants to take the company in a dangerous direction. He wants to get a lot more aggressive." Hunter seemed impatient at having to explain, but he did it anyway. "We're not mercenaries. Not technically. Mercenaries will go on offense as well as provide defense. We're security contractors—defense only. Maybe that's not a distinction that means much to the general public, but it means something to me. And it means something to the guys I work with, the guys I recruited to be a part of a certain kind of company. Bentick wants to change that, and Wendy wants to stop him."

"So Bentick's bad, Wendy's good. That's what we're going with."

"Bentick's bad," Hunter said firmly. He sounded a lot less confident when he said, "Wendy's better." He sat up quickly, his head grazing the bunk above him as he put his feet on the floor and stared at Christian. "But the whole situation's bad, and dangerous, and fuck it, Christian, you need to get out. Whatever the fuck Wendy is up to? That's her game. You do *not* have to play it."

"I thought I wasn't allowed to quit? Bentick would come after me, and all that?"

"Fuck Bentick. If he can't find you, he can't hurt you. It's not my specialty area, but I know the basics... pay cash for everything, keep moving, don't contact anyone from your old life—"

"That last part'd be easy. But I don't have the money to go on a cash-only road trip, Hunter. And for how long? You have no idea when this is going to end."

"What about your dad? He's got to have some serious contacts, and some money too. You could give him a call."

"No," Christian said. It was that simple.

"Why the fuck not? You need help, Christian. I can give you some cash, but I couldn't put too much together all that fast, and it's important that once you get out of here you don't have any contact with me, nothing that would let them trace you. I could give you enough to start, and then your dad—"

"No," Christian said again.

"It'd be kind of embarrassing, is that it? Calling him up after all this time and asking for help? It'd be a hell of a lot better to go cruising home with a nice car and a good job or whatever, I get that, but—"

"You don't get it." Christian knew it was pathetic that this still got to him, but what the hell, he could just add it to the list of ways he was a loser. "Let it go."

"This is life and death. If there's a chance of him helping you out, why the hell wouldn't you give it a shot?"

Christian wished they weren't stuck in the room together. He didn't need much, just a little bit of space. But Hunter wasn't giving it to him. And maybe Christian should stop being such a little drama queen about it all. Yeah, maybe he should just explain himself, like a normal person would.

"My mom died when I was twelve," he said. He kept his voice calm and controlled. If he was going to do this, he *needed* the control. "Drowned in the hot tub one night. She was a drunk, and she took a lot of pills, so... nobody was too surprised." There, that was the way to do it. Just the facts. "I didn't know she was out there when I left for school. I just figured she was passed out in the bedroom. I got home from school and my dad was there, which was a bit weird but not totally crazy, and he sent me out to put my bike away; I'd left it in the backyard days before, and he liked things tidy. So I found her in the tub, and she'd been in there all day." That was all Christian was going to say about that. All he was *ever* going to say about it.

But he could finish the story without giving any more details of the discovery. "The cops came and my dad said he'd gone to bed before she was even in the hot tub. He had no idea she was there, and in the morning when she wasn't in bed, he was in a hurry and just figured she'd passed out on the couch or something." Christian wanted to look at Hunter but couldn't bring himself to do it. "The thing is, I *heard* him in the hot tub with her the night before. My bedroom was right above the patio, and I heard them. I don't know if he pushed her under or if he just left her in there when she was fucked up and then tried to cover up his carelessness when something bad happened.

I don't know. I know she was an embarrassment to him, and I know he'd just been passed over for a promotion he should have gotten, and he blamed her drinking for it. But I don't know whether he killed her or not. What I do know, though, for sure... he *absolutely* knew she was in there when he sent me out to get my bike, and the damn bike had been out there for days already. Why the fuck was it so important that it get put away right fucking then?" Why did he have to be the one to find her, the one to see the effects of the heat and the water...

He sat up, not because he wanted to look at Hunter but because he was unable to lie still. "So, no, I'm not going to ask him for help. Fuck him." He pushed himself off the bed. "I'm going for a run. That's allowed, right? It's not going to break one of Wendy's rules?"

"I'll come with you," Hunter said. He rolled to his feet. Christian wanted to argue, but he didn't have the mental energy.

So they ran, their strides easily matching, their breathing synchronized to their bodies and therefore to each other. Neither of them knew the area, so they explored, their surroundings shifting from industrial to something near farmland and then to residential. By the time they made it back to the bunker, it was dark out and Christian had regained his equanimity.

And as soon as he stepped inside the building, he lost it again. Because Hunter was right *there*, and he smelled like clean sweat, and back when things had been good they'd so often take a break right after their run, nothing too involved, just making out a little, maybe jerking each other off if they felt like it. So easy, so good. So gone.

He could tell Hunter was thinking about the same thing. They'd been almost friendly while they were running. Well, they hadn't said much, but Hunter had seemed relaxed for a change, and it had been nice. Now, though, his shoulders were high again, and he was gripping the corner post of his bed as if it were the only thing keeping him from falling off a cliff.

"I think I have towels," Christian said, trying to think about something other than Hunter's sweaty body, the tiny growling grunts he'd made when he was really turned on, the way he'd burrow his nose into Christian's neck and inhale his scent, the way.... "Towels!" Christian said, far too loudly. "Yeah. In that box, maybe. Hang on." He clawed at the packing tape, trying to get inside, trying to focus on anything but the demands his cock was making, the magnetic pull his whole *body* was subjected to. "Yeah, here," he said, and he stood up quickly

Too quickly. Hunter had been trying to get by him, heading for the bathroom, and when Christian stood up he ended up right in Hunter's path. They both had good reflexes but they were also both in the middle of a pretty serious fight with their bodies and that slowed them down a little. Not a lot, just enough that Hunter ended up having to step back to stay balanced and his foot hit the sill of the bathroom floor and he tripped a little and Christian reached out to steady him.

That was all it took. Christian's hand on Hunter's forearm. They both stared at the connection, and Christian knew he should draw his hand back, but how could he? He was touching *Hunter*.

And Hunter wasn't moving away. They both stood there, staring, their ragged breathing the only sound in the room.

Christian made himself do it. Not because he wanted to, but because Hunter deserved better. His hormones shouldn't trap him for the second time. So Christian straightened his fingers, slowly, watching as they trembled from the strain, and then he pulled his hand back and tucked it against his stomach. "Sorry," he whispered.

"Fuck, Christian." Hunter stayed still for a moment longer, then moved fast, making it into the bathroom in one long stride and then slamming the door behind him.

Christian was left in the main room, his pulse racing, his cock hard and demanding. *Hunter*. It was hard to ignore the pull, the desire, but he'd certainly tried. Hard to forget the way he'd felt. The warmth, the safety. The affection. And then the panic. He'd wanted to protect Hunter, but he'd wanted to protect himself too. He'd known the game they were playing, tucked away in the forest, wasn't something that would still make sense after it was exposed to the real world. But he hadn't wanted to see it shattered and destroyed. Better to run away than stay there and watch as everything fell apart.

He leaned against the wall next to the bathroom door. Hunter. He was in there, just past the thin wood partition. He still wanted Christian; that much was as clear now as it had been three years earlier. But lust was common; countless men had wanted Christian's body, for as long he could remember. If Hunter could just keep things separate—if he could just remember that lust and love were two very different things— then maybe it would be safe to give in to their instincts. But Hunter couldn't be trusted. Oh, in some ways he could. Christian would stake his life on Hunter to do the honorable thing; Christian *was* staking his life on it. But Hunter couldn't be trusted to make sense, to follow the patterns other men had followed. He either didn't know the rules or he broke them without letting anyone know what he was up to.

Falling in love? No. Christian shook his head. Hunter hadn't fallen in love, he'd just gotten confused, and he'd tried to drag Christian into his mess then, just like he'd dragged Christian into his mess now. Christian needed to keep the hell away from him, for both of their sakes.

His resolve completely disappeared as soon as the bathroom door opened. Hunter was standing there, still in his shorts but with his shirt off; he'd been standing on the other side of the door, clearly having an internal debate pretty similar to the one Christian had been having. From the expression on his face, it was clear that his brain had come to the same conclusion Christian had, but the hand that shot out and grabbed Christian's shirt made it pretty damn clear that Hunter's brain wasn't in charge right then. He yanked on the shirt and Christian didn't resist. He stumbled forward, expecting to be met with one of Hunter's deep, wet kisses, but instead found himself being spun, shoved, arranged.. oh, yeah. Hunter pressed his hard cock into the cleft of Christian's ass and wrapped one arm around Christian's torso, hip to shoulder, pulling him in tight, controlling him. Christian gasped and arched his back, grinding his ass into Hunter wantonly. Common sense was *gone*. This needed to happen.

"You've got stuff?" Hunter growled in his ear.

Everything Christian owned was boxed up and in the room; there must be condoms and lube somewhere. But where? He tried to make his brain work, tried to think of anything but Hunter's hot body, his strong arm and demanding cock. His toiletries kit. There were condoms in there, and he'd seen it in the same box as the towels. "There." He managed to gesture.

But instead of leaving Christian on the wall and getting the stuff himself, Hunter kept playing his control game. He kept one arm wrapped around Christian's body while the other hand took a firm grip on his hair, and then he eased them both out of the bathroom and bent Christian far enough over that he could reach the box, Hunter's body off to the side enough to let Christian move. Did Hunter think Christian didn't want this? Did he think he had to use force? No, Christian realized. It was just easier to do it this way, to make it about dominance and submission instead of about feelings. That was fine by Christian.

It took only a moment of frantic burrowing to find his prizes, and as soon as he began to straighten Hunter jerked him upright and spun him back around, shoving him against the wall like a cop about to search a suspect. "Give it to me," he ordered, and Christian extended his hand backward. He felt Hunter stretch away a little—dropping the stuff on the bathroom counter. Then he was back, his hands rough as he pulled Christian's T-shirt up over his head. Christian raised his arms obligingly, and Hunter twisted the shirt around his wrists, tying them together. Christian could have gotten loose if he wanted to, but he didn't bother trying. He was too distracted by the way Hunter's hands swept back along Christian's wrists, then his biceps and shoulders. "Keep your hands up there."

Their bodies were so close, so tight, lined up from head to toe, and when Hunter wrapped his arm back around Christian's chest and pulled them tighter, Christian finally let himself inhale deeply. The smell of their mingled sweat, their matched desire was overwhelming, and his whole body trembled. Hunter felt the reaction and tightened his grip as if he thought Christian might be cold, or scared. Or maybe he thought Christian might try to get away. He was wrong on all three counts, though, and he damn well should have known it.

Everything happened fast after that. Hunter wasn't rough but he wasn't gentle, either. No long, slow kisses—no kisses at all. The way he stripped them both down would have felt coolly efficient if Christian hadn't been able to hear Hunter's gasping breath. He was a constant, overwhelming presence, and he never stopped touching Christian; even when he pulled away to deal with the condom, he half turned and kept his hip braced against Christian's ass. Was he still worried Christian would try to escape, or was he, like Christian, just craving the contact, the reminder that after all this time they were really back together and this was really happening?

Christian wanted to turn around, but he was pretty sure that was against the rules. Hunter was in charge, and for all Christian's trembling, Hunter clearly wanted this as anonymous as possible. Maybe *because* of his trembling. So Christian closed his eyes and kept his head turned obediently away. He'd spent enough time appreciating Hunter's cock in the past, he could imagine it now just fine. Long and thick and hard, only a little darker than the rest of his body, the head distinct and proud, with its strangely delicate ridges. It felt perfect as Hunter ran it along the crease of Christian's ass, and even better as he lined up and eased forward.

Blunt pressure, then the familiar burning, stretching, invading. The first push always made Christian's body rebel, and he could feel his muscles trying to resist, trying to reject the intrusion. A deep breath, a reminder to his body that it was going to be very happy in a few moments, and Christian started to relax. Hunter returned his arm to its home around Christian's chest, pulling him in closer. It wasn't a hug, it was just one more way for Hunter to control Christian's body. He never stopped pushing, didn't give Christian a real chance to adjust, but he kept it slow. Just a steady, irresistible force finding its way inside Christian, deeper and deeper.

"Fuck," Christian gasped. He clenched his fingers against the painted wall, trying to find something to dig into, and arched his back involuntarily, pushing his ass back for more punishment, more impossible stretching. When Hunter finally bottomed out, Christian hoped there'd be a moment to collect himself, but Hunter started moving immediately. Almost all the way back out so that the head of his cock stretched Christian's opening, then all the way back in, harder and faster this time. Long, powerful strokes, driving Christian up onto his tiptoes, then leaving him achingly empty before filling him again.

It was overwhelming, and Christian just needed a minute, he needed it to stop for just a tiny bit so he could get his self-control back. But Hunter didn't stop. Harder, faster, more demanding, one hand still wrapped around Christian's chest, the other on his hip, changing the angle to suit his needs, maximize his pleasure. *Hunter's* pleasure. This wasn't about Christian, or at least not about making him come. Hunter wasn't making love, and he wasn't Christian's *partner*. He was fucking him, using him, taking what he wanted with no concern for Christian's needs.

How many times had Christian been fucked like this? How many johns had pushed him up against the wall in an alley or a motel room or the back of a bar and *used* him like this? But somehow, this was different. This was Hunter. He wasn't renting Christian's body, wasn't stealing anything; he was just taking what was his. And that was exciting in a way Christian couldn't quite understand.

Hunter's thrusts were getting wilder, his arm around Christian's chest gripping almost too tight. With every thrust his breath was a ragged, wet explosion on Christian's neck, a beautiful complement to Christian's own gasping. Even in his darkest, most self-destructive days, Christian had never had unprotected sex, but he was wishing for it now, wishing that Hunter's orgasm would explode inside him and coat him, soak him, mark him. But the condom was there, and when Hunter's rhythm finally stuttered, when he made his last few impossibly deep strokes, Christian just had to imagine that there would be something left behind.

Hunter sagged against him, Christian the strong one now, holding them both up. But only for a few breaths before Hunter straightened and pulled away. But he didn't go far. He did his trick with his hip again, holding Christian in place while he took a moment to get organized. Then he quietly said, "Turn around."

Finally. But Christian was disappointed; Hunter didn't look that different. He still looked tense, almost angry, and he was frowning at Christian as if this was all somehow his fault. Then his gaze dropped to Christian's erection, hard and leaking and desperate, and his face softened just a little. "Lean against the wall," he ordered. "And bring your hands down. Lock your fingers together behind your head."

Christian felt a little ridiculous, but he did as he was told. He was exposed and vulnerable as Hunter stared at him, inspecting his body like he was for sale and Hunter wasn't sure if he was worth his price. *You already own me*, Christian thought, but he didn't say it. Maybe Hunter wasn't sure he wanted to keep him.

But finally, mercifully, Hunter reached down and wrapped his fingers around Christian's cock. His grip was tight. Almost too tight, but Hunter knew what he was doing. Christian wasn't afraid of pain, and Hunter's rough grip was just what he needed to get back into himself and focused on his body. "Keep your eyes open," Hunter ordered. Christian hadn't even realized his lids had drifted shut, but he obeyed the command instantly. "Look at me."

That was too much. The fucking, the pressure on his cock— it was all intense, but he could handle it. But looking at Hunter? He'd wanted it so bad before but now he knew he'd been a fool. Seeing Hunter as Hunter saw him like this? It was too intimate, too much. But Hunter's hand stilled, his grip relaxed, and he repeated, "Look at me."

Christian tried. A quick glance was enough to get Hunter's hand to tighten, but he wouldn't move it, wouldn't give Christian what he needed until... there. Fuck, he did it, he looked Hunter in the eyes. And once Christian looked he couldn't stop. Hunter's hand moved, tight and hard and fast, and he stared at Christian as he did it.

It wasn't fair. Hunter had come apart in private, Christian's face turned to the wall. But now that it was Christian's turn, Hunter was staring at him, making him stare back, and it was far too much. Letting Hunter see inside him as his orgasm built, as his universe shrank and expanded, as he lost control of his body and his mind. He shouted as he came, some words he couldn't recognize echoing off the cold bathroom walls, and Hunter's free hand braced on his chest, keeping him from falling over or completely coming apart.

They stood in silence, afterward, Christian's body starting to relax as the come on his chest cooled.

Then Hunter said again, softly, "Look at me."

Christian hadn't realized he'd closed his eyes. There was no bribe this time, no threat, but Christian made himself look at Hunter anyway. Hunter had saved his life, and Christian had repaid him with betrayal and pain. If Hunter wanted to get a little revenge by invading Christian's privacy, Christian couldn't object.

But Hunter didn't seem angry anymore. He didn't seem like he was looking for revenge. He just watched Christian's eyes for a while, then said, "I'll shower first, then you can take your time."

He pushed away, leaving Christian cold without him. Hunter stepped into the tiny shower stall and Christian let his knees buckle, sliding down the wall to the floor. He stayed there while Hunter showered, and for quite a while after Hunter got out. It wasn't as if he had anywhere else to be.

CHAPTER FOURTEEN

Hunter was either asleep or pretending to be when Christian got out of the shower. Good. Christian wasn't sure what the hell he was feeling and didn't want to deal with Hunter until he'd figured it out. He checked the locks on both doors, then climbed into his own bunk and fell asleep more quickly than he'd expected.

He woke up to Hunter moving around the room, using his phone as a flashlight in the darkness and trying to be stealthy. "You can turn the light on," Christian mumbled.

Hunter didn't reply, but a moment later the overhead bulbs glared down into Christian's dark-sensitized eyes. Damn, the room *was* well lit.

After they'd both taken a moment for their eyes to adjust, Hunter started moving again. He was getting dressed. Christian pulled out his arm to see his watch. It was past eight in the morning; he'd slept like the dead. "Where are you going?"

"Meeting," Hunter grunted. And that was all.

Christian swung his feet over the side of the bed. "With who? And what am I supposed to do? I mean, can I go with you? Or can I go out on my own?" He'd left his motorcycle in the basement of Hunter's apartment complex, but he could walk somewhere, do *something*.

"Stay put."

Well, it wasn't like Christian had expected sex to lead to flowers and hand-holding, but was it possible that fucking Christian had made Hunter even *more* sullen and grumpy? Christian looked around the little room. There was nothing to distract himself with. There was room for some basic calisthenics, maybe, but it'd be hard to do a real workout. He was just supposed to sit there, worrying about everything but not able to *do* anything. "For how long?"

"Until I come get you."

"Fuck that, Hunter." Christian stood up. Not being able to sit and think was a part of his weakness, but the desperation it caused made him strong. "I'm not sitting around like a princess waiting to get rescued. I need to—"

"You need to do as you're fucking told!" Hunter's whole body was tense, and Christian watched as he tried to make it relax. "This meeting could take care of things. It could end everything, get you out of this mess. But there's no point in me doing it if you end up getting yourself killed while I'm away. So, please, Christian, give me one less fucking thing to worry about, okay?"

"Who's the meeting with?"

Hunter clearly didn't want to say, but he just as clearly knew that Christian wasn't going to be obedient if he didn't get at least a little more information. "Bentick," he finally grunted, his eyes on his feet, the door, anywhere but Christian's face.

"What? He called you directly? Okay, Hunter that's the trap, right? He doesn't need to use me to set it up if he goes directly to you. You can't go, Hunter!"

"I called him," Hunter said. He was dressed now, ready to leave, staying only long enough to make sure Christian was under control.

"Why did you call him?" Christian tried to sound calm. "What are you thinking?"

"I'm thinking he can do whatever he wants to with the

fucking company. Hopefully I can negotiate an exit for myself, but if I can't, at least I can make sure he leaves you alone."

"What? Hunter, no! That would mean he *wins*! It would mean the whole thing *worked*, using me to control you!"

"He can win," Hunter said softly. He was looking at Christian now, finally. "If it keeps you safe, he can win."

There were arguments to make. If it worked this time, Bentick would know it would work the next time too. The only way to deal with a bully was to stand up to a bully. There were real reasons Hunter hadn't wanted to agree to Bentick's plans, and those reasons hadn't changed. But Christian couldn't bring himself to focus on any of that. "Why?" he finally said. "I mean... okay, I was your first gay sex, and you liked it. A lot. I get that. You kind of got lust and love mixed up. That's why I had to get out of there, to give you a chance to clear your head. But you've been... okay, sorry if it was supposed to be the-sex-that-never-happened, but last night... you knew what you were doing. You knew exactly what you were doing. You've been having lots of gay sex, Hunter. It's not like you've been sitting off in the forest pining over me. So what the fuck? You're doing all this because you feel guilty, or something?" It was the only thing that made sense. "Remember what I told you? You're the one who saved my life. You don't have to feel guilty about it getting a bit messed up now."

Hunter was back to looking at the door, his longing to use it clear in every line of his body. But he forced himself to stay. "I've had lots of gay sex," he agreed reluctantly. "I didn't pine in the forest. I came back to the city, started working again, and went out every night, fucked every guy I could find." He looked at Christian now, his eyes blazing with fierce truth, and with something else. "I knew the difference between lust and love when we were together, and I sure as hell know it now." He held Christian's gaze for a long moment, making sure his words were heard and understood.

Then his voice was softer when he said, "Remember what you told me about chasing the dragon? The first time you do heroin is the sweetest thing ever, and then every time after that is just like an echo? A pale imitation? But the first time was so perfect that you keep chasing anyway, like you couldn't stop yourself...." He looked at Christian and said, "Remember that?"

"I remember," Christian whispered.

"It's not about guilt," Hunter said. He moved a little closer now, staring at Christian, willing him to understand. "I'm a grown man and I know what I felt and what I *feel*. I couldn't make you love me then and I can't change the way you feel now, but for me? Last night wasn't the-sex-that-never-happened, it was the sex I've been wanting for three fucking years."

Christian's mouth was dry, but he forced words through it. "You could have... last night... you could have done that with anybody. That was all *you*."

"The motions? The actions? Sure, with anybody. I mean, I *have* done it with anybody. And it never felt the way it felt with you." Hunter pushed away suddenly, took two steps toward the door, and caught himself. "I don't expect you to understand. But I figured I should say it—"

"I understand," Christian blurted. "I mean, not all of it. A lot of it I'm pretty confused about. But that part... the way it felt different... I understand that part. Completely." And Hunter was being so brave, making himself be so open, that Christian knew he had to go a little further himself. "Before. At the cabin. I panicked, and it was a chickenshit thing to do, and I'm sorry to you. I'm sorry to Hayley. I'm fucking *sorry*. But *it wasn't about not loving you*."

Hunter stared at him for quite a while, then nodded, hard and jerky, like his head was on a string and the puppeteer had just dropped it and then grabbed it back again. "Okay," he said. "Okay, for now. I've got to get to this fucking meeting and get things back on track." Then he gave Christian the ghost of a grin, his expression tentative but hopeful. "But I'm telling you, Christian, both of us had damn well better make it out of this mess alive, because I want to hear a *lot* more about what you just said. I want fucking *details*."

Christian felt his shoulder muscles unclench for what felt like the first time in days. He felt brave enough for a quick smile of his own. "Yeah, okay. Details. Hell, I can act some shit out for you if you want."

And there it was. The fire in Hunter's eyes, lust and amusement and affection, all mixed up together and all for Christian. He hadn't realized how much he'd missed it until he had the chance to see it again. To feel the way it spread warmth down through his chest, all the way to... well, he needed to not think about that. They were in a bad situation, and Hunter had a meeting to get to, so Christian really needed to keep control of himself. "Don't shut me out, okay? If this meeting... if it doesn't feel right, or if you think you're in danger or if Bentick's pushing too hard or if *anything* isn't perfect, get the hell out, okay? Come back here and tell me what's going on, and we'll figure something else out."

Hunter didn't say anything. He just stepped forward, two big strides, and he grabbed Christian, one strong hand behind his head, the other gripping his bicep, and his mouth found Christian's with ferocity and power. Christian stumbled backward, surprised and dazed, and Hunter followed, his lips demanding an answer to a question he hadn't yet asked. Christian knew the answer, and he kissed it back with intensity to match Hunter's. *Yes*, he kissed. *Of course, yes. Then, and now, and always.*

When Hunter finally pulled away, Christian had to grab hold of the bedpost to keep himself from following. Hunter caught the motion and smiled, a real, sweet, *Hunter* smile, the kind Christian had taken for granted when he was staying at the cabin. "To be continued," Christian said hopefully.

Hunter nodded. "Absolutely. With sequels and spin-offs and reboots."

"Okay." Christian could accept that. He was pretty sure he could accept all of this. "Okay. I'll stay here so you have one less fucking thing to worry about. But I'm going to be going crazy, so you need to call me as soon as you can. Okay? You said you'd keep me in the loop. You need to do that."

"Yeah," Hunter agreed. He'd let go of Christian when he moved away but he stepped back now, spreading his hand along the back of Christian's neck as he leaned in for a quick, warm kiss. A kiss good-bye. "I'll call," he promised, and with that he was gone.

Christian flopped back onto his bed. Then he stood up, paced around the room, then flopped onto *Hunter's* bed. That was a bit better, at least. He burrowed beneath the covers, trying to chase any of Hunter's warmth, his scent... anything. When he finally gave up on that he stood up and started figuring out ways to exercise. If the mom in *Terminator 2* had gotten that ripped working out in a cell, Christian could at least wear off a bit of tension doing the same thing.

He managed to keep his anxiety at a constant level, at least. That was something. And when he'd exhausted his creativity, if not his body, with every exercise he could think of for such a confined space, he got rid of a little more tension in the shower thinking of Hunter's strength, his smile, his eyes, his damn hands wrapped around Christian's cock like he *owned* it. Yeah. Christian leaned against the shower wall as the water washed away the evidence. Jerking off to thoughts of Hunter was good, but it would be a hell of a lot better when Christian could get his hands back on the man himself.

He'd just pulled clothes on and was toweling his hair when he heard heavy feet on the stairs. More than one set. The door was locked, and Christian had an exit, but what the hell was going on? His cell rang and he grabbed it, hoping it was Hunter, but he answered a call from an unknown number instead.

"Christian, it's Wendy. Things have gone wrong. I've sent a couple men to help you. Let them in, do what they say, and I'll contact you as soon as possible."

"What? Wait, what's gone wrong? Is Hunter okay?"

"I'm not sure. I'll get back to you when I know more." And with that, the phone went dead. The men were banging on the door. Maybe they knew something?

Christian opened the door and two men strode inside, both big and bulky, both wearing suits that made them look like gorillas playing dress-up. One of them grabbed the phone from Christian's hand, pulled the back cover off and slipped the battery out before returning the phone to Christian. "They can track you through your GPS," he said

"Let's go," the other one said. "They may have already tracked you here. We need to move."

Christian was bewildered. He let himself be herded out the door, up the stairs, and into the waiting SUV. "Do you guys know what's going on?" he asked. "Hunter—Jack Hunter—do you know him? Is he okay?"

"There was a shooting at company headquarters," the man in the passenger seat said. "That's all we know."

Christian stared at him. "Like, random shots? Or somebody *got* shot?"

"We don't have information on that. As soon as we know more, we'll tell you."

Christian needed more than that. He needed to talk to Hunter.

"Can I have my battery back for just a second? Just long enough to get a number out of the phone, and then you can take the battery back and I'll use one of your phones to make the call?"

"Too risky."

They were moving, but they were still in the city. There'd be a stoplight, or a corner; Christian could take the opportunity to get out of the vehicle, and he could definitely outrun either of these clowns. But where would he run to? How would he find Hunter without their help *and* without a functioning phone?

So he sat, trying to control his fear, as the SUV worked its way through city traffic. He sat up straighter when he realized where they were going. "Wait. I can't... I'm not going anywhere. And Hunter made it completely clear—I'm not supposed to get on a plane. I can't leave the country. Is that what you think we're doing here? No, sorry. Also, no passport."

The man beside him punched a few buttons into his phone and then said, "We're at the airport. He doesn't want to get on a plane."

Then he handed the phone over to Christian. A thrill of hope, the possibility that maybe he was about to hear Hunter's voice, was dashed when Wendy said, "Christian. I'm sorry. I was hoping to come down to see you in person but things are still very out of control. That's why we want you out of the way. Please do as the men say. They have paperwork for you—everything you'll need. We'll try to get you back as soon as things have settled down."

"I need to talk to Hunter. I'm not going *anywhere* until I talk to Hunter."

There was a long pause and then a shuddering sigh over the line. "Oh, my dear boy," she said, and for a change she didn't sound sarcastic. "I'm so sorry. Hunter was in a meeting this morning. I have no idea what he was doing there, why he was talking to Bentick, but it was a trap. He was shot. I'm sorry, Christian; Hunter is dead."

PART THREE

CHAPTER FIFTEEN

As soon as Hunter saw the bunker door standing open, he knew something was wrong. He'd gotten back as soon as he could, and Bentick had seemed agreeable, interested in letting Hunter find a way to make things work.

But the door was open. Christian was a scatterbrain, but he wasn't stupid; he knew to keep the door closed. Hunter approached carefully and wished he had a gun. The company had set up shop in Canada partly *because* of its restrictive gun laws; even at the very start they'd realized that they'd get along better if they weren't armed in meetings. It wasn't that hard to get hold of one when needed, but people weren't packing heat as part of their daily routine, and it generally worked well. But right then, Hunter really wanted a gun.

"It's me, Hunter." Wendy's voice came from inside the room, and Hunter relaxed a little and strode forward.

"Where's Christian?"

"We had to move him," Wendy said. "Things were getting too complicated."

"Complicated? How? And where'd you move him to?"

"He's safe," she said with maddening calm. Then she cocked her head to the side and added, "And I think you *know* how things were getting complicated."

Hunter tried to understand, and failed. "What are you

talking about?"

"Your meeting with Bentick?" she prompted. "Your *betrayal* of the alliance you and I had formed?"

He felt cold. "No. I didn't betray anything. I just needed to de-escalate. I needed to find a way for—"

"For Christian to be safe," she said. "You didn't care about letting Bentick win, as long as precious Christian was all right."

He squinted at her. "You were listening to us. This place is bugged."

"Of course it is, Hunter." She shook her head in affectionate disgust. "You know me well enough to know that I always want information."

"Where's Christian?" Hunter demanded. "I swear to God, Wendy, if you do anything—"

"I told you, he's safe." She glanced down at her watch. "And on his way to a lovely vacation in a warm, somewhat arid climate."

Would Christian do that? Would he get on a plane, after all the warnings Hunter had given him? But how many times had Hunter told him to trust Wendy and do what she said? Of course Christian would believe her. "What do you want?" he growled.

Wendy smiled. "I want your loyalty. Your vote on the board, your service in the field."

"That's... that's all long-term stuff. You can't seriously think you're going to keep Christian wherever you've sent him forever? And I'll just keep being your puppet for the rest of my life, without ever even seeing him?"

She smiled. "Based on what I heard this morning, you smooth-talking romantic, I think maybe I could expect exactly that." She shrugged. "But I don't think I need to go that far. You've always been a good ally, Hunter. The only reason you've run into trouble is because Bentick has *pushed* you into trouble. As Christian said, you're letting Bentick win."

Hunter wanted to grab her, shake her, *make* her stop being so smug. Make her give Christian back. But he kept himself completely still. Waiting.

She seemed pleased by his self-control. "So all it takes to make this better," she said, "is getting rid of Bentick. Allen will fall into line, and the rest of them? I can control them. It's Bentick who's causing all this trouble." She leaned forward a little, her expression calm and sincere. "You kill Bentick, and Christian can come back and we go back to normal."

Hunter stared at her. "You want me to kill another board member. Murder him. Here in Canada, where we're supposed to be so civilized and keep things quiet."

"I've got it all set up," Wendy said. "You're meeting with him again this afternoon, right? That's the plan? You just stick to it. Tell me where you'll be, and I'll make sure there's support as needed. You kill him, my people take care of the body, and we move on. There's no crime if there's no evidence."

"You're crazy."

"Don't act like you haven't killed before, Hunter."

"In self-defense, or in a war zone! Not like this."

"Well, there's a first time for everything." Wendy pulled out her phone and glanced at the screen, clearly reading a message that had just arrived. She frowned. "We're being tracked, possibly listened to. I'm clean; I was swept before I left to come here. What are you carrying? Is your phone turned on?"

"My phone? It's clean."

"You spent the morning with it in the office of the man in charge of surveillance for our entire company, and you're still confident of that?" For the first time, she sounded as if she wasn't having a pleasant chat over tea. "Give it to me."

Hunter pulled his phone out reluctantly. He looked down at it, then back at her. She had Christian. He'd do whatever she said. He reluctantly handed her the phone.

Then he said, "I need to know Christian's okay. I'm not doing anything until I get some evidence."

"Hunter. Your evidence is that you're dealing with *me*. You know I wouldn't do anything rash. As long as you're cooperating, I'll keep him alive. But we need to move. Now."

It felt wrong. It *was* wrong. But Hunter followed her out of the room anyway. She was his only link to Christian, and that meant he wouldn't let her out of his sight.

Christian kept moving. The goons had taken him to a smaller terminal, not the main airport. It had been easy to walk away from them, but harder to lose them entirely. They hadn't expected the initial escape; he'd been sitting quietly in the car as they dealt with whatever they were doing on the tarmac, and then he'd just opened the door and walked away. He wasn't sure where he was going, exactly, but he knew damn well he wasn't leaving the country.

Maybe there was still hope for Hunter. Wendy had *said* everything was chaotic, so maybe she was reporting something she hadn't personally seen, or maybe she didn't really *understand* how tough Hunter was, how impossible it was for him to be.... No, there'd been a mistake. Hunter was okay. Maybe he was in trouble, maybe he was back at the bunker getting pissed off at Christian for leaving, maybe... maybe anything. He wasn't dead. That was absolutely unacceptable.

And even if he were, even if the universe was *that* cruel and had taken Hunter away just when Christian was maybe going to get a second chance... even if that had happened, Christian still wasn't going anywhere. No. He was going to stay in Vancouver, and he was going to figure out what had happened and who had caused it, and then he was going to make somebody pay.

The goons were behind him, one on each side maybe ten feet behind him, like he was the speedboat and they were his wake. One of them had sent a text as soon as Christian had slipped away, while the other had trailed Christian, but now they were both back there. He knew they were trying to herd him back toward the plane. He was pretty sure that if they cornered him they'd grab him and do what it took to *get* him on the plane. So they were kidnapping him. Wendy had sent men to kidnap him.

It was the best realization Christian could have had. Wendy had sent kidnappers, so Wendy couldn't be trusted. And the only reason to believe that Hunter was dead was that Wendy had said so.

Christian saw a doorway into the building, an exit from the vast expanse of tarmac he'd been striding across, and he headed for it. He saw the men behind him break into a jog, and he felt a wave of elation. They were *chasing* him. They needed to stop him before he got any farther, because they knew Hunter was alive and they thought they could stop him from finding out. He actually laughed, then skipped into a sprint, his lean body powered by pure joy. Hunter was okay. He *had* to be okay.

The door Christian had seen was locked, but there was a group of employees not far away, and he ran to join them. The goons hung back.

"Long story," Christian said quickly to the closest stranger, "but I need to get out of here. Is there a cop or a real security person around? Like, not a mall cop—someone with a gun and connections to the government? Can you tell me where they'd be?"

"Customs and immigration," the guy said, eyeing Christian and the goons curiously. "Over there."

Christian ran the first half of the way, then looked over his shoulder and saw that the goons weren't following. They were walking away, one of them punching a message into his cell phone. Yeah. Send *that* message to Wendy.

His elation faded as quickly as it had arrived. Fuck. Of course they'd send the message to Wendy. So she'd know he was loose, and she'd do what it took to keep Hunter from finding out. And Christian's damn phone had no battery.

It was such a stupid, inconsequential problem. How would someone have solved it *before* cell phones? But before cell phones, people probably wrote down phone numbers instead of storing them in their phones.

So Christian needed a battery. But he didn't have his wallet; the goons hadn't given him time to grab it. So he didn't have any cash. Which was okay—he'd shoplifted before and he'd do it again if he had to. But would a battery fresh off the shelf even be charged? How much time could he afford to spend on this?

He redirected himself away from the immigration door; he had no identification and wasn't sure how things would work if he couldn't prove he was Canadian. He could try to tell the whole story to the cops, but would they believe him? Would they just get in the way of finding Hunter? And what was Hunter up to, anyway? Christian had never been completely sure of the legality of it all, and he didn't want to find out by getting Hunter in trouble.

So he turned back the way he'd come. The goons' car was gone now, and Christian headed for the gate they'd entered through. It was just a tollbooth, a single bar that raised and lowered to let vehicles in, but there was a man behind the glass and he didn't look too impressed to see Christian coming on foot.

Christian grinned when he got close enough to be heard. "Bachelor party pranks," he said. "Those assholes." He didn't give the guy time to respond, just ducked under the gate and started walking. He glanced back when he was near the first turn and saw the guy talking into a telephone. As soon as he was around the turn, he sprinted. He had no idea if he was breaking rules and didn't have time to wait around and find out. When he saw flashing lights in the distance, he dove to the side of the road and lay in the drainage ditch as an airport security car raced by. Not good.

If he could make it to the main terminal it would be easy to get lost in the crowd. Easy to get a cab too, although he wouldn't be able to pay for it. But he could run out on the fare if he had to. Spread the misfortune around a little. But how the hell was he supposed to get to the main terminal?

No. The municipal road was just ahead, and it was busy enough to hitchhike. So he jogged ahead, keeping an eye out for cops, and stuck his thumb out. The fifth car stopped, a middle-aged man leaning across and asking, "Where you heading?"

Excellent question. This was a working man, driving a pretty old car. He wasn't heading downtown, or to one of the richer suburbs. "Just downtown Richmond," Christian guessed, and the man nodded.

"I can get you most of the way."

Christian climbed in and heard the radio playing. "You didn't hear anything about a shooting, did you? Somewhere in Richmond?"

The man shook his head. "No. Didn't hear about it. Just today?"

"Maybe," Christian said, trying to hide his relief. Wendy was a liar. Hunter was okay. Christian just had to keep it that way. He wondered if he was pushing his luck, but he decided to give it a try. "Don't suppose you have a Samsung phone, do you? My battery's dead, and if I could borrow one for a second my life would get way easier."

The man shook his head. Probably he had a different kind of phone, but maybe he just figured he'd done Christian enough favors. Fair enough. So they drove, Christian jittering every time the car slowed down, even though he wasn't quite sure where he wanted to get to. Then he realized where they were. "I can get out here!"

The man turned to look at him, then pulled over. "Thanks," Christian said, and then he took off running. He was so close. A couple kilometers, and he was out of breath and sweaty but he didn't care as he burst through the front door of the company's main office building. Both of the guards stood up, but Christian ignored them. "Jack Hunter," he practically shouted at the receptionist. "Is Hunter here?"

She smiled robotically and checked her computer. "I'm sorry, no."

Who else? Damn it, Bentick or Wendy? Was there no one else? "There wasn't a shooting here today, was there?"

The receptionist looked at him, then shook her head. "Do you think we'd all be sitting around like this if someone had been shooting?"

"No." He'd thought he was sure, but then it didn't make sense for him to be feeling so relieved now. So, good. Hunter was okay. At least he hadn't been shot. Christian grimaced at his own indecision, then said, "I need a phone battery." He held up his phone.

The receptionist looked at him for a moment, then said, "Company business?"

"Yes! Absolutely. Company business."

She held out a well-manicured hand, then hit a few buttons on her keyboard and spoke into her headset. "Front desk needs a battery for...." she turned Christian's phone around and read the make and model out loud. "For employee Christian Manning."

Shit. He wished too late that she hadn't announced his name. But if he got a battery out of this, he'd accept the loss of anonymity.

It was only a few moments before a casually dressed man stepped off the elevator and approached the desk. "Christian Manning?"

"Yeah!" Christian held his hand out greedily and practically grabbed the battery out of the man's hands.

"That's charged for now. Do you have a charger?"

Christian tried to pay attention to what the guy was saying, but not until he'd jammed the battery into place and heard the chimes of the phone starting up. "A charger. Uh, somewhere, I don't know." At the bunker, he supposed, but he wasn't sure it made sense to go back there. "If you have one, I'll take it."

The man handed it over. "And to what account should I invoice this?"

"What? I don't know. Do I have an account? You can take it off my paycheck, or I can pay you back in cash... I don't care."

"We don't normally supply items for personal use...," the man started.

Christian nodded dismissively. "You did this time." He leaned in to whisper, "If the company doesn't like it, they can fire me." Then he strode outside so he'd have some privacy for his call.

He hit the buttons and held the phone so tight to his head that his ear was squashed. And then he heard a robotic voice offering to take a message. Shit. Still, it was better than nothing. "Hunter, hey. It's Christian, about... about two in the afternoon, and I'm fine. But Wendy's guys tried to put me on a plane. They told me... they told me you were dead. You had better not be, you asshole. I don't think you are. I'm pretty sure. But, fuck, I'd really like to hear your voice, if you could manage to call me back. Yeah, call me. And don't trust Wendy. She's playing you." What else was there to say? "Hunter. Fuck, Hunter. Please be okay." He disconnected the call.

He needed to do more, but wasn't sure what. Fuck it,

he needed to be decisive. So he strode inside and asked the receptionist, "Is Willem Bentick here?"

"I'll check," she said. She seemed to have cooled a little since the battery theft. She typed something into her computer rather than calling, waited a few moments, then said, "He'll be right down."

Christian really, really hoped he hadn't made a mistake, and he wasn't exactly soothed when Bentick appeared and marched toward him. "Where the hell have you been?" he demanded.

Christian stared at him. "When?"

"You didn't show up for sparring today."

"I...." *Was busy getting kidnapped?* Christian had no idea what to do with the accusations that were apparently being thrown his way. "Sorry. It's not really a fixed schedule. But, look, I need to find Hunter. Do you know where he is?"

Bentick stared at him for a long moment, then said, "I'm on my way to meet him. You can ride with me if you like."

Christian knew the rules on that one. But kidnapper-Wendy had been the one to make up those rules, so he wasn't sure they needed to be followed. Except Hunter had apparently thought they were a pretty good idea. "Maybe you could just give me the address and I'll meet you there."

"It's a private meeting," Bentick said. "I'm not going to give you the location ahead of time so you can broadcast it to all your friends."

"I really haven't got many friends."

"You ride with me or you don't come." And there was the oily shininess in Bentick's eyes again. He was up to something, but he was also the only way for Christian to find Hunter.

Easy choice. Christian nodded his agreement and followed Bentick out to his car.

CHAPTER SIXTEEN

It was pouring rain, more than the usual Vancouver autumn mist, and Hunter's only hope was that somehow the rain would obscure the images recorded by Wendy's cameras. Not that she'd *mentioned* cameras, but that was all Hunter could come up with to explain Wendy's plan. She'd insisted on knowing the meeting place ahead of time, and there had to be a reason for that. And she'd said that she wanted Hunter's cooperation long-term, which made sense, but she couldn't expect to hold Christian hostage indefinitely. She'd know Hunter would try to track him down, and there was always the chance Christian would escape, or the political situation where he was being held would change, or he'd get sick and die and Wendy would be unable to show Hunter proof of life and Hunter would kill her slowly. No, using Christian was a good short-term tactic, but Wendy wasn't a short-term thinker.

So she'd film the murder and use it to blackmail Hunter into doing what she wanted. She'd be able to hold it over him for the rest of his life.

Hunter could live with that, if he had to. Wendy would give Christian back to him if Hunter was cooperating with her. And Bentick was a thug; just because he hadn't pulled the trigger first didn't mean he hadn't been the one to put the bullet in the gun by recruiting Christian.

Wendy would win, but Hunter didn't care. He'd been

willing to let Bentick win if it meant saving Christian. He didn't care about their games, not anymore.

He looked down at the SIG Sauer Wendy had supplied. Standard issue, nothing distinctive, but like all guns, it would have a unique ballistics pattern. And his fingerprints were all over it. He bet her guys would want to collect the gun at the same time they picked up the body. They'd return the gun to Wendy, bury the body somewhere they could find it again if needed. Yeah, Hunter was being set up. And he was going to go ahead anyway.

He saw Bentick's sedan approaching, lights on in the gloom, and checked the clip in the gun. They were meeting behind an empty warehouse in an industrial area; the noise of the shot would probably go unnoticed. Wendy had said to pull the trigger and walk away, and Hunter couldn't see any point in doing things differently. He was ready.

The sedan pulled up and Bentick got out. Hunter didn't want to talk; he just wanted to do this. He took a deep breath, exhaled... and froze as the passenger door swung open. It was hard to see through the rain, but Hunter felt an unmistakable jolt of recognition. The height, the ranginess, the way he moved. Christian. *Bentick* had him? But Christian didn't seem to be restrained at all. He was walking toward Hunter with a crazy grin on his face, looking almost dizzy, almost drunk.

"You're alive," he said. "I knew you were, but I really, really wanted to see you."

Hunter had questions. A lot of them. But he didn't ask any of them, he just stepped forward and grabbed hold of Christian, each of them hugging the other with all their strength, and there was no breath left for talking. "I thought Wendy had you," Hunter finally managed to whisper.

"Only for a bit. I think I was supposed to be so overwhelmed that I just did what they said. But I didn't believe her. I knew you *had* to be alive."

That was when they heard the shot, the distinctive crack of a sniper rifle. Hunter moved first, but Christian was right behind him, both of them flattening themselves against the wall as they watched Bentick's body crumble.

Jesus Christ. Apparently Wendy had set up a plan B for disposing of her rival.

Hunter calculated the angles. "He's on the roof... there!" He had the SIG, but the distance made a handgun shot really unlikely to work. Luckily, the sniper was moving, heading for the exit. "We need to get out of here."

"Where's your truck?"

"Wendy dropped me off."

Christian nodded, looked at Bentick's body and then at the roof, and then, before Hunter knew what was going on, Christian was sprinting. He reached the body and had his hand in Bentick's pocket before Hunter caught up to him. He pulled out the man's keys and said, "You drive, or me?"

"You. I need to make some phone calls." Hunter froze. "Fuck, have you got a phone?"

"She take your battery?"

"Took the whole thing."

"Damn," Christian said. "That'd be even worse."

Hunter wasn't quite sure what Christian was talking about and there wasn't time to figure it out. Christian handed over his phone as they jumped into the front seats of the car, and Hunter was already dialing as Christian guided them out of the parking lot. "Which way?" he asked.

As if Hunter knew. As if he was any good at this. He was the one who *executed* plans, not the one who made them. Without Wendy's voice in his ear, he felt lost. "East," he said desperately. West was the ocean, north was the mountains, and south was the border. They'd go east.

So Christian drove while Hunter called his sister. He'd given her a heads-up the day before and asked her to be a little extra careful, but they were way past that now. If Wendy didn't have Christian, but she hadn't had her sniper take Hunter out, it might mean she was still planning to control him somehow. And the most likely remaining target for that was Hayley. "You at home?" Hunter demanded as soon as she picked up the phone.

"No. You told me to stay at a friend's, so I did, and now I'm at the mall."

"Which mall?"

"Pacific Centre. Jack, you're freaking me out. Is something really happening? This is real?"

"I think so. I'm sorry, Hayley, but I need you to take the SkyTrain to Metrotown, okay? You don't go anywhere there isn't a huge crowd of people, and you don't go anywhere with anyone until me or Christian shows up."

"You or *who*?"

"I'll explain later."

"Yeah, you will!"

"Okay. Get on the SkyTrain, okay? If we aren't at Metrotown in half an hour, call this number back, and if we don't answer, call the cops. Tell them you think the same people who killed the guy in East Van are after you, and then tell them everything you know. It won't be enough, but tell them anyway. Everything you've got. Okay?"

"Be careful, Jack." Her voice was shaky, but she didn't sound out of control.

"Yeah, I will."

He hung up, and Christian said, "We're going to Metrotown?" It was a central area, with shopping and offices and apartments and a huge transit station; it was always crawling with people, and in the right direction for them to be going. It was the only place Hunter could think of.

"Yeah," he said, and Christian took care of the driving. It was a relief to have a partner Hunter trusted, and even better to have that partner be Christian. Hunter could keep an eye on him *and* take advantage of his skills.

Hunter's next call was to Miriam. She didn't answer. Not her cell, not her home number. He called information to get the clinic's number and tried there, but she wasn't working. Damn it. He could feel the fear starting to creep in. What if Wendy had her? Hunter had brought all of this down on everyone he cared about. If one of them got hurt, it was completely his fault.

He tried to keep his head in the game. His mom was on vacation in Europe, and Hunter didn't even know what country she was in; hopefully Wendy wouldn't be able to figure that out, either. But Miriam was missing. Maybe she was just somewhere out of cell range; there were enough places like that up in the mountains, for sure. But maybe it was something more serious.

So Hunter's next call was to the police.

It was hard to listen to, but hearing Hunter on the phone made Christian better understand why Hunter hadn't called the police earlier. He'd gotten some pretty immediate attention when he'd tried to report the murder, but they wanted him to come in to give a statement in person, and when he tried to explain why he couldn't do that, he clearly didn't get a lot of respect. Christian focused on driving while Hunter tried to persuade the police to pass the message to the Kamloops detachment. He wanted Miriam protected, but the police were clearly looking more at solving the crime that had already happened rather than preventing a hypothetical one in the future.

"No, I don't *know* his immigration status," Hunter practically shouted into the phone. "He's South African. I assume he was here legally, but I don't know. What I *do* know is that he's dead and Dr. Miriam Greaves may be in the hands of the same people who had him killed. Or she may still be fine, but walking around not knowing that they may be coming for her. She needs to be contacted, and she's not answering her phone."

Christian pulled the car into the Metrotown station and started scanning the crowd, looking for Hayley. It would be a lot easier if they could just call her, but with only one phone between them....

Then Hunter hit the button to end his call with the police. "Fuck it," he growled. "We'll find Hayley, try Miriam again, and I'll call the cops back." He was dialing Hayley's number as he spoke. "I wasn't getting anywhere with them anyhow."

"What are we doing with Hayley when we find her?" Christian was happy to let Hunter run the show, but that didn't mean he didn't want to know what the plan was.

"Keeping her safe," Hunter said. His eyes were bleak when he looked at Christian. "I have no idea what that's going to mean." Then his call connected and he gave a few directions, and soon Christian picked Hayley's frowning face out of the crowd. He pulled the car around and she jogged to meet them, staring incredulously at Christian as she came.

The door was barely shut behind her before she said, "I swear, I thought I misheard. What the fuck is he doing here, Hunter? Are you insane?"

"Probably," Hunter said tightly. "But let's focus on a few other details right now. Christian, keep us moving, please."

Christian pulled out into traffic. "We going to Kamloops?" he asked quietly.

Hunter looked at him, then nodded. "Fuck. Yeah, let's head in that direction." He was dialing the phone again, trying all the numbers for Miriam, and Christian was meeting Hayley's glare every time he looked in the rearview mirror.

"Sorry," he said quietly to her. "For before."

"You don't need to apologize to *me*, asshole! You need to apologize to *Jack!*"

"Yeah, I already did." Christian frowned in Hunter's direction. Just how much had the man told his little sister? But as Hunter had said, that was a conversation for another time.

Hunter was punching numbers into the phone with increasing agitation, and Christian softly said, "If you break that, we'll be even more fucked than we are now. Get Hayley to keep trying Miriam on her phone, and you can call the cops. Or maybe you can call Wendy. Maybe she's not that pissed?"

Hunter looked startled by the suggestions. "Fuck. Yeah, good. Hayley, you have Miriam's contact information, right? I need you to try to get in touch with her, any way you can. Text, e-mail, phone, call any of her friends and see if they know where she is. If they can reach her, get her to go to the police station and wait there. Okay? Tell her it's an emergency."

Then he looked at Christian. "I don't know if it'll do any good to call Wendy. I can't trust anything she says, so what would change if I talked to her?"

It was a good question, and Christian wished he had a better answer. He liked the dynamic, Hunter asking for his opinion and treating him like he might actually have something to contribute, but at the same time, it made it clear just how little he knew. "Maybe nothing," he admitted. "Hey, do you *know* any of the Kamloops cops? Like, is there someone on the force up there who might trust you? Who might care about Miriam?"

"They're RCMP—they transfer around a lot. And the one guy I know...." Hunter looked a bit sheepish. "He already thinks I'm a bit off my rocker. I've been a bit... volatile lately."

Hayley snorted angrily in the backseat. "I wonder what set *that* off?"

"Don't start, Hayley." Hunter looked slightly embarrassed.

Probably best to keep the conversation on business. "Calling him might be better than nothing? Hey, maybe you could make it sound like *you're* the one threatening Miriam, and then he'd at least go find her and make sure she's safe." Christian thought about it. "But they might just end up getting in our way, pulling us over before we can get to her and arresting you, and then she'd be loose, and...."

"Yeah," Hunter agreed. "But I'll call him, and see what—"

He stopped talking when the phone in his hand rang. He looked down at the call display, then lifted the phone to his ear as if he was worried it might bite him. "Hello, Wendy."

"Hunter. Why am I not surprised to hear your voice on young Christian's phone?"

"I don't know. I guess you must have heard that he didn't make the flight for his vacation. What a shame, after all the trouble you went to."

"I'm just glad you're both happy and safe."

"I'm sure you are."

"I'm concerned about your decision to involve the police, though. Do you think that was wise? This is all company business, Hunter." Of course she'd heard about that. Hopefully because her spies had seen police cars go to the site of the killing, but maybe because she had Christian's phone bugged, or the car, or... so many ways for her to gather information.

Hunter tried to concentrate on the conversation. "You had one of the board members killed, Wendy. That goes outside business as usual."

"That's a serious accusation. Where is your proof that I was involved? And, really, where is your proof that Bentick was even killed? I've been trying to call him and I haven't gotten through, but that doesn't mean too much, surely. Actually, the company plane left this morning, heading for Africa—I'll have to check the manifests and see if he was on it."

And of course he would be, if that was what Wendy wanted. "I *saw* him killed."

"Where's the body, Hunter? When the police go to the location you specified, are they going to find *anything*?"

Of course they wouldn't. She'd had a team ready to deal with the body before he'd even been shot. Hunter knew he was being outsmarted, but he struggled to think. "Well, they'll find blood, at least!"

"In this rain? Oh, I'm sure they might find *something*, eventually. The world is a dirty place, after all. But enough to suggest *murder*? Seems unlikely."

Hunter was tired. "What do you want, Wendy?"

"I want you to remember the company you serve. Stop stirring up trouble with the police, stop running around like a chicken with your head cut off. Come back to the office and we'll talk. We'll sort it all out."

He was so used to doing what she said. So used to trusting her to guide him. "If I do, everyone's safe? If I come back, if I do what you say, you'll leave everyone else alone?"

He wasn't prepared for Christian's speed. One second the phone was at his ear, the next it was being tugged out of his hands.

Hunter stared as Christian lifted the phone to his mouth and said, "Go fuck yourself, Wendy. He's not coming in. And if you come after him, it's not going to be just him you're messing with."

There was a pause as Wendy said something, then a bark of laughter from Christian. "I'm not talking about fighting. I'm talking about *publicizing*. I've already got this all typed up and on a delayed send from an e-mail I set up just for this job—if I don't go in tonight by midnight and delay it, it goes. Media all over the country, members of parliament, defense department, police, foreign governments... every fucking place I could think of. And while I'm sitting here driving, I'm thinking of new addresses to add to the list. If anything happens to Hunter or to anyone he cares about, I send it, and if I'm not around to do it, it goes on its own."

Hunter didn't need to hear the words on the other end of the line to know what they were. Wendy accused Christian of bluffing.

And Christian smiled confidently. "Think so? Try me." And he ended the call.

There was silence in the car, and Hayley leaned forward to hear better.

"Did you really do that?" Hunter asked.

Christian glanced away from the road and said, "Hell, yeah. After I left the airport and before I hooked up with Bentick, I stopped at a library and used their computers. Set up a whole new account. Should be hack-proof, since they won't be able to find it." Those were the words he said, but as he spoke he was shaking his head from side to side, clearly negating it all. Apparently Hunter wasn't the only one thinking they might be bugged.

"That's too big of a risk," Hunter objected. "You can't... I can't let you take that chance. I need to go in and—"

"Nope," Christian said. "You're not going in. We'll take care of this." He was smiling calmly. Then he gave a quick look over his shoulder to Hayley and said, "Sorry, I guess I should have checked with you first. I shouldn't have made that decision for you."

"No, good call," she said, just as calm as he was.

"Okay, good." Christian looked at Hunter. "Do you have

your wallet? I could use something to eat." But he was pointing at a garage on the side of the highway, a place advertising car rentals. Damn. The kid was thinking.

"Sounds good," Hunter agreed, and Christian guided the car to the next exit.

Christian was driving, in more ways than one. Hunter supposed he should have resented it, or worried about it, but somehow he didn't. Hunter was a soldier. A grunt. Sure, he could improvise when he had to, but he wasn't a planner. He sure as hell wasn't a spy. When something went wrong on one of his jobs, he had to hotwire an ancient truck or survive in the wilderness for a while or fight some angry locals; he didn't have the option of renting a different car whenever he felt like it.

Hunter's brain was stuck in a rut; Christian's seemed to be working pretty well. So Christian was in charge. Hunter leaned against the door and looked toward the driver's side, and Christian grinned back at him. "I'm glad I didn't waste time decorating the bunker," Christian said.

"Yeah. This whole thing would have been really aggravating if it forced you to walk away from a decorated bunker."

"That's what I'm saying," Christian said, nodding in satisfaction.

Hunter stared at him, then glanced back at Hayley when she stirred.

She'd been watching him. Seeing him as he watched Christian. Now, she shook her head gently. "I hope you know what you're doing," she said, and Hunter knew she wasn't talking about the way he was handling Wendy.

"Doesn't matter if I do or don't," he replied. "I couldn't change anything anyway." And he settled back to watch Christian some more.

Damn, he was beautiful. Lord knew the kid had never had any baby fat, not while Hunter knew him, but there had still been a sort of softness to his face back then. It was completely gone now. Even with the jokes and the smiles, the man before him was the same hard creature Hunter had seen that first night in the alley, strong and confident and in control of himself. Hunter had loved the boy, but the man? The man was something else entirely, something even more fascinating and seductive. And therefore dangerous. Not to Hunter's body, but to his heart, maybe even his sanity.

But as he'd told his sister, it didn't matter. There was nothing to be done. Hunter was strapped in for the ride, and he wouldn't be able to get away even if he'd wanted to. So he watched, and he tried to memorize every expression, every gesture. Christian might not be around forever, and Hunter wanted to have *something* to comfort himself with when he was gone.

CHAPTER SEVENTEEN

It was dark by the time they reached Kamloops in the rented SUV, and the rain had changed to sticky, slushy snow. Hunter had spent most of the drive on the phone with one police station or another, trying to get anyone to believe his story or offer any help. But apparently Wendy had been doing her job better than him, as usual, and had already contacted the Vancouver police with a tale of concern for a coworker who seemed to have grown paranoid and was making wild accusations about conspiracies and murders. Vancouver was a safe city in a safe country, and Hunter found it working against him; the police just didn't seem to be able to accept that maybe things weren't quite as secure as they seemed.

He knew that Hayley was hearing more about the details of his work than she ever had before, but he couldn't think of any way around it, and he figured maybe he owed her that information anyway. If she was getting dragged into it all, she deserved to at least know what it was. And she didn't seem too shocked by any of it; she was still working away, endlessly trying every number she could think of for Miriam. But she got no answers at Miriam's numbers, and no one she spoke to knew where the doctor was. Apparently she was taking a long weekend, something she'd scheduled in advance, but no one knew of any plans she'd had to travel.

The only comforting thing was that Wendy hadn't mentioned having Miriam, and surely she would have. And if Hunter and

Hayley were having trouble finding her, then Wendy's people would have the same problem.

"We should try my place," Hunter said. "It's the only place we haven't checked, and if she's out there, her cell might not be working."

Christian was quiet for a moment, then asked, "Is that... does she... she spends the night at your place? Is that usual?"

His tone was too careful, too deliberately neutral and nonjudgmental. He spoke like he knew he had no right to ask, maybe not even any right to care. But Hunter felt like maybe it was time to *give* Christian that right. "Not when I'm there," he said, and he waited a moment to make sure Christian understood. "But she's talked about using it as a bit of a retreat sometimes. People have a hard time accepting that a small-town doctor gets any time off."

"The snow's getting pretty bad," Christian said. He was changing the subject, but his voice was more relaxed than it had been. "Has either of you checked the weather?"

Hunter called up the function on Christian's phone. "Shit. Yeah, looks like it's going to last all night, into tomorrow. They're calling it the first storm of the season."

"So if we go out there, we might get stuck. If we find her, that's great—snow will keep us in, but it'll keep everyone else out too. Right?"

Hunter nodded. "But if she's not out there...."

"We're stuck, and it's somewhere we can't even get a signal to keep calling her."

"She *has* to be there," Hayley said from the backseat. "I've called every other place I can think of."

"Okay," Hunter said. "Let's try it."

"Is there food? If we get stuck?"

"Not much."

"It seems wrong," Christian said, "but maybe we should make a quick stop for groceries." He shrugged. "Hell, maybe we'll see her at the grocery store."

"If we do, I'm gonna kick her ass for not answering her phone all afternoon," Hayley said.

It did feel wrong, but they needed to eat. They left Christian in the SUV, idling just outside the entrance, while Hunter and Hayley practically sprinted around the store, grabbing enough food to get by, although possibly not enough to have well-crafted meals. It was in the checkout line that Hayley finally had time to say, "You guys are back together? Are you serious? After last time?"

"Not *together*," Hunter hedged. "I mean, we're physically together, obviously. Working together." What else were they? What could he say with certainty? "I trust him. I don't mean in terms of a relationship. I mean I trust him with my life. With yours. He's on our side."

"Yeah, that's great, but—"

He held up his hand to stop her. He knew what she was going to say. It hadn't worked before, and he'd spent the last three years trying not very successfully to get over it. There was no real reason to believe things would end differently this time. By his own admission, Christian still struggled with addiction; making Hunter take the key to his motorcycle had been a pretty good sign of that. And if Christian didn't have that under control, then maybe he didn't have anything else under control either. It was all true, and Hunter wasn't denying it. But he also couldn't deny what he'd already told his sister. "I really can't do anything about it, Hayley. I have to spend time with him in order to help keep everyone alive. And if I'm spending time with him... I feel the way I feel. I can't help it."

"You can't trust him, Jack. On personal stuff? You *can't*."

"Okay," he said mildly. He knew it was true. He had no reason to believe Christian was going to stick around once this was all over. No reason to believe he wouldn't leave Hunter in just as much pain as he had before. "I won't. No trust, no expectations. This time, I won't be surprised when it happens." He shrugged at her dismayed expression. "That's all I can give you, Hayley."

They paid for their groceries and headed for the door. On the way, Hayley said, "I can't decide. I mean, he's an asshole and he's hurt you before and he's almost certainly going to hurt you again." She shook her head and smiled sadly. "But you're running for your life, your career is dissolving around you, and you've been betrayed by someone you thought was on your side in all this, and you're *still* in a better mood than I've seen you in for the last three years."

"Nothing's ever simple," he said.

Except it seemed like maybe things *were* getting simpler, because when they finally arrived at the cabin, after a trip made slow and dangerous by the increasing snow cover on the roads, Miriam's car was in the driveway. And when they got inside, she seemed surprised to see them, but not alarmed. At least not until she saw who the third member of their party was.

"Holy shit," she said, and she sat back down in the chair she'd just stood up from.

Christian looked embarrassed.

"He's returning to the scene of the crime," Hayley said.

"Enough." Hunter supposed he appreciated Hayley's protectiveness, but they had more important things to worry about. Starting with explaining all this to Miriam. "Sorry to invade, Miriam, but... I fucked up, and you and Hayley might get dragged into it." He turned to Christian and Hayley. "I think we should stay here for the night. The road's going to be impassable pretty damned soon, so we should be safe. It'll give us a chance to regroup."

They didn't object. Christian said, "I'll bring the groceries in."

"And I'll find the smelling salts for Miriam," Hayley said pointedly.

Christian ignored her and Hunter tried to follow his example. Miriam was looking more than a little confused, and he pulled off his shoes and went to sit by her. "Let's talk about the life-and-death stuff first," he said. "You can yell at me for the rest later."

Hayley followed Christian outside when he went to get the groceries. He wished she'd been serious about the smelling salts, if only so she'd leave him alone. But she stood there as he pulled groceries out of the back of the car, then said, "I changed my mind. You *should* apologize to me."

"I already did," he said mildly. "But, okay. I'm sorry."

"Not for the sex," she said. "Not for fucking me under false pretenses. That was... it was sleazy and gross and you're an asshole for doing it, but I'm not talking about that."

Oh. It had occurred to her too. Christian hadn't realized it until just a few moments ago, not until he'd heard Hunter say that *he'd* fucked up and dragged the women into it. "Yeah, okay," he acknowledged. "I'm... I'm really sorry, Hayley. If I'd gotten on the damn plane you never would have been involved in this. I was thinking about Hunter, and I guess about myself. I wasn't thinking about what Wendy would do if she couldn't use me. I fucked up. I'm sorry."

"What?" She wrinkled up her face as if his words smelled bad. "No, asshole. I don't think you should have to be sorry because someone Hunter works with turned out to be a psychopath. I'm talking about the last three years. You should be sorry because you turned my brother into a... a self-destructive, bitter... zombie."

He stared at her. He had no idea what to say. She was

exaggerating, obviously. "I think that might have had more to do with getting dragged back into the company, don't you?"

"Dragged back? He went *running* back. He didn't even make it through Christmas vacation up here before going down and jumping back into it all. He was out of the country on a job by New Year's, and he's been working his ass off ever since, not here for more than a week or two at a time before heading off on some other job, some new way to get himself killed."

No, Christian wasn't going to think about Hunter getting killed. Better to respond to the motivation than the possibilities. "Well... it's hard to retire, I think. I mean, harder than maybe he thought it would be. They...." Christian shrugged. "They make you feel like you're special. Like you're part of a team. He probably missed that."

"You're an idiot," she said, and she grabbed a few bags of groceries and headed for the door.

He didn't follow behind her too closely. Maybe better if everyone had a little space. It wasn't like he could blame her for being pissed.

And he wasn't sorry to have a bit of time to adjust to everything himself. Being back at the cabin, with the snow falling, the smell of wood smoke coming from the chimney, the warm yellow glow of lights coming from inside: it reminded him of how he'd felt here the last time. Yeah, when he left he'd burned the bridge and scorched the earth, but maybe somehow he'd swum back across the river, stumbled through the wasteland, and found his way home.

It was only temporary, he reminded himself. He couldn't get comfortable. That had been part of the problem before; he'd let himself take things for granted, thought they could just keep going as they had been without Hunter complicating it all, without Hunter wanting to say things that shouldn't be said.

The door to the house eased open, and Hunter stepped cautiously out into the snow. "You okay? I thought maybe

Hayley stabbed you with an icicle and left you to die."

"Not quite," Christian said. "And I don't blame her for being pissed."

"No. Neither do I." Hunter stepped forward cautiously. "You fucked up. No way around that. And she... she hasn't got quite the same incentive to forgive you that I do."

Christian frowned. *Incentive to forgive?* "Well, she kind of does." He wasn't sure he and Hunter were on the same wavelength. "I mean, I owe you my life, and she's your sister... it extends, right? I mean, I'm committed to her safety." Hunter was looking at him strangely and Christian started scrambling. "Miriam too. I mean, I know I'm not as good as your other guys, the guys you work with, but whatever I can do, I'll do it. Absolutely. Not just for you. For the whole... team. I owe you, so I'll do everything I can to protect her."

Yeah, Hunter was not loving what Christian was saying. But what was wrong? What was Christian missing? Jesus, what did Christian have to say to make it clear that he was committed to this, that he wanted to stay there at the cabin, where he'd once belonged and where he wanted to belong again and where *Hunter* was? What more was Hunter looking for? "Your mom? I mean, I've never met her—"

"Shut up, Christian." Hunter sounded like he meant it. He really wanted Christian to stop talking. So Christian tried.

He lasted about ten seconds. "I'm confused," he finally said.

"You don't owe me anything." Each word sounded like it was being dragged out from under a pile of rocks in Hunter's chest. "If that's all you're doing this for... I mean, you need to stay, I think. If you won't call your dad—and I know, you can't call him, I get it. But if you can't get away you're kind of stuck with me, I know. But that's... you shouldn't be here because you think you owe me something."

Christian had no idea where to go with that. "Well... yeah,

okay. I mean, I'm here. That's the fact. So you can have your reason for me being here, and I can have mine, and it doesn't really... we don't have to agree on that, do we?"

Hunter was frowning as if *he* was the one totally confused by this conversation. "We're just trying to stay alive," he said.

"Yeah. We'll worry about the rest of it later." Christian stepped forward, mostly just trying to see Hunter's face a little better, but Hunter stepped back like Christian was waving a knife. Apparently even the possibility of physical contact was repugnant.

Christian had no idea what had gone wrong, but it was pretty damned clear that Hunter wanted nothing to do with him. Christian was willing to die for Hunter; what more could he say? What else would match that level of commitment? Whatever Hunter had said in the bunker, he'd obviously had second thoughts. A good fuck had scrambled his brains, but only temporarily, and now his judgment had returned. Christian forced himself to smile. It probably looked pretty horrible, but luckily Hunter was refusing to look at him. "I'd better get the groceries in before they freeze," he said, and Hunter nodded vaguely.

When Christian opened the door, Miriam and Hayley stared at him from the sofa, where they'd been talking. Pretty clear what they'd been talking about, and from the suspicious looks on their faces it was pretty clear what conclusion they'd reached. Yeah. Fuck. Christian had been fooling himself. He'd swum back across after burning the bridge, but the people on that side of the water didn't want him there. They'd keep him for as long as he was useful, he supposed, as long as he could shoot a gun or at least take a bullet. He looked down at the bags in his arms. Maybe as long as he could make them something to eat. But he didn't belong there. He'd been the only one to see it three years ago, but now it was clear to everyone.

Everyone except maybe Hunter. Hunter was the wild card

in all this. And he was the one who really mattered. Sure, Christian loved the cabin, but it was *Hunter* who made the cabin what it was, Hunter who'd made the damn *bunker* Christian's favorite place to be. And Hunter was outside, standing in the cold, trying to cool down after whatever the fuck Christian had said to piss him off.

Christian had no idea whether he should try harder or just shut up and keep his head down. He was probably screwed either way.

Hunter felt like an idiot, but he couldn't quite understand where he'd gone wrong. That morning—God, was it only that morning?—in the bunker, hadn't Christian said.... He'd said that he'd screwed up before, but it hadn't been about not loving Hunter. That was what he'd said. But Hunter had read too much into it. Christian had been talking about the past, not the present. And, really, the double negatives made the entire statement unclear. Christian had meant it one way, and Hunter, fool that he was, had taken it way too far in a whole other direction.

He supposed it didn't really matter His love for Christian had never needed to be returned. It just was. The sun rose in the east, gravity kept things from falling into space, and Hunter loved Christian. For three years of anger and loneliness and despair, Hunter had loved Christian; it wasn't going to just go away now that they were back together.

He took a few deep breaths of the cool air. The snow was still falling, wet and heavy, the kind of snow that knocked down trees and took out power lines. It wasn't blowing much, at least. But nobody was going to be moving, not in weather like this.

That didn't mean he could allow himself to get distracted, though. He needed a plan, a way to get them all out of this alive. He was pretty sure Christian's bluff had held the seeds of a good idea, but he wasn't sure it was enough to keep Wendy at bay. Had she believed him? If she had, how worried would she be? She was a planner, a thinker. No emotions, just cold reason. Lucky bitch.

So if she was coming for them, Hunter had to prepare for that. If she *wasn't* coming for them... what then? Did he just turn everything around, drive back to town, and go to work?

No. The crazy fantasies he'd allowed himself to entertain in a few stolen moments that afternoon might be lost—he wasn't going to find a beach somewhere and live with Christian, fishing and eating coconuts forever. But he wasn't going to go back to the company, either, not after everything that had happened. So at best he needed an exit strategy.

He thought about Christian's bluff. It was probably a pretty good plan. Hunter might not know enough to put Wendy in jail, but he could absolutely give the company the kind of exposure it did *not* want. Even just letting Canadians know that there was a private military company recruiting, training, and running missions out of their country—yeah, that'd be enough to cause some trouble. Legal or not, people didn't like mercenaries, especially that close to home.

He'd be ruining the company that paid him dividends every quarter, but he was well past worrying about money. Even if he just told the board members what Wendy was up to, without involving the public... that might be enough. He needed to do *something* like that.

And of course, now that he had the beginnings of a plan, he had no way to do anything about it. No phone, no Internet. The snow was still coming down; not a storm with howling winds, just a big, heavy dump of snow. The tracks left by the SUV were already filling in. Even with four-wheel drive, it wouldn't get far. They were stuck there, for sure.

It should have been peaceful, but Hunter just felt restless. He needed to be doing something. God, how perfect would it be to go inside and find Christian and... well, not take him upstairs to the open loft, not with the ladies below. But maybe the guest room, or maybe just there in the kitchen, nuzzling in behind him like they'd used to do, kissing his neck, smelling him, touching him. It didn't have to be sex, just... anything. With Christian, Hunter would take anything.

But not if Christian was just giving it out of a sense of obligation, thinking he owed Hunter a fucking favor. No. Not like that.

So he headed inside and refused to let himself go into the kitchen, where Christian was. Instead he found the key hidden under the bathroom sink, opened the gun locker, and pulled out his hunting rifles and the shotgun. He laid them on the dining room table and went to find the ammunition in the back closet.

When he returned, Christian was running his fingers thoughtfully over the barrel of Hunter's bear gun. The women were standing silently behind him. The guns had refocused everyone, reminding them they weren't at the cabin for a tea party. Good.

Christian looked at him, nervously chewing his lip. "I've never... targets, yeah. I know how to shoot. But I've never shot a person."

Hunter made himself smile. "Well, I sincerely hope we can keep it that way. But if we can't, you just have to do it. Do it, and sort out how you feel about it later."

Christian snorted softly. "Yeah. *That* advice has never gotten me in any trouble before."

"This time, you're already *in* trouble. We're trying to get ourselves *out*."

"Yeah." Christian didn't sound too sure, but a moment later he nodded and said, "Yeah," again, this time with a little more enthusiasm.

He'd be okay, Hunter was pretty sure. If it actually came

down to it, the kid would pull the trigger. One more reason Hunter was glad to have him around. Not that he really needed any extra reasons.

CHAPTER EIGHTEEN

The couch wasn't comfortable. Or maybe Christian just *thought* it wasn't because it wasn't where he wanted to be. The women were sleeping in the guest room, Hunter was upstairs in his own bed, and Christian.... Christian was on the damn couch. There hadn't even been a question about it. They'd started talking about bed, the ladies had said they'd go to the guest room, and Hunter had looked at Christian and said he'd find a pillow and blankets for the couch. Hayley and Miriam had smiled like it was a welcome return to the natural order of the world, and Christian... well, Christian had kept scrubbing the dishes, his neutral expression glued on his face.

But now, with Hunter *right there*, not even a wall between them, there was nothing neutral about his reaction. He was in the wrong goddamn place, and the right place was *so close*. Maybe he should go up. Not sneakily; not a good idea to sneak up on an armed, nervous man who'd been trained to kill. Just calmly. Like it was the most natural thing in the world, which, seriously, it pretty much was. Because Hunter wanted Christian. That much was clear. The rest of it was confusing and scary and best not thought about, but the desire was there. And Christian absolutely wanted him back. So why the hell weren't they in the same bed?

Maybe because it would have been a distraction. And, really, they were in a pretty good position for combat, the way they were spread out now, with Christian on the ground to draw the enemy's fire and Hunter elevated and ready for sniping. But nobody was coming, not through that snow.

No, there was no real risk of attack that night. Christian wasn't in Hunter's bed because Hunter didn't *want* him in his bed. That simple. That frustrating. Christian spun around, putting his feet where his head had been and trying to get comfortable *that* way. It didn't do any good, of course, but the movement made it clear that Christian's brain wasn't the only part of him that had been hoping for some attention from Hunter. He reached down and eased inside his underwear to wrap his fingers around his hard cock.

He remembered Hayley's words from earlier. Sleeping with her had been sleazy and gross. He wondered if it was more or less sleazy and gross to jerk off in someone's living room when that someone was sleeping in a loft separated only by a wooden railing.

Well, he might as well find out. It wasn't like he was going to get any sleep if he just lay there, hard and aching and lonely.

Not, not lonely. Scratch that. Hard and aching. Sleazy and gross. Christian could be *those* things. But loneliness wasn't a sensation he could allow himself to acknowledge. So he ran his clenched fingers down his shaft, tight and hard, just the way Hunter had done the night before. Yeah, that was good. He let his eyelids drift shut and thought about the way Hunter had touched him, the way Hunter had *fucked* him, as if he'd *needed* Christian, as if he'd tried to resist and still didn't want to do it but just couldn't keep himself away. Christian wouldn't let himself think about what had changed in twenty-four hours, wouldn't get distracted from his memories.

Hunter had fucked him. It had felt right. Whatever was going on now, whatever happened the next day or ever in the future, nobody could take that away from him. He swallowed a groan, thinking about Hunter's hot, demanding gaze as he'd jerked Christian off. Hunter hadn't just fucked him, he'd *claimed* him. Or at least, it had felt like he had. Christian's rhythm faltered at that thought, but he tightened his grip and got back into it. For the purposes of the current fantasy, Hunter had claimed him. Christian would worry about how that related to reality some other time.

It had been bad enough listening to the bastard tossing and turning. Now Hunter had to listen to him tossing one off? Because that was what was going on downstairs, Hunter was pretty sure. At first he'd thought it was his own feverish imagination, but....

No. That soft, sliding noise? Barely audible, but the acoustics in the cabin were peculiar, amplifying sounds from below, and the rhythm was distinct. Like Hunter hadn't been in bad enough shape to start with.

Fuck it, he should just storm down there, bend Christian over and take his ass like he had the right before. Christian had liked it then and he'd like it now too; after all, he had a history of being pretty indiscriminating about his sex partners.

Hunter felt guilty for thinking it, then shook the remorse off angrily. The kid had been a whore when Hunter met him; no point in pretending otherwise. He'd been fucked by a lot of guys, and just because Hunter hadn't paid him didn't mean he was anything more than the latest link in a long, long chain. Anything special Hunter *thought* they'd found had been nothing. Christian had proved it three years ago when he went after Hayley, and proved it this time with all his bullshit about owing him.

Owing him. Hunter hadn't even realized his hand was wrapped around his cock, but he tugged it now, rough and graceless and impersonal. Christian thought he owed Hunter a favor; no, more than that, his life. A debt like that, from someone who gave his body away for a few dollars? Yeah, Hunter could absolutely go down the stairs now, and whether Christian actually wanted him or not, Christian would be happy to oblige. Because none of it mattered. It was all just sex, like Christian had tried to tell him years ago.

The faint sounds from downstairs were speeding up, and Hunter let his own hand match the rhythm. It was just sex. It didn't mean anything. His body responded better with a little extra stimulation, that was all. More than just his hand. His ears, his imagination. Picturing Christian sprawled out on the couch, completely naked, legs spread wantonly, staring at Hunter, because in this fantasy Hunter was down there in the armchair and Christian was putting on a show for him. He was showing Hunter how much he wanted him, trying to convince him that they should fuck, trying to earn the touch of Hunter's cock. Yeah, in the fantasy Christian was desperate, and he was making noises, keening sounds that made him sound completely lost in his lust. Not the near-silence of real-world Christian, not in Hunter's imagination.

Then there *was* a sound from below. Nothing loud, just a deeper, gasping, shuddering breath, and the sounds of movement changed. Hunter was close, and he let himself change the fantasy, let himself remember how perfect it had felt to drive into Christian's tight, warm body, how pliant and obedient he'd been, how Hunter had driven him on his toes with every thrust. And how he'd stared at Hunter when Hunter made him come, how his gaze had seemed so honest, so brave. As Hunter came, he could see Christian as *he'd* come the night before, the ecstasy that had swept away all the doubts and insecurities.

Hunter relaxed back into his mattress. He wiped his hands off on his underwear; he had extra clothes in the dresser, and he supposed he could loan some to Christian if he had to. He'd fill them out better than he had when he first came to the cabin, but Hunter bet it would give him the exact same thrill to see the other man wearing them.

The same glee at the familiarity of shared clothes, the same possessive pride at having provided something his mate needed.

The same tenderness at the idea of keeping Christian warm and protected, even if it was only fabric doing the job.

Yeah, Hunter was still in love.

Damn it.

Christian woke up in the darkness, but didn't move. Something had *woken* him up, he was pretty sure. Some sound…. There it was again. A rustle of movement. Someone was sneaking around in the kitchen. The back of the couch blocked Christian's view, and if he moved he'd make his own rustling noise and be discovered.

Then there was a gentle thump and a familiar, if muffled, grunt of pain. Hunter.

"Stub your toe?" Christian asked quietly.

"These fucking stools," Hunter answered after a brief pause. "They're never where they're supposed to be."

"Neither are you, I guess. Something wrong with your bed?"

Another pause, and then Hunter said, "I thought I'd start breakfast."

There was no need to be quiet anymore, so Christian raised his wrist and hit the button for his watch to light up. "It's four thirty in the morning. What the fuck are you planning to cook?"

There was no answer and Christian sat up and peered over the back of the couch. Hunter was shirtless, his sweatpants falling low on his hips, and Christian felt a surge of desire. It was *Hunter*. He was back in Christian's life after too long away, and maybe it was just temporary, but that didn't mean it wasn't real.

Christian stood up slowly. "Having trouble sleeping?" he asked gently. He was wearing only underwear, since Hunter hadn't bothered to offer him anything else to sleep in. Hunter didn't answer, so Christian eased around the couch and took a few slow, cautious steps toward the kitchen. He wasn't afraid of anything, but he didn't want to spook his prey. "Anything I could do to help with that?"

They were close enough that Christian could hear the shudder in Hunter's chest as he exhaled. Yeah, this was going to work. Christian smiled and took another few steps, then held out his hand. "Come on," he said. "Let's go upstairs."

Hunter stared at him, eyes wide, then wordlessly reached out and took Christian's hand.

His tractability lasted until they hit the foot of the staircase, where it was as if he suddenly came awake. His fingers tightened around Christian's, and then he tugged, twisted, and turned. Christian could have fought it. He would have lost, eventually, but he could have resisted for a while, if he'd wanted to.

Instead, he let himself fall. Hunter caught him before his back hit the hard wooden stairs, breaking his fall enough to make the landing rough, but not actually painful. And Christian wasn't too worried about pain anyway, not with Hunter dropping his body down on top of him, twining their legs together, and then finding his mouth with a bruising kiss.

Christian gasped and opened his mouth, letting Hunter as far in as he wanted to go. He wrapped his arms around Hunter's neck and pulled himself up, pulled Hunter down... he didn't care about the actual directions, as long as they were together as close and as tight as they could be.

Hunter's groan was familiar; Christian didn't realize how much he'd missed hearing it. He was making his own sounds, he realized, almost whining with need and desire. Hunter drove his leg between Christian's, and Christian pushed back with his own. His body arched without his command, demanding more, more, more.

They made it up the staircase one step at a time, Christian's ass hitting each step, Hunter half lying on him, half kneeling, both of them struggling and dragging and grinding against each other with each increase in altitude. By the time they finally reached the top they were both vibrating with need, senseless and clumsy with desire. Luckily neither of them was wearing anything with zippers or buttons. A few quick tugs and they were both naked.

It was Christian who pushed them down on the bed, and he made sure he landed on top of their little pile. Then he forced himself to pull away just long enough to get a good look at the man beneath him on the mattress. Hunter's body was hard and tough, his skin scarred in several places, smooth and warm elsewhere. His eyes were wide, as if he was surprised by how much he was feeling, and his mouth was open, lips slick with their shared spit. Yeah, Christian wanted to remember this.

But then Hunter shifted just right and Christian's brief moment of self-control was gone. He dropped down, his full weight pinning Hunter to the mattress, and they were kissing again, hungry and demanding. Hunter's hands were everywhere, running over Christian's body like he knew he had a right to all of it.

For the briefest second Christian thought about taking charge, finding a condom and rolling it onto his own dick and claiming Hunter the way he'd shown his ownership of Christian in the bunker. But it wasn't really what Christian wanted. He *wanted* Hunter to own him, even if it was only temporarily. So he let Hunter roll them over, and when Hunter made a desperate lunge for the bedside table and then returned, Christian raised his legs and hooked them over Hunter's shoulders without a moment's hesitation.

Hunter's entry was no gentler than before, but this time he waited a moment, his body still and steady as Christian writhed and fought to relax. Christian looked up and saw Hunter staring down at him, his expression unreadable. "Fuck me," Christian ordered, and Hunter's hips moved as if they were responding to the words reflexively, with no need for Hunter's brain to be involved at all.

Neither of them lasted long. Barely time to set a rhythm, and then Hunter's hand was tight around Christian's cock, giving him completely unneeded encouragement. They strained together and they came together, their gasping moans echoing off the rafters and dropping like snow to the ground beneath them.

They lay joined together for a few moments. Then Hunter rolled off to the side. Christian thought about rolling after him, snuggling up, but something, either cowardice or instinct, kept him still. When Hunter spoke a few breaths later, his voice was level. "Don't go to sleep up here. The girls will come in for breakfast, and it'll be more complicated than it needs to be if you're not where they expect you."

Christian didn't respond. There was nothing to say. He took a deep breath, then rolled out of the bed and scanned the floor for his underwear. This was nothing new. Nothing to be upset about. If he was going to start crying about every guy who'd kicked him out of bed after sex, he'd end up dehydrated.

He leaned over to grab his boxer briefs and didn't bother putting them on. Not there, with Hunter watching. Or, even worse, *not* watching. Maybe he didn't even care enough to keep his eyes open.

Christian refused to turn around to check. It was sex. That was all. He'd gotten off, and now it was time to go to sleep. That was the way things worked.

He headed down the stairs, underwear gripped tightly in his hand, and he didn't look back.

The snow stopped falling overnight, and as Christian puttered around the kitchen, working on breakfast, he kept an eye on the road. Still too early for anyone to be coming through, he knew. The thermometer outside the window said it was a few degrees above freezing, so the snow would be melting, but it would take a while for it to clear up enough to make driving possible. Not that long, though.

He heard movement behind him. Hunter. Christian refused to have any emotional reaction whatsoever to the other man's presence. Instead, he engaged intellectually. "Have we got a plan?" he asked. Then he filled a coffee mug and carried it over to where Hunter was standing, because this was his kitchen, after all. "Still take it black, right?"

"Yeah," Hunter said. He seemed a little disoriented, which was weird, because he used to be pretty quick to wake up. "Thanks." He wrapped his hands around the mug and sank into a chair at the kitchen table.

"A plan?" Christian prompted. If he was going to keep things business as usual, Hunter needed to help him out a little. "Have we got one? Or are we just going to stay on the defensive and react to what they do?" He topped up his own mug. "Assuming they do anything. It'd be pretty funny if this whole thing was just a big overreaction on our part."

"Bentick's dead," Hunter said. "Wendy might have erased the evidence, but don't forget what you saw. Don't forget what we're up against."

Christian nodded. "Yeah. Okay." Good reminder, but still no answer to his original question. "So what're we going to do?"

Hunter looked frustrated, then sighed. "I don't know. This isn't my area. But we've got everyone safe now. We didn't come up here to hide, we just came up to pick up Miriam. So I think maybe it's time I went on the offensive. I should talk to the other members of the board. They'll believe me about Bentick, and obviously they'll want to take action if one of us is arranging the assassination of others. And if that doesn't work, I can go to the cops in person, if that'll make them take me seriously. You can keep an eye on Miriam and Hayley, right?"

"We could just bring sleeping bags and camp out in the lobby of the police station," Christian said. He wasn't a big fan of cops, not with his background, but he was on the other side of things now and supposed they could be useful.

"Yeah," Hunter agreed. "So, I guess that's the plan. We go back to town, I talk to the board, talk to the cops, try to expose this whole thing. Even if Wendy doesn't get arrested, hopefully the board can get her under control." He shrugged, not casually, but more like he just didn't have any other suggestions. Then, reluctantly, he said, "Or we could... no. *I* could. If we go this way, it's all me, and you're not involved."

"I don't like it already."

Hunter's expression was strange, as if he simultaneously liked and disliked Christian's response. Then he shrugged again. "It'd be a last resort, I think. But I don't think she's got a lot of allies, or a real leadership team or anything. So if we can't get her to back off, maybe I just have to take her out. Self-defense. Get to her before she gets to me or mine."

"*Take her out*," Christian said softly. "*Get to her*." Hunter wasn't being deliberately evasive, he was just using the terms they used around the company. Christian had heard them lots of times, in stories about some mission or another. "Kill her," he said. "Murder? Yeah, I think it'd be murder. I mean, I understand why you'd have to do it. But the cops would call it murder, right?"

"Yeah," Hunter said heavily. "I'm not a lawyer, but I expect they would."

"And these are... these are logical ways to respond. We're not overreacting or going too far or anything. Right?"

"I think they're logical," Hunter said.

Christian nodded. "Yeah." He didn't have Hunter's expertise in the field, but he was pretty sure he agreed. "So if it's a logical plan, Wendy's probably already thought of it, right? I mean, she's smart. She'll know she's vulnerable. She'll know...." He didn't want to say the next words, and Hunter's expression made it pretty clear that he didn't have to.

"She'll know she has to stop us," Hunter said slowly. "She'll know that if we get out of here, she's lost."

"So she'll be desperate," Christian said. He tried to find a bright side. "She may not even know we're here. But...."

"It's not a secret that I have this place. She's obviously had surveillance on it before, since she knew about you and me."

Christian frowned. "She may have the place bugged." It seemed paranoid, but in a world where snipers shot people from factory roofs, maybe it wasn't too far-fetched.

Hunter stared at him, then nodded slowly. "She might," he agreed. "I had it swept a few years ago, but I haven't really thought about it since then. I guess I didn't really care what they heard." He looked around as if thinking he might see a wire dangling from a light fixture, then returned his gaze to Christian. "Wendy," he said softly. "If you're listening? This ends now. We'll drive out of here, and I'll call you. That's the only deal I'm offering you. You back off, let this end peacefully, and I'll call you when I get out, and we can see what we can work out. But if you fuck with us... if you try to stop us from leaving... it's on. It's war."

Christian grinned. "Kinda funny if the place *isn't* bugged. She's got you talking to the furniture."

"Yeah, well, the furniture had better not fuck with me either," Hunter said fiercely. He held his expression for a moment, and then he grinned.

The emotion hit Christian like a surprise wave at the beach. He didn't have a word for what he was feeling. Well, there was a word, maybe, but he thought of that as being something warm and sweet and safe, not this overwhelming, joyful, almost *savage* thing that was swelling in his chest. He stepped forward without thinking, caught Hunter's head in his hands and pulled them together. Christian's mouth was hungry, needy, and hot. Hunter's was... inactive.

Christian froze. He released Hunter's face and stared at him. "Sorry," he managed to say, but then it was Hunter's turn to step forward and catch Christian, one hand on his jaw, the other on his waist.

This kiss was more controlled, but Christian could feel the passion, the desire. Hunter was savoring what Christian had tried to devour, but they were both just as hungry.

That was when they heard it. Not loud. Not yet. Just a distant thrumming, low and powerful and menacing. A helicopter.

"Might be nothing," Hunter said, but he was running for the door, grabbing a rifle on the way. "Get warm clothes on."

Hunter skidded to a halt when the door opened and Hayley appeared, Miriam close behind. "Is it coming for us?" Miriam demanded.

"Maybe," Hunter growled. He looked at Christian, then spoke to the walls of the room. "If it's coming for us, it's war."

CHAPTER NINETEEN

"We might be able to make it through the snow," Christian said. "Maybe."

"They'll have an ambush set up on the road," Hunter replied. "At least, they should."

"So we're stuck?" Christian tried to make it sound like it wasn't a big deal.

"Snowmobiles," Hunter said. He'd thought of them the night before and made sure they were gassed up and ready. There were two machines, each big enough to hold two passengers. But they'd be easy to track with a helicopter. "Hayley and Miriam, you guys take one sled. Get your asses to town and see if you can send help. We'll distract them here for a bit and follow you when we can."

"We can stay," Hayley said. She was pale, but looked determined. "We both know how to shoot."

"No," Hunter said firmly. "You need to get the message out." And she needed to stay alive. He couldn't have *everyone* he loved caught up in this battle.

Hayley looked indecisive. Hunter grabbed the SIG off the table and handed it to her, then handed the shotgun and a box of slugs to Miriam. "Anybody gets in your way...," he said in a low voice.

Miriam looked torn, as if she too wanted to stay. Hunter

looked at her pleadingly. *Please, get Hayley out of this.* Miriam winced, then grabbed Hayley's arm and dragged her to the door.

The helicopter sound was louder now.

"Maybe it's the cops," Christian said. "Or search and rescue or something."

"That'd be nice," Hunter said, but he was distracted. All the planning, all the scheming, it was over his head. But this, right now, the boots-on-the-ground, getting-dirty-but-getting-it-done stuff? This was his game.

He grabbed two boxes of ammunition for his deer rifle and the gun itself and shoved it all into Christian's hands. "Go to the ridge behind the house," he whispered. The gun had a good range and enough power to take care of a human, as long as the target wasn't wearing armor. And Christian was a good shot. "We're trying to buy time for the women, distract the helicopter, let them get away. Then it's our turn. We'll draw them out, then try to get to the snowmobile, but if things go bad, you can run through the woods for a long time. You know the terrain."

Christian looked like he was thinking about arguing, but he gave a jerky nod. "Where will you be?" he whispered.

"Mobile." Hunter grabbed the bear gun and its ammo. It didn't have the range of Christian's gun, but it had a lot more power at close range. And Hunter definitely wanted to keep Christian as far away from it all as possible. The helicopter was closer now, a booming sound that reminded Hunter of too many jobs in too many foreign countries. He wished he was as well-armed now as he normally would be on a company job, but he'd make do with what he had. "Go!" he ordered. Thankfully, Christian went.

And Hunter followed him, at least as far as the door. But as soon as he was outside he started moving on his own. He slid around the back of the garage in time to see the snowmobile enter the forest, and then he busied himself scouting the terrain.

He'd thought about how he'd use this terrain before. He'd been training and fighting for almost twenty years of his life, and evaluating a site was second nature to him. But it had just been idle speculation, and he'd never considered a helicopter attack. He would have to improvise a little.

There was a moment, when the chopper first came into sight, that he thought maybe Christian had been right. Maybe this was a false alarm. Because it was just a civilian helicopter, the kind used to drop heliskiers off on mountains. It was flying low, sure, but it wasn't a gun ship.

Then he realized that even Wendy wouldn't have been able to get her hands on a fully militarized helicopter in Canada. Not overnight. And as the chopper drew closer, then hovered over the trees, Hunter saw the ropes drop. Two on each side, and then four men in forest camouflage rappelled out and dropped to the ground. They were about 500 meters out. Too far for a shot with any of the guns Hunter kept at his cabin, but close enough that the men wouldn't take too long to reach him. And as he watched, a second wave dropped. Eight men on the ground.

Eight against two. Not great, not if the eight were as well-trained as Hunter assumed they would be. He wondered briefly whether he'd been the one to train any of them, whether he'd worked with them before, whether they even knew who they were attacking or why. Then he dismissed the thought. He couldn't afford to worry about any of that.

Especially as the helicopter dropped its lines and then, instead of flying away, came closer. There were still two men in the back, Hunter realized, both armed with what looked like M16s. Wendy might not have been able to get her hands on a military helicopter, but she'd still found some firepower. And the house was in a clearing, all of Hunter's careful work to maintain his view of the lake giving the damn thing room to maneuver.

He glanced over to look for Christian, hoping the kid had sense enough to find cover. A part of Hunter's brain was screaming at him, telling him to grab Christian and run, get him to safety, not let him get hurt. But his discipline held. Christian wasn't stupid, and he wasn't weak, and running away wouldn't do either of them any good if they were trying to outrun a damn helicopter.

The chopper was almost directly overhead, now, and a new sound was added to the heavy thrum of the blades: the rattle of M16 fire, in short bursts. The first target was the truck. The shooter wasn't too precise, but with a gun like that he didn't need to be. The tires went, and there were enough rounds in the engine that Hunter doubted it would even start. He wondered how the rental company was going to feel about that.

The next target was the snowmobile. Bullets bit through the metal and plastic, tearing holes and destroying the track. Then the helicopter turned, and Hunter realized that they'd seen the tracks leading into the woods. They were going to follow Miriam and Hayley.

He'd taken cover behind a tree, but now he leaned out, found his target, and fired. The man behind the M16 jerked and stopped firing. Hunter didn't think he'd gotten a direct hit, but hopefully he'd wounded the guy, at least.

But he'd also given away his location, and the chopper was rotating, bringing the door with the other shooter around in Hunter's direction. Damn it, he needed to move. A quick dodge farther back into the trees, but then bark was flying around him and he had to find another big tree. He tried to pull all parts of himself behind the trunk, but he could hear the chopper moving, changing angles. Tracking him.

Then a crack of rifle fire from a new direction. And another. And another. Christian. Firing on the helicopter, aiming, firing, aiming, firing. Methodical, disciplined. Perfect. The chopper's engine whined as it gained altitude, and Hunter dared a quick peek, then stepped out, aimed, and fired. He saw the hole in the glass canopy, saw both doors empty, the shooters either injured or taking cover, and then the damn thing was flying away. Retreating.

Hunter resisted the urge to give a war whoop. Instead, he scrambled through the forest and found a spot about twenty meters from Christian. "Eight guys dropped out of that thing," Hunter yelled. "Watch for them."

"Yup," Christian answered. Hunter wasn't sure if the guy was being stoic or just wasn't feeling that talkative. Unless.... "You hurt?"

"They didn't even shoot in my direction," Christian said. "Did you think I stubbed my toe?"

Okay, yeah. Hunter needed to stay focused and not let his paranoia get out of control. Christian was okay, but there were still eight men incoming on foot. And the helicopter had lifted off enough to be out of range of even Christian's rifle, but it hadn't left their area. It was up there, watching them and reporting their locations to the men on the ground. Not ideal.

"We need to move," Hunter yelled. "Stay under cover, try to find a dense canopy where the chopper can't see you. They'll be able to track us in the snow, but they won't know where we decide to stop and ambush them."

"Check," Christian yelled, and then, without hesitation, he turned and sprinted into the forest.

Hunter wanted to follow him, but it made more sense for them to maintain some distance and split up the enemy forces. Hunter just hoped the men would be able to see who was who and would choose to follow him. There was no way he'd be able to handle it if he came out of this and Christian didn't.

But that was another one of the thoughts he couldn't allow himself to have. So he tamped it down and found his own route into the forest, running at an angle to the path Christian had laid. He found a dense thicket and moved through it, circling around as far as he could without exposing himself to the helicopter. And then he waited.

Christian needed to stop trembling. He wasn't afraid, he was pretty sure. Well, yeah, he was afraid, but that wasn't causing the shaking. And he wasn't cold, although he wished he was wearing winter boots and maybe a thicker jacket. But it wasn't that cold of a day, and he was moving.

But he'd shot a man. He'd aimed for him, he'd pulled the trigger, and he'd seen the man's body jerk and then fall. Dead? Christian hoped not, but he had no idea. He'd needed to do it in order to get the helicopter's attention off Hunter, and he had no regrets. But it was still an enormous thing, and his body seemed to be reacting in a not totally productive way.

He kept moving, hoping the exercise would wear off some adrenaline. But he didn't want to get too far from Hunter. The evergreens were dense over his head, and he figured if he couldn't see the helicopter it couldn't see him, so surely he didn't need to go too much farther. So he found a fallen tree with a hollow in the snow behind it, and he settled in to wait. And tremble. Damn it, he couldn't lose his cool.

He let himself think about Hunter. The bastard in the helicopter had been spinning around to shoot at Hunter, and that meant Christian had to stop him. It was that simple, and nothing else mattered. He brought the rifle up to the top of the log and sprinkled a little snow along the barrel to make it look less glaringly black. The snow melted immediately, the barrel still hot from the bullets that had traveled down it. So much for that bright idea.

He was almost done shaking when he saw them coming, and then the trembling started again. It was different this time.

Two of them, clearly following his trail in the snow, moving cautiously, but unable to really take cover, not if they wanted to have any chance of ever catching up to him. It was an ambush. They weren't about to shoot at Hunter, they were just walking along.

But if they kept walking, they'd find him, and then they'd kill him, and then they'd find Hunter and kill *him*. And that was not acceptable.

Christian waited for the men to get closer. They were wearing body armor, he realized, its bulky outline visible beneath their light jackets. His rifle wouldn't pierce body armor. Which meant... God, it meant he had to aim for the head.

He couldn't do it.

He had to.

But a human being, a *face*, maybe one Christian knew, and he was going to... how could he?

They were close now. Too close. Christian had left it too late and he needed to act *now* and it was already probably too late and—

The shot rang out from somewhere to his right, and one of the attackers fell. The other turned, aimed, and Christian fired. Head shot, not that hard from this close, and the man fell. He'd been aiming at Hunter. He had to be stopped.

Christian was pretty sure he was going to throw up, but then Hunter was there beside him, tugging him to his feet. "It's okay. I know, I know. But it's okay. And we need to move. There's six more of them."

Fuck. Six more. Christian didn't know if he could pull the trigger *once* more. But his training kicked in enough to let him reload the rifle, and instinct made him follow Hunter.

He knew enough to not look behind him. He couldn't let himself see those bodies in the snow, not if he wanted to keep going. Couldn't let himself wonder about the men they used to be, the hole that would be left in someone's life now that they were gone. He thought about Hunter instead. The man *he* was, and the endless, gaping chasm that would never be filled if anything happened to *him*. Christian needed to focus on that.

So he stumbled along behind Hunter and eventually realized they were circling back toward the cabin. Christian didn't know the strategy and didn't think he cared. He could hear the helicopter overhead, but it sounded even farther away than it actually was, and when Hunter turned and said something, Christian saw his lips moving as if they were in slow motion, and his voice came out garbled and blurred, as if he were talking underwater.

Then something cold and wet got shoved into Christian's face and ground in until he stumbled backward and raised his hands in protest.

"You need to stay with me," Hunter growled, shaking the remaining snow from his hand. "Keep it together, Christian."

Christian blinked hard. Yes. Hunter. Stay with him. Forever. "I'm okay," he croaked.

Hunter didn't look convinced. "We can keep moving, head toward town. Hopefully the cavalry's on the way."

That sounded perfect. Christian didn't want to be a soldier anymore.

"But I don't know where they all are. You need to be ready to shoot, Christian. I'll try to take care of it, but...."

"I can," Christian said. "If I have to, I can."

Hunter looked at him for a long moment, then nodded. "Yeah. You can. Okay. Stay low, and move fast." Then his gaze flickered behind Christian, and he whispered, "Freeze."

There was a tree at Christian's back. Hunter had stopped there on purpose, Christian supposed, somewhere there was a little shelter. But it didn't feel like enough, not when Christian couldn't look behind him to see the threat, not when he could imagine the bullets flying toward him, toward Hunter....

"Two coming," Hunter whispered. "On three, you drop, roll, and take out the one at my two o'clock. You understand? You can do that?"

If Christian didn't, Hunter might get shot. "Yes," he whispered.

Another long look from Hunter, then a quick, sad smile. "You're doing good, kid. Keep it up." Then, "One... two... three."

Christian dropped, rolled, heard Hunter's gun ring out, found his own target, moving now, and fired. He saw red fly from the man's shoulder, but it wasn't enough Christian took aim again, this time at a target that was stumbling and searching for cover. He pulled the trigger and then stared at the results. Oh, God. He'd done that.

Hunter was pulling on his shoulder again. "Come on. We're moving. If they catch us again, you'll have to do it again."

Good motivation. Christian made his feet move, made himself stumble along behind Hunter. He just needed to follow Hunter.

Following Hunter. That was what Christian needed to remember. As soon as he had it at the top of his mind, it was as if a strange peace descended on him. Not the sense of being submerged and lost that he'd felt before. Just a calmness. He wasn't shaking anymore, he noticed. And he was seeing everything around him in almost amplified clarity. They weren't going anywhere. This was his home, and maybe his grave. Okay. That was the way it was.

He smiled. "Okay. What's next?"

Hunter didn't think it was shock. Christian had been in

shock after the first kill. Totally natural, totally expected. And he'd functioned well, considering. Hunter could barely remember his own first combat experience, overwhelmed as he'd been with it all, and Christian was no different. But now, this new calm? It wasn't shock. But Hunter wasn't sure just what it was.

And he didn't have a lot of time to figure it out. "We'll go on foot," he said. "The same route Miriam and Hayley took, but keep off the path until we're sure we're clear of it all. Watch for ambushes. We'll head for town. If we make it, we win."

Of course, town was forty kilometers away. Forty kilometers of wet, heavy snow to trudge through. They could try to make it to the road to hitch a ride, but at this time of year and with this weather there wouldn't be much traffic, and what there was might be hostiles. Safer to keep to the bush and hope Miriam and Hayley made it through and came back with help.

"Okay," Christian agreed. He was still far too calm. "Split up, or stay together?"

"Stay together."

"Excellent." Christian waited expectantly, and after a moment's hesitation, Hunter started moving. He wasn't sure what was up with the kid, but he certainly seemed capable of functioning.

They moved cautiously. The snow was a blessing and a curse; the hostiles could track them, but Hunter could track the hostiles too. As long as Hunter kept them moving, as long as he kept scanning the snow ahead of them for any signs that hostiles had passed, they should be okay.

It should have worked. At least, it could have. But it didn't.

Hunter felt the shock before he heard the crack of the rifle. He fell forward into the snow and felt Christian drop beside him, then rise to his knees and fire. Then another shot from Christian, and then silence. Hunter couldn't hear anything but his own breathing.

Then he heard Christian. "Fuck, Hunter, no! No." The kid was frantic, grabbing Hunter's thigh where the blood was gushing, his eyes wild and staring. But he'd gotten his shots off first. Good.

Christian was still fumbling around, pulling off his jacket and his belt, then lifting Hunter's leg. Hunter gasped, but the pain brought him back to himself. He saw what Christian was doing. Field dressing, first aid, applying pressure to the wound. Good stuff. Christian was doing well.

And Hunter let him. The pressure would slow things down. It would give him more time, and that meant it would give Christian more time. That was all that mattered. "He came straight from the 'copter," he said through gritted teeth. It was important that Christian understand that. "They didn't all go to the house. You can't trust the tracks."

Christian nodded, but he didn't seem to really be listening.

Hunter grabbed his arm. "You hear me? Don't trust the tracks."

Christian looked up at him, his face pale, and swallowed hard. "Yeah. Got it. Can you move? Like, if I help?"

Hunter supposed it was worth a try. There was no way he could make it all the way to town, but there was also no point giving up before he had to. He could still be another set of eyes, another gun; he could help get Christian a little farther down the path.

That was when they heard the new noise. The helicopter was still overhead; too close, Hunter realized. It had spotted them and must be relaying the information. So the hostiles would know what they were trying. But that wasn't the main concern. Christian straightened and looked around, his gaze locked on Hunter's.

"Snowmobiles," Christian said, his voice dead calm. "Sounds

like they're coming down the road?"

"Sounds like," Hunter agreed. And that meant there was a new threat, and they needed a new plan. Hunter was pretty sure it wasn't going to involve both of them getting out alive.

CHATPER TWENTY

"Okay, snowmobiles," Christian said. He looked at Hunter and tried to ignore the man's paleness, the way the muscles of his face were all drawn in pain. They needed to get out of this mess, and then Hunter would get to the doctor and get fixed up and everything would be fine. "We can't outrun that."

"Terrain," Hunter grunted. "Get off the trail, stay in the deep forest. Go up and down cliffs. You can't go in the open. They'll catch you in the open."

"Okay," Christian said. "Yeah, okay. We can do that." He reached down and grabbed Hunter's shoulder, helping him get upright. He tried to ignore the red stain on the snow where Hunter's body had lain and the dark, wet patch spreading down his pant leg. "Let's move."

He kept to the forest, as Hunter had directed. He moved as quickly as he could, but he could hear what was happening around him, and he knew he wasn't fast enough. The snowmobiles had spread out, a few working their way along the path beside Hunter and Christian, but at least two others racing ahead. Looking for an opportunity to cut them off. And there were still at least three men on foot behind them, probably closing fast now that the helicopter had picked up their location. It wasn't going to work. Even with Hunter at full strength, it wouldn't have worked.

"Go right," Hunter gasped, and Christian obeyed. Another

few minutes of painful progress, and Christian could tell that he was doing more and more of the work. Hunter was weakening, losing too much blood. "Up there," Hunter managed, feebly raising his arm to gesture to a spot halfway up a rough slope.

"That's a dead end," Christian said. "I could get us there, but we'd be stuck."

"Defensible," Hunter said, and Christian had to admit he was right. And there was no way they were going to make it forty kilometers to town, not the way they were going, not chased by snowmobiles. "And the terrain bottlenecks here. Everyone has to come through that pass."

But there was only one set of tracks, the ones Hayley and Miriam had left. "They haven't come through yet."

"They haven't figured it out yet. Trust me, it's the only way."

"Okay," Christian said. It wasn't easy dragging Hunter up the slope, the snow and loose shale slipping beneath their feet, Hunter grunting in pain with every step. But Christian did it because he had to. "Okay," he gasped when they'd arrived. He had to admit, it was an excellent location. He would have trudged right by it, but Hunter knew his land.

"If I can stop the snowmobiles, stick to the path," Hunter said, his voice tight. "If I can't, stay in the trees. Don't even worry about getting to town, just keep moving wherever they aren't."

Christian frowned. "What? You said we were going to defend *this* spot. We're staying *here*, aren't we?"

"Just me," Hunter said. "You're going."

"No." It wasn't even worth getting upset about. It just wasn't going to happen. "I'm staying with you."

"No. This is it. I'm done. You still have a chance. You're going."

Christian shook his head vigorously. It wasn't worth fighting about him leaving, but he would damn well object to the *I'm done* part of that sentence. "We just need to hold out for a bit. They'll send help from town. You'll get to a doctor and you'll be good."

"Fuck, Christian, we don't have time. If that's true, great. I'll still be here whether you stay with me or not. If it isn't true… you still have a fucking chance, here!"

"I'm staying. Here, scoot over a bit, and I'll wedge in—"

"No," Hunter grunted. "You say you owe me, right? Fine. You need to pay me back by getting the hell out of here and making sure this gets seen through. You need to take Wendy down. The legal way, with the cops. That's what I want."

"Hunter." Christian smiled. "You know Miriam and Hayley will be way better at that. You know they won't give up." He was feeling calm again. This was okay. Yeah, he was a bit scared, but he was with Hunter. He wished they'd been able to get away. There was a lot of stuff he'd wanted to do. Some of it naked, but a lot of it just… living. He scooted down so he was lying next to Hunter, rearranged and tightened the bandage on Hunter's leg, and listened to the sound of a snowmobile approaching. "I think we should get an aquarium." he said softly. If he was going to pretend they were getting out of this, he might as well pretend they were living together too. "A big one. But just with nice fish, ones that all get along. Okay?"

"Christian," Hunter said, but he was losing his strength.

That was going to be the hard part. Christian wasn't all that afraid of dying, himself, not if Hunter wasn't going to be around either. But he wasn't sure he could just sit there and watch the man slip away.

"I love you," Christian whispered. "I'm sorry I fucked up. We could have had three years." He swallowed hard. They could have had three beautiful, glorious years. Or maybe more, because maybe Christian could have talked Hunter out of going back to the company, and then none of this would have happened. But that wasn't the game he was playing. "An aquarium," he said. His voice was a bit rocky and the tears running down his cheeks were a distraction, but he could keep going. The snowmobile was close now. "And maybe a dog. We could take it on runs with us. A big one. And he'd jump on the furniture when we weren't around. Yeah. Let's get a dog."

"Please, Christian," Hunter said. "Please, go."

"I don't know about cats," Christian said. "A cat might eat the fish." The snowmobile was…. His head jerked up. He half stood, trying to hear without the echo from the cliff. The snowmobile was….

He leaped over the lip of the ledge they were on and slid down the cliff on his ass. Scrambling, rolling, finding his way to the bottom just in time to launch himself in front of the snowmobile, the one coming *toward* the cabin site, not away from it.

Hayley dodged him, her eyes wide, and Miriam leaped off the seat. "Christian!" she yelled. "We couldn't leave you guys. We came back to help!"

"Hunter's hurt." Christian wouldn't think about whether there was enough time. There *had* to be enough time. "I'll bring him down. You guys take him to town, and I'll slow them down behind you."

He didn't wait for agreement, just sprinted back up the slope. It was so much easier to make it without Hunter's weight, and with just a little bit of hope.

He tried not to notice that Hunter was barely conscious, and he wasn't too careful dragging him down the hill.

Miriam knelt beside him, checking the injury, and Hayley stared, wide-eyed.

"Hey!" Christian yelled. "Hayley, hey! You can do this, right? Turn the sled around. If you wedge him between you and Miriam, there won't be much room, but you can do it. You can get him out of here. Hayley!"

She tore her eyes away from her brother and stared at Christian for a moment, then nodded jerkily. "He's not...."

"He's still alive. But you need to fucking *move!*"

And she did. She got the sled turned around, Christian lifted Hunter into place, and Miriam slid in behind him. "We could try to carry four," Miriam said desperately.

Christian shook his head and grinned at her. "Nah. I'm good." There was barely room for three, and even if Christian *could* fit, the extra weight would slow them down. "I could use the walk."

"So is it over now?" Hayley locked hopeful as Miriam arranged herself on the sled. "We're safe?"

It was tempting to say yes. It'd be easier. But they had to know what was going on so they'd be able to make good decisions and tell the police what they needed to know. "At least four guys on snowmobiles. Three guys on foot. And that fucking helicopter." He saw Miriam realize what that meant. They were far from safe, and Christian wasn't going to be taking a little walk. He made himself grin at her. "I'll trade you guns? I'll take the shotgun, you take the deer rifle." He didn't need the range, and he wanted the power.

She handed the gun over wordlessly. Christian wanted more time. He wanted to be able to say good-bye to Hunter. But Hunter needed to live, and that meant there *was* no time. "Hurry," Christian said.

And Hayley did. The snowmobile sped down the path, heading for town and safety, and Christian turned and started back up the slope. The bottleneck was still a good tactical location. It still made sense for one of them to stay behind and defend it, keeping the others from being followed. Christian would do that. He would buy them time. It was all he could do.

"You're okay," Hunter heard. The voice was familiar, cutting through the panic, but it wasn't enough. He *wasn't* okay. He kept struggling, trying to free himself from whatever trap he was in.

"Hunter, stop!" Miriam's voice again. "Trust me, Hunter. You're okay. You need to lie still or they'll sedate you. We don't want that."

Sedate him. He was in a hospital. Miriam was there. What had...? Oh, God. "Christian?" Hunter managed to open his eyes, half sat up, and looked wildly around the room. "Christian!"

Miriam put her hands on his shoulders. "They're still looking for him," she said. "They want to talk to you as soon as you're able, but you need to make sure you're not going to injure yourself. I won't let them in until you're calmer. Do you understand?"

"Looking for him *where*?" It was coming back to Hunter, but the pieces were jumbled, and he couldn't remember the ending at all. Couldn't figure out how he was in the hospital, or why Christian wasn't there with him.

"In the forest. They say...." Miriam shook her head as if dismissing the possibility of tears, and when she spoke again her voice was stronger. "Apparently it's quite a mess. The spot where we picked you up. Christian... he stopped them. Kept them from coming after us."

"Where *is* he?" Hunter demanded.

"They're sorting it out," she said softly.

"Sorting out...." He stared at her. Sorting out the bodies. If Christian was alive, he'd just... he'd just give them his name. There'd be no *sorting*. "No...."

"They don't know," Miriam said.

Hunter struggled again to get upright. He looked at the tubes connected to his wrist and reached for them, only to have

Miriam catch his hand. "You lost a lot of blood. You're fixed up for now, but if you start moving around, you'll start bleeding again. If you somehow made it up to the site, you'd just be a distraction. People looking after you won't be able to spend their time looking *for* him. You'll do no good, and you could do harm. Stay put."

"While he's out there...."

"They've got an army of people up there," she said. "This place is like a war zone. Maybe they didn't take you seriously before, but that many bodies, a crashed helicopter—"

"A *what*? The helicopter... it crashed?"

Miriam nodded. "We saw the explosion from the trail. Maybe fifteen minutes after we picked you up."

"*You* picked me up? And Christian... he was with me? Why didn't he come?"

"No room on the sled, and...." She smiled sadly. "He knew they needed to be slowed down. He was in a sort of bottleneck, and he had a perch way up on a slope."

"That was where *I* was supposed to stay." Hunter didn't know how to deal with this. He'd been prepared to die. He hadn't wanted to, not now that Christian was back in his life, no matter how tenuous that might be. But he'd been prepared for it. But somehow everything had gotten turned around. The world was backward, and Hunter didn't think he could accept that.

Miriam gave him a moment to collect himself, then seemed to realize she was waiting for something that wasn't going to happen. Her voice was gentle as she said, "There's someone here from... I'm not quite sure. The government. Some sort of counterterrorism unit. I checked him out with the RCMP, and I told them you might still be in danger. They're taking it seriously now. But this counterterrorism guy wants to talk to you and start figuring it all out."

"Counterterrorism?"

"I don't think they're quite sure what to call this."

Hunter didn't care what it was called, he just wanted to get out of the goddamned bed and go find Christian. But Miriam was right; he'd just get in the way. "They're looking for Christian?" he said.

"They are."

Hunter lay back on the bed. He stared at the ceiling and tried to calm himself. Christian wasn't dead. Hunter had been in battle zones so many times he knew how confused things could get. Christian was okay. He was fine. They'd find him, and bring him in, and he'd give Hunter that cocky grin and say something annoying, something about.... Hunter frowned as a flash of memory came to him. Something about getting a dog. Christian wanted them to get a dog. Together? "We need to find him," he said.

"They're working on it. You're okay talking to the terrorism guy?"

"Okay," Hunter agreed. Maybe it would help. Maybe the guy could help him find Christian.

Christian's shoulder was numb. Which was excellent, because before it had been numb it had been throbbing in agony with every step he took. And he'd taken a lot of steps. Some of them had been stupid; he shouldn't have gotten lost, should have been able to figure things out better. But there'd been some rough patches, a few times when he'd sort of drifted out of it all. It had gotten dark, and then it was daytime, and then it got dark again. He'd kept moving, though, through it all. He'd been determined to keep putting one foot in front of the other. That was all he let himself think about. Keep moving, keep getting closer to Hunter. Too damn bad if his brain shut off sometimes and led him farther away. He'd kept moving. He hadn't given up.

And he was still moving, now. Through all the cars, staggering into one and setting off its alarm, stumbling forward, away from the racket, still walking. He needed to find Hunter. He needed to know if it was worth it to keep fighting, or if he could just lie down and die. And he couldn't know that until he found out if Hunter had made it.

The lights burned his eyes. And everything was hard and sharp, not like the blurred outlines in the forest. The air changed, a warm whoosh as he stumbled forward, and then new smells. Antiseptic, and other things. Worse things. He was inside. He'd found the right building. But he kept moving.

Then there was yelling. Angry voices, loud words, and none of them made any sense. He raised his hands to cover his eyes, tried to cover his ears as well, but he kept moving. One foot in front of the other. Trudging on, not stopping. Not until he knew.

But then something hit him. Someone, he supposed. Tackling him from the side, knocking him down, and everything was confused. His hands were wrenched behind his back and he howled, not because his shoulder caught fire again, although it did, but because they were stopping him. He had one thing to do, and they were keeping him from doing it. Too many to fight, and he was too weak, but he kept trying. He needed to know.

"Christian!" That was his name. Someone, a woman, saying his name. "This is Christian Manning," she said. That sounded right. Christian tried to look at her, but someone was holding his head, pressing it into the hard floor. "He's injured and he needs help. Get off him!"

Christian really liked this woman.

The weight shifted off his back and he struggled to get up. His hands were joined together, though, and it was hard to stand without pushing off the ground. "Uncuff him," the woman ordered.

That didn't happen, though. There was a buzz of conversation, arguments, and Christian managed to roll onto his side, then lever himself slowly, painfully upright. Good. He started moving again. One foot in front of the other.

"Christian. We can help you. Where are you going?" The woman's voice was gentle, her slim body standing in front of him, and he let himself look at her. His eyes were raw from walking in the sun and snow, and the light burned, but he could see her. Miriam. She would know about Hunter.

And now that the answer was so close, he was afraid to ask. Hunter had been so pale. And there had been so much blood, stark red against the white snow. He stared at her, and after a moment, her confusion faded. "Oh, sweetie. He's upstairs. He's okay." She smiled sadly at him. "We need to get you fixed up. We need to...." She frowned again. "Oh, sweetie. Christian... shit, somebody help me, please!" Christian knew he was falling, sliding down her body as she tried to catch him. He was going to end up back on the floor, but that was fine. Hunter was okay, and that was all Christian needed to know.

Hunter stared at Christian. Objectively, he looked like shit. There was a huge white bandage on his shoulder, where they'd had to dig the bullet out, and the skin of his face was red from sun, wind, and cold. One of his eyes was blackened and his hands were raw, with bandages covering frostbitten patches. He was beautiful.

Miriam had pushed their beds together so Hunter could keep an eye on him without having to get out of bed, and that was great, but it wasn't enough. Christian needed to wake up. Exhaustion and hypothermia, blood loss and a mild concussion, and Hunter knew the best treatment for all that stuff was rest in a warm, soft bed, so he didn't want Christian to *stay* awake, necessarily. But just one little smile, just... just *something*.

A nurse jangled into the room to check whatever the hell it was nurses checked, and she made a face after looking at Christian's chart. "He's going to want morphine," she said matter-of-factly.

"If he does once he's awake, you can give it to him." That was what Miriam had said. It wasn't forbidden for addicts to have opiates, they just had to be careful about it. She would supervise things closely, if that was what Christian wanted. But it needed to be his decision.

"He's going to want it." Now the nurse was almost smug, as if she knew something about Christian that Hunter didn't. "There's going to be a lot of pain," she explained, as if it weren't obvious.

"He walked forty kilometers through the snow without proper gear, *with* a bullet in his shoulder. I think he can handle pain if he needs to."

"Hey," came a muffled, mumbled voice from the bed.

Hunter practically launched himself across the metal railings between their beds. "Christian? Hey, Christian? You in there?"

"Hunter?" Christian squinted against the dim light of the room.

"Yeah. It's me. You're good, okay? Everybody's good."

"You're okay?" Christian was looking in his direction but still seemed to be having trouble focusing.

"Yeah, I'm okay." The nurse was still there, waiting expectantly, and Hunter sighed. "Hey, Christian? They can give you something for the pain, if you want. Miriam says she'll watch to make sure there's no risk of addiction. Do you want that?"

"Something?"

Hunter sighed. "Morphine. They say morphine's the best

thing. I'm enjoying a little of it myself, to be honest."

"Better not," Christian said.

"Are you sure? Apparently you're going to hurt a lot. I can see if Miriam can come talk to you about it."

"No," Christian said. "I don't want... it takes me away. I don't want to go away. I want to stay with you."

Hunter tried to control his voice, but he wasn't completely successful. "Even if it hurts?" he asked.

Christian nodded slowly, as if rediscovering the use of his neck muscles. "I'm not scared this time."

"Okay," Hunter said. The nurse left, and Hunter worked his hand through the bars of their beds so he could wrap his fingers around Christian's, and they lay together like that until they both fell back to sleep.

CHAPTER TWENTY

"You're sure he's okay to go home? We're not rushing it?"

"Hunter." Miriam didn't look impatient, exactly, but she wasn't pretending she hadn't already heard the question. "Are you worried about what happens when he gets out? I mean, medically, his injuries are no more serious than yours, and given the location of the injuries, you're more likely to pull your stitches and end up back in here. There's no *medical* reason to keep Christian in the hospital."

Hunter nodded. "Okay. Yeah."

"And the cabin's been cleaned up The cops are out of there. He's got somewhere to go. And between the two of you, you should be able to look after each other: he does the moving around, you do things that require two hands...." She caught his expression and slapped his shoulder. "I'm thinking about cooking and cleaning, you pervert."

"He's got somewhere to go," Hunter agreed, once he'd brought himself back from thinking about things he and Christian might want to do with two hands. "As long as he wants to be there."

"You think he might leave."

It seemed dangerous to put it into words, as if saying it might make it real. So Hunter shrugged. "Maybe," he said. "I mean, it's happened before."

Miriam nodded. "Yeah, it has. And I don't know, Hunter. I guess it might happen again. I don't think... this is not a medical opinion, you understand that? This is just me being a... I don't know. Probably me being a nosey parker. But, whatever. The thing is, I don't think he really knows how to love." She raised her hands when she saw Hunter's expression. "I don't mean he can't love, I don't mean he *doesn't* love. For what's it's worth, I think he's *crazy* in love with you." She gave Hunter a moment to try to hide his reaction to that idea, then smiled indulgently before saying, "I just don't think he knows *how*. He doesn't know how it's done, doesn't know the rules, doesn't know how to handle emotions that are so intense. I think they scare him. Maybe he feels like he's losing control, maybe he's afraid of loss... I don't know. But, the thing is... he can *learn*, Hunter. You can teach him."

"*I* can teach *him*? Like I'm an expert?"

"You're a few steps further along the trail than he is, I'd say." She smiled. "He's brave. In the forest? When we picked you up? He was so strong. He knew what was coming, and he faced it head-on, because he wanted to protect *you*. And then he walked into town, all that way in all that pain, because he wanted to be with *you*. Hunter, if he leaves again, it won't be because he wants to. You know?"

They were standing outside the door of Christian's room, Miriam holding a clipboard, Hunter balancing on crutches. He'd checked out the day before, over Christian's objections, and gone out to the cabin with the investigators to run through it all again. He felt like he'd told the story a million times, dredged up details of every meeting he'd ever been in with Wendy, but still they wanted more. The board members wanted more too, but Hunter was still ignoring their calls. He'd have to sort it out eventually, but didn't feel inclined to rush. He'd already shared all the information he had, so there was no practical reason for Wendy or anyone else to want to silence him. And Wendy wasn't the sort of person to allow herself the luxury of revenge.

So Hunter didn't need to worry about her anymore, and that was a good thing, because he'd much rather focus on Christian. "He doesn't want to leave," Hunter said softly. "And I don't want him to leave. So, fuck it, he'll just have to stay."

"On the plus side, he's still really sore, so he's not going to be wanting to move around much."

"I took my last Percocet this morning," Hunter said, "so I'll be pretty sore too."

"I prescribed a week's worth," Miriam said with a frown.

"I told them to only give me a few. I don't want to take them around him, not when he can't have any."

"That's...." Miriam shrugged, clearly reminding herself not to get too involved. "That's your decision. Go in and help him get dressed. I'll send a nurse down to help with the rest of the checking out."

"Okay," Hunter said. But he watched her leave, and stood outside the door for a moment longer. He'd found that he needed to brace himself before seeing Christian these days. Too many emotions hit him every time he looked at the other man. Love, sure, but also fear, and insecurity and some residual anger. Definitely frustration. A tentative, delicate sense of hope. All of it mixed up together into something too powerful to experience without a little preparation. So, he took the time to make sure he seemed calm, then pushed the door open.

The bed was empty. Then someone moved in the bathroom, and Hunter looked in that direction. Christian was standing in front of the mirror, the jeans Hunter had brought from the cabin baggy and hanging low on his lean hips, the muscles of his bare torso even more defined than usual after a couple of days in the wilderness without food, followed by almost a week of hospital fare. The bruises on his face had faded and his skin was smooth again, but he didn't look too pleased with what he was seeing in the mirror.

"You okay?" Hunter asked. "You need some help getting a shirt on?"

Christian nodded reluctantly. "Yeah. Sorry. I think I could have managed a T-shirt, but not the buttons on this one."

"I thought it would be warmer," Hunter said as he crutched his way into the bathroom.

"Yeah, it's great. It's a good shirt. Thanks for lending it to me. I'll wash it, for sure."

Christian was worrying about laundry? This wasn't good. "The cops pulled everything out of the bunker for evidence. I don't know what the hell they're thinking they're going to find in any of your stuff, but they say they want it. If you're up to it, we can stop off at the store on the way to the cabin and buy whatever you need, but you can borrow my stuff too."

Christian's smile was a little bitter. "You have to look after me again. This time, you're hurt yourself, and you still have to look after me."

Hunter stepped closer. If Christian was feeling that way, then Hunter needed to say something to make him feel better. "I don't have to look after you. I could leave your skinny ass here and they'd have to keep you around or throw you out on your own. But I wouldn't do that. Not ever. Not because I'm a good guy, or because I owe you anything, although I owe you my *life*, Christian, and I haven't forgotten that." He was still afraid of the next part, afraid that it would set Christian off just like it had the time before, but he was pretty sure he needed to say it. "I'd never leave you, because I love you, Christian. I love…. No, Christian, look at me." He waited until Christian finally turned his head. "I love you. I want to be with you, and I want to take care of you. And when you're feeling better, you'll take care of me." He edged a little closer. "And we'll get a dog. A big one that jumps on the furniture when we're not home. And a fucking aquarium, apparently. Maybe a cat, if we can be sure it won't eat the fish. Okay?"

Christian squinted at him. "Wait. You remember that? You were really out of it."

"I remember. I remember what you said, Christian. You said you loved me. You said it, and I heard it, and I remember." Hunter took a deep breath before asking, "Were you lying?"

Christian was pale and he'd turned his face away again. "No," he said quietly. "I wasn't lying."

Hunter let out a breath he hadn't known he was holding. "Pretty terrifying, isn't it?"

Christian's head jerked in his direction.

Hunter snorted. "You think it's just scary for you? Fuck it, Christian, you tore me apart last time, and I'm diving back into the same mess again, and you think I'm not scared? Really?"

"I...." It was Christian's turn to edge closer, and now he was staring at Hunter as if he was afraid everything would disappear if he blinked. "I won't do that again. I promise. I mean, obviously not the *exact* thing. Hayley wouldn't be down with that. But I won't... you know. I promise. I'll screw up, probably, but it'll be something different. Something *less*, hopefully. And I'll... I don't know, I'll try really hard not to do it. Or I'll try to give you some warning, and then, I don't know, you can beat me up and handcuff me or something, try to keep me from—"

He stopped, his eyes wide, when Hunter reached out and touched his face. "Okay," Hunter said quietly. "I heard *handcuffs*. We can definitely explore that, if you want."

Christian snorted. "You heard the rest too? You know I'm not... I'm not a good bet, Hunter."

"I don't have a fucking choice in the matter." That was the truth of it. Hunter wasn't picking Christian. "I'm stuck with you." He smiled to show that he wasn't really complaining about that. "I love you. You...." Maybe it was pathetic to be fishing for the words, but Hunter didn't think he cared. He'd give Christian anything in the world, anything he had or anything he could beg, borrow, or steal. He just needed Christian to give him this one thing. "In the forest. You said it, but... it was kind of a weird situation. Is there any chance of hearing it once more?"

"Hunter...," Christian started. He was looking at the goddamn sink again. But then, without prompting, he nodded, as if he'd just given himself a mental talking-to and was agreeing with what he'd said. "Fuck it," he muttered. Then he turned and looked Hunter straight in the eye. "I love you," he whispered.

It was enough. It was all Hunter needed. But it made him want more. "I think I said I wanted to *hear* it, not read your lips."

Christian looked startled for only a moment before his face relaxed into a beautiful smile. He'd made it through, and now he could celebrate. "Was it a little quiet?" he asked. "Yeah?" Then he tilted his head back and bellowed, so loud the rails on the bed vibrated, "I love you!"

"Shhh," Hunter whispered frantically. "Hospital! Sick people!" But he was laughing, and Christian smiled at him, and their kiss was warm and sweet enough that Hunter was pretty sure it was sending out healing energy waves to every bed in the damn building.

Eventually, a nurse interrupted them and Christian let Hunter help get his shirt on, and then they worked together on his shoes. Then Christian was bullied into a wheelchair and Hunter crutched down the hall beside him, heading for the exit. They were battered and bruised, but they were free. And they were together.

"You shot down a helicopter." Hunter had his fingers entwined with Christian's, and it was hypnotic to watch them moving, shifting, but never letting go. Christian was only partly listening to Hunter's words. "With a shotgun."

"Slugs," Christian said sleepily. He didn't want to be asleep, but he didn't want to wake up all the way, either. They were lying on the mattress Hayley had dragged downstairs to spare Hunter's leg the climb to the loft. There were blankets, and a fire in the fireplace, and best of all Hunter, leaning against the back of the sofa, one arm wrapped around Christian's bare chest and the other... yeah, the other playing with Christian's fingers. Like they were trying to learn sign language, just making it up together. "And it was really close. Still, I just got lucky."

"We both got lucky," Hunter said seriously.

Christian shifted around a little. He could feel Hunter's erection pressing against his lower back, and his own was clearly visible beneath his soft sleep pants, but neither of them seemed overly concerned about the situation. They'd probably do something about it eventually, but there was no rush.

"We're good, right? I mean, it's over?" Christian would fight again if he had to, but he really, really didn't want to.

"It's over," Hunter said. He kissed the top of Christian's head. "I'm pretty sure. Don't get stupid, don't be careless, but... the company's in lockdown. The board's scrambling, trying to figure out how Wendy got access to all that information and equipment. The personnel weren't even from our firm. At least they don't think so. The cops are combing through all of it, sorting it all out. They're on top of it now."

"But they haven't found Wendy.' Christian didn't want to be a nag, but he needed to know what was going on if he was going to make sure Hunter stayed safe.

"She's gone," Hunter said slowly. "Disappeared. They won't find her unless she wants to get found. She's too good at all this."

"Will she find *us*?"

"Revenge isn't logical. Poking her head out, risking exposure, now? Everything I know, I've spilled. There's nothing more I can do to hurt her or help her, so she'll have lost interest in me. She'll have moved on to the next person to use and manipulate."

It sounded plausible, but Christian squirmed around to look Hunter in the eye as he asked, "And that's all you know. And if anything comes up, anything that worries you even a little, you'll let me know? We'll handle it together?"

Hunter smiled at him and leaned in for a gentle kiss. "Together," he agreed, and they both watched, satisfied, as their fingers twined and danced together.

About the Author

Kate Sherwood, Cate Cameron, Catherine Dale... and probably a few new names, eventually. They're all one person.

One person who's lucky enough to get to live a bunch of extra lives through all the characters in her books, and who's trying desperately to keep all the lives organized into some sort of categories... so each name writes a different type of story.

But really, beneath the genre categories? All the stories will have some kind of humour, even in the darkest times. They'll all show characters who are far from perfect, but who are trying to be better.

Basic bio stuff? Kate/Cate/Catherine lives in Cottage Country, the water-filled world north of Toronto, Canada, the land where summers are sunny and crowded with visitors and winters are snowy and isolated. She loves it there. Not that she doesn't sometimes miss the city, especially when her internet is acting up or she wants something delivered!

She works full-time at a non-writing job but would love to shift into a more writing-centred life. There's a five-year plan. It might work....

OTHER BOOKS BY KATE SHERWOOD

For details, see www.booklives.com

Writing as Kate Sherwood (m/m)

All That Glitters – contemporary romance

Long Shadows, Embers, Darkness, Home Fires – four book contemporary action

Feral, Lap Dog, Twice Shy, Pure Bred – four book NA contemporary romance

Sacrati – fantasy/alt history

In Too Deep – NA contemporary romance

Chasing the Dragon – angst and adventure!

Mark of Cain – contemporary romance

The Fall, Riding Tall – two book contemporary romance

The Shift – contemporary fantasy novella – monster hunters!

Room to Grow – contemporary romance novella

The Pawn, The Knight – two book futuristic romance with plenty of angst

Poor Little Rich Boy – contemporary romance

More than Chemistry – light contemporary novella

Dark Horse, Out of the Darkness, Of Dark and Bright – three book contemporary romance with extras

Shying Away – NA romance

Lost Treasure – contemporary romance

Writing as Cate Cameron (m/f, YA)

The Billionaire's Forever Family – contemporary romance

Center Ice, Playing Defense, Winging It, Breakaway – contemporary YA hockey romance

Just a Summer Fling, Hometown Hero – contemporary small town romance

Shining Armor – contemporary romance (originally published under "Kate Sherwood")

Writing as Catherine Dale (YA, contemporary fantasy, general fiction—everything but romance!)

Dark Houses – Speculative YA